MEANT FOR STONE

Ryleigh

Growing up in Hollywood, I was surrounded by liars and phonies.

So when I got my law degree, I knew I wanted to work as a district attorney.

Busy days turned to long nights—I was on my way up the ladder.

Then he happened.

Bullied his way into my life as if there was no choice.

Suddenly everything I thought I wanted wasn't as important.

Stone

I had one thing on my mind and that was never going to change: The game.

The only goal I had was beating the records set by my family.

I didn't have time for anything else.

Until she walked in the room.

The earth shifted, just like the stories said it would.

I said it wouldn't happen—not to me.

I didn't have the time, but now she was the only thing on my mind.

I knew it was her.

Now I had to convince her.

BOOKS BY NATASHA MADISON

Meant For Series
Meant For Stone
Meant For Her
Meant For Love
Meant For Gabriel

Made For Series
Made For Me
Made For You
Made For Us
Made for Romeo

Southern Wedding Series
Mine To Kiss
Mine To Have
Mine To Hold
Mine To Cherish
Mine To Love
Mine To Take
Mine To Promise
Mine to Honor
Mine to Keep

The Only One Series
Only One Kiss
Only One Chance
Only One Night
Only One Touch
Only One Regret
Only One Mistake
Only One Love
Only One Forever

Southern Series
Southern Chance
Southern Comfort
Southern Storm
Southern Sunrise
Southern Heart
Southern Heat
Southern Secrets
Southern Sunshine

This Is
This Is Crazy
This Is Wild
This Is Love
This Is Forever

Hollywood Royalty
Hollywood Playboy
Hollywood Princess
Hollywood Prince

Something Series
Something So Right
Something So Perfect
Something So Irresistible
Something So Unscripted
Something So BOX SET

Tempt Series
Tempt The Boss
Tempt The Playboy
Tempt The Hookup
Tempt The Ex

Heaven & Hell Series
Hell and Back
Pieces of Heaven
Heaven & Hell Box Set

Love Series
Perfect Love Story
Unexpected Love Story
Broken Love Story

Mixed Up Love
Faux Pas

STONE FAMILY TREE
SOMETHING SO, THIS IS ONLY ONE & MADE FOR FAMILY TREE!

SOMETHING SO SERIES
Something So Right
Parker & Cooper Stone
Matthew Grant (Something So Perfect)
Allison Grant (Something So Irresistible)
Zara Stone (This Is Crazy)
Zoe Stone (This Is Wild)
Justin Stone (This Is Forever)

Something So Perfect
Matthew Grant & Karrie Cooley
Cooper Grant (Only One Regret)
Frances Grant (Only One Love)
Vivienne Grant (Made For You)
Chase Grant (Made For Me)

Something So Irresistible
Allison Grant & Max Horton
Michael Horton (Only One Mistake)
Alexandria Horton (Only One Forever)
Something So Unscripted
Denise Horton & Zack Morrow
Jack Morrow
Joshua Morrow
Elizabeth Morrow

THIS IS SERIES
This Is Crazy
Zara Stone & Evan Richards
Zoey Richards
Stone Richards (Meant For Stone)

This Is Wild
Zoe Stone & Viktor Petrov
Matthew Petrov (Mine To Take)
Zara Petrov

Southern Wedding Family Tree

Mine To Have

Travis & Harlow

Charlotte

Theo

Mine To Hold

Shelby & Ace

Arya

Mine To Cherish

Clarabella & Luke

Zander

Mine To Love

Presley & Bennett

Cadence

Charleigh

Mine To Take

Sofia and Matty Petrov

Mine To Promise

Stefano Dimitris & Addison

Avery

Mine To Honor

Levi & Eva

Cici

Mine To Keep

Grace & Caine

Meadow

SOUTHERN TREE

Southern Family tree

Billy and Charlotte
(Mother and father to Kallie and Casey)
Southern Chance
Kallie & Jacob McIntyre
Ethan McIntyre (Savannah Son)
Amelia (Southern Secrets)
Travis

Southern Comfort

Olivia & Casey Barnes
Quinn (Southern Heat)
Reed (Southern Sunshine)
Harlow (Mine to Have)

Southern Storm

Savannah & Beau Huntington
Ethan McIntyre (Jacob's son)
Chelsea (Southern Heart)
Toby
Keith

Southern Sunrise

Emily & Ethan McIntyre
Gabriel
Aubrey

Southern Heart

Chelsea Huntington & Mayson Carey
Tucker

Southern Heat

Willow & Quinn Barnes
Grace (Mine To Keep)
Charlie

Cover Design: Jay Aheer
Photo by Wander Aguiar Photography
Editing done by Karen Hrdicka Barren Acres Editing
Editing done by Jenny Sims Editing4Indies
Proofing Julie Deaton by Deaton Author Services
Proofing by Judy's Proofreading
Formatting by Christina Parker Smith

meant for
STONE

NATASHA
MADISON

ONE

STONE

I LOOK OUT the window at the city below us. "Flight attendants," the captain announces on the speaker, "thirty minutes until landing."

"Are you done with that?" I look over at the flight attendant, her finger pointing at the glass of water on my tray table.

"I am." I hand her the almost empty glass. "Thank you." She nods at me as she moves along to the person behind me. After putting my tray table up, I look back out the window at the city bustling below me. Leaning back in the seat, I watch as the city comes closer and closer before the plane jerks as we land. Pulling my phone out of the pocket in front of me, I turn it off Airplane Mode. The captain comes on the speaker. "Welcome to Dallas." He continues to tell us what the local time is and all that stuff. The phone vibrates in my hand, and I see a text coming in from my cousin Christopher.

Christopher: *What time do you land?*

He sent the text about an hour ago.

Me: *Just landed, on my way to the gate. You?*

Christopher: *An hour ago. When you said let's surprise them together, you didn't mention you would be arriving an hour after me.*

I laugh at his message, shaking my head.

Me: *I told you my flight number. It's not my fault you didn't look it up.*

Christopher: *You're a dick.*

Me: *See you soon. I think it said gate 83, but I'm not sure. I could have misheard.*

Christopher: *I'll meet you at baggage claim. I'm the one holding up the Welcome Back from Prison sign.*

I'm about to answer him when the ping for the seat belt light turning off sounds, and everyone stands. I get out of my seat and turn to open the overhead bin to grab my black duffel bag, waiting for the door to be opened. The phone vibrates in my hand again, and this time when I look down, I see it's my sister, Zoey. She's named after my Aunt Zoe, but my parents added a Y. When she was young, everyone used to call her Zoey with a Y, so that's how she's stored in my phone.

Zoey with a Y: *Remind me never to travel with Mom and Dad again.*

Me: *Why?*

Zoey with a Y: *I caught them making out when I went to the bathroom. It looked like he was going to jump her. I threw up a little in my mouth.*

Me: *He always looks like he's going to jump her.*

Zoey with a Y: *You aren't helping. I need to pour*

tequila in my eyeballs.

I'm about to answer her when the sound of the door opening makes me look up. The two people in front of me move to disembark the plane. "Thank you." I nod at the two flight attendants who smile at me before walking out and feel the heat hit me right away. My white T-shirt sticks to my body as I make my way down the gray carpet toward the gate. As soon as I step into the terminal, an announcement is made about some flight as I look right to left and see the Baggage Claim sign.

Besides New York, I've been to this airport the most in the past couple of years. It's probably because the family is spread out in two places: New York, where I was born and raised. My Uncle Matthew played for New York and then became the GM. His first big deal was acquiring my father from Dallas. The deal was easy, especially for my father, who fell in love with my mother, Uncle Matthew's younger sister. Their love story is one for the books, really. I'm reminded of it every single time I walk into our family home because it's framed on the wall in the middle with our family pictures around it. They didn't meet in the conventional way people meet. Nope, not with my mother. My mother decided to tweet him to crash her ex's wedding, following up with hashtags that will forever be ingrained in my brain; #myexhasapencildick was my favorite.

He was traded to New York, and that's where he retired. I lived there until I was sixteen years old, when I was drafted to the Ontario Hockey League. Moving from my home to Canada was definitely something I wanted but actually having it happen, and then being away from them, was a tough time. I want to say it didn't show on the ice, but I would also be lying. My game suffered, but not that much. The scouts still noticed me, but that had to do with my name and the dynasty surrounding it. Not only was my father top dog but it also didn't hurt that my grandfather was the best thing that happened to the sport. He held all the top records—well, most of them. My cousin Dylan was giving him a run for his money. Needless to say, I finally got my groove back the year after, and I was drafted to Las Vegas. I opted to go back to school instead of going straight to the NHL. I attended the camp, and even though they were ready for me, I wasn't ready. Luckily, I had everyone's support until the year later when they traded me to Nashville. It was the name of the game. I've seen a couple of family members being traded over the years, so I knew it was always a possibility. I've been with Nashville for the past six years, and I have two more years left on my contract.

I spot Christopher looking down at his phone while I walk down the stairs toward him. "Where is my sign?" I question, and he looks up at me and glares.

"I've been waiting an hour for you," he huffs before he pushes on my shoulder.

"Ouch, that hurt," I joke with him. "Have you been hitting the gym?"

"Don't even," he sneers at me. "Now let's get the car."

"You had an hour," I mumble, walking out with him. We're dressed almost the same in jeans, a T-shirt, and, of course, the staple we always wear, our baseball hats backward. We walk toward the corner, and I look up. "What are we doing?"

"We have to take a shuttle bus," he grumbles, looking at his watch. "They come every ten to fifteen minutes." I clear my throat, trying not to laugh out loud as he hisses.

"How about I rent the car, my treat?" I offer, and his head snaps up. "I'll even put you down as a co-driver."

"When was the last time you ever rented a car?" Christopher asks.

"Umm." I look up at the sky. "I think a couple of years ago when we decided to go backpacking in Europe."

"Do you even know how to rent a car?" he asks, and I laugh.

"It's an airport." I stretch my arms to the sides of me. "You're telling me they'll be sold out of all cars?"

"Yeah," Christopher gasps, "that's what I'm saying." He shakes his head and pulls out his phone. "You had one job," he mumbles as he puts the phone to his ear. "Yeah, should we use a car service or take a cab to Gabriella's house?" Gabriella is the only reason we're here. She has a huge night tonight, and we have come to support her. Christopher has no choice since it's his sister, but since we grew up together, we all feel like siblings.

"Who is that?" I whisper, and he puts his phone on speaker.

"Where are you guys?" The sound of my Uncle Matthew's voice fills the air.

I slap his arm. "Why? Why would you do that?" I hiss, pointing at the phone in his hand.

"Stone and I are at the airport," he says as I shake my

head.

"Of all people, why would you call him? I could have called Zoey," I ask, and he presses the mute button.

"Because he knows everything," Christopher states. "Is it better for us to get an Uber or get a car service from the airport?"

"It's better to get an Uber," he says. "No way can you schedule a car service now. Amateurs." He chuckles right before he hangs up.

"You had to call him," I hiss, pulling out my own phone. "I'll get the Uber." I pull up the app. "What's her address?"

"How?" Christopher puts one hand on his hip. "How did you even get here?"

I laugh at him. "I can book a plane ticket to just about anywhere," I inform him and check the email my cousin Gabriella sent out a month ago, inviting us to her housewarming party. "Also, I got the address," I gloat, putting it in. "You're welcome."

He doesn't say anything to me as we get into the SUV that arrives four minutes later. "Isn't this better than renting a car, anyway?" I look over at him. "Now we don't have to return anything."

"Whatever," Christopher responds as he looks down at his phone, texting someone.

We pull up to the house. "Damn." I get out, grabbing my bag from the trunk. "This place is huge for two people."

"You have a five-bedroom home," Christopher points out, "and a condo in Florida, as well as a condo in

Montreal and…" He lists off all my real estate properties.

"They're called investments," I snap. "It's residual income."

"Did you just try to school me because we own practically the same properties?" I don't bother answering him. Instead, I walk up the steps to the house and walk in.

I stop when I see Gabriella and Abigail, who is her twin, with her husband, Tristan, in front of me.

"Surprise," I say, shaking Tristan's hand before walking over to hug Abigail. Gabriella comes over to me and gets on her tippy-toes to hug me.

"Did you come with your parents?" she asks, looking behind me to see if my parents are here.

"No." I shake my head. "They don't know I'm here." I smile at her and then look over her shoulder at a girl I've never seen before in my life. All I can see is this woman in front of me, and my feet are moving before I even realize it. The smile stays on my face as I walk over to her. "I'm Stone, and you are?"

"Off-limits," Romeo, Gabriella's boyfriend, grumbles, and everyone laughs. He's an up-and-coming actor, who has shifted his focus to producing movies. His father is one of the biggest action stars at the box office.

"You're shacking up with my cousin." I point at Gabriella. "I don't see why she would be off-limits."

"My brother is half wrong," the woman states. I take in her long black hair with her green eyes that look like they have some blue in them. "I'm not off-limits, but I'm also not interested." She smiles at me, and I put my hand on the middle of my chest, as if she just shot me.

"Ouch," I gasp, still smiling, "that hurt."

"It'll hurt a lot more if you touch her," Romeo threatens, puffing out his chest.

"I just introduced myself to her." I hold up my hand. "If two single people somehow spark a conversation…" I shrug. "It's on them."

"What do you do for work?" she asks. I can see the twinkle in her eye as some specks of blue start to form, making me want to keep her smiling to see how blue they get.

"I play hockey for Nashville," I say, and she snaps her fingers.

"Shucks," she deadpans, "I already scratched that profession off my list. Besides, Chicago and Nashville are very far apart."

I just stare at her, still not knowing her name, when the doorbell rings. "That must be my parents," Romeo says. Everyone moves to the side as I walk over to stand next to the woman.

I lean against the doorjamb. "So am I going to get a name or am I going to have to follow you around all night long, hoping someone says your name?"

She turns to face me. "My parents said not to talk to strangers." She winks at me.

"I'm in your brother's house," I point out, "and you know my cousin." I smirk at her. "I don't think that would put me under the column of a stranger." Her head moves to the side as she takes in my words. "Besides, all I have to do is google your brother, and I'm sure there is mention of you somewhere on his Wikipedia page." She throws her head back and laughs, and only then do I see how blue her eyes can get.

"That's a good point," she concedes. "I'm Ryleigh." She extends her hand as if we just met.

I take her small hand in mine, moving it up and down for way too long, not ready to let it go. "Ryleigh, it's a pleasure to meet you."

TWO

One Year Later

"RYLEIGH!" MY NAME is being shouted from somewhere in this monster of a house. "Ryleigh," again my father calls my name. I smirk at the cereal bowl in front of me as I wait for him to find me. "Ry?" His footsteps come closer and closer to the kitchen, and then he's walking in. "I've been calling you." He huffs as he walks over to the massive stainless-steel fridge, pulls it open, and grabs a bottle of sparkling water. I've been here for two days because my brother is premiering the first movie he produced with my father in the starring role. It's going to be a huge night for them both.

"I answered you," I lie to him, and he leans back on the granite counter. "It's not my fault you rented Buckingham Palace." I look around the ridiculous kitchen the size of my whole condo back in Chicago. "I got lost going to the bathroom"—I grab another spoonful of cereal—"in my bedroom."

He shrugs as he takes another pull from the water bottle. "Why are you eating now?" He looks over at the stove to check the time. "We're leaving in an hour and a half, and there will be food at your brother's house."

"You act like I've never been to a Hollywood shindig before." I take another bite full of the granola cereal. "It's always the same thing: little pieces of food that no one eats because they will look like they are bloated on the red carpet." My father has been a sought-after action actor since before I was born. My parents met on one of those press tours. From what I read and was told, they hated each other until, well, they didn't.

"Have you met Gabriella and her family?" He chuckles as he puts the bottle of water down. "They could give a shit. They ordered enough food to feed an army." Gabriella has been dating my brother for a little over a year, maybe even two. They actually dated for eight months before he was a dipshit and did her dirty. Finally, he pulled his head out of his ass and went to get her back. Some may say she is a doormat, but you love who you love, and no one should judge someone else's relationship.

"You might be right," I agree but finish the cereal.

"There you two are," my mother states, entering the kitchen. "The hair and makeup people are ready for us." She walks over to my father and wraps her arms around his waist as he slips an arm over her shoulders. "How are you feeling?"

"Good," he replies, but I can see he's a bit nervous.

"The movie is amazing. I think people are going to really enjoy it."

"Now that's the supportive dad we all love." I point my spoon at him before I finish the cereal and walk over to the sink to rinse out the bowl and place it in the dishwasher. "Shall we go and glam ourselves?" I wink at my mother. She smiles up at my father, then kisses his lips.

"I'll call Romeo and see if he's okay," my father tells my mother, and I internally groan. "It's his big day."

"He's a big boy," I remind him, walking to the fridge to grab a water bottle before making my way out of the kitchen toward the massive entryway and to the winding steps to go upstairs.

"Caw, caw," I call as my voice echoes through the house, and my mother laughs behind me as she follows me up there.

"Mom, seriously." I look over my shoulder. "This is a bit ridiculous." I wave my hand around the house.

"It's because we're having everyone over here after the movie," she informs me, and I gasp.

"What do you mean by everyone?"

She finally reaches the second-floor landing, pushing me to the bedroom where they have set up the glam station. "To celebrate the big day, we thought it would be better to do the party here rather than go to some restaurant and not have any privacy. You know how the paparazzi can be."

"So, like, all of the million family members Gabriella has?" I have to say I love her family, but you really need name tags on people. Also, every time you look around, someone else is pregnant or just had a baby. I think one of her cousins even has like six or seven kids.

"That would be correct." She taps my nose like she did when I was younger. "Now, let's get ready."

I sit in the chair next to my mother as someone starts on my hair, and then I close my eyes when the makeup people begin. "What color is your dress?"

"Black," I reply, "like my soul."

"Ryleigh," my mother hisses.

"Just keeping it real." I giggle a bit. "I want my makeup as natural as you can make it." I open one eye, and the girl nods at me. "Just make sure the circles under my eyes are covered, and I look semi human." An hour passes and no one says anything until we are both done. I open my eyes, seeing my makeup in soft tones of pink and gold, and my hair is slicked back but loose, exactly how I wanted it. "I look fierce," I declare, turning to the side to see how the back of my hair looks.

"Go get into the dress," the hairdresser tells me, "and then we'll put the final touches on you."

With a nod, I leave the room and go to my bedroom, where the black dress hangs in the closet. Slipping out of my skirt and top, I grab the black lace thong pinned on another plush hanger in little clips, and I have to laugh at the craziness of my real life back home in Chicago compared to this. Back home, my closet is half this size, and all my panties are in a drawer together. Once my thong is on, I glide the lace dress off the hanger before stepping into it. I slide my arms through the delicate lace

16

sleeves that fit snugly on my upper arm and then widen from the elbow all the way down to over my fingernails, which are also painted black. I reach to the back to zip up the zipper to the waist before I walk out of the room and head to get help. I stop at my parents' closed door, knocking once. "I need help with the zipper. Are you two decent?"

"Yes!" my mother shouts from behind the closed door. Even though she said yes, I still poke my head in before opening it and seeing no one is in the room. I find them in the walk-in closet.

"Hi," I say, spotting my father zipping up my mother's black gown. She looks over at me and puts her hand to her chest. "I need help."

"Um." My father looks at me for a second. "Um, the front."

"Yes." I smile at him. I look at the front that plunges down to my navel in a V. "Isn't it pretty?" I turn around. "Can you zip the back?"

"Why is there more material on the back than the front?" he mumbles as he zips up the see-through lace that covers the back.

I turn to check in the mirror to get the final look. The top has the illusion that it's nude under the bodice, but there is a skin-colored material, so I'm not showing off the girls. It goes tight at the waist and around the hips until it kicks off mermaid style. "I've seen this dress before."

"I hope you have." I turn to him. "I took it from Mom's closet."

"Oh my God." He puts his hand in front of his mouth. "Yes."

"I hope it's not the one she wore when she caught you having sex with someone in the bathroom." I wink at my mom while my dad hisses.

"I didn't touch her." He holds his hands up. "I would never do that."

"Was it the dress she was wearing when she caught you holding hands with your co-star?" I tease him some more.

"Stop reading the fucking tabloids." He walks over to his black suit jacket and snatches it off the hanger.

"I didn't read that in the tabloids. Mom told me." His head whips around to look at my mother.

"What?" She cocks her hip out to the side and folds her arms over her chest. "She asked me how we met." She raises her hand in the air, waving it. "And I had wine!" she shrieks, turning to pretend that it's not a big deal. "We were bonding."

"Yeah, she told me all the details." I fake gag. "You attacking her in the elevator after you made out with that girl."

"I didn't touch her." He points at me. "She was all over me like an octopus." He pulls out his cuffs as he arranges his jacket. "Besides, I only had eyes for your mother."

"Is that why you called your co-star to fuck it out?" I mimic my mother, cocking my hip out.

"Is nothing sacred?" He raises his eyebrows at my mother. "Did she tell you there was that one reporter who was all over her ass?" My father points at my mother, and I cough, trying not to laugh.

"Um, yeah, and how you got so jealous that you were, like, peeing all over her leg but still tried to bang your co-star." I shake my head. "Anyway, it's time to go. I have to get my shoes and do last-minute touch-ups on my lips."

I run back to my room to grab the black heels, purse, and a little bag that holds a pair of flip-flops for after the red carpet. We take about twenty minutes to get on the party bus and make our way over to Gabriella and Romeo's house.

The driveway has an insane number of party buses parked in it. "This is going to be a circus."

"Yup," my father agrees. "Try to be nice."

I gasp. "I'm a ray of fucking sunshine," I say, walking out of the party bus and toward the house. I don't bother ringing the doorbell because there is no way they are running around naked with a million people in their house. They own two homes—one here and one in Dallas, where they live the majority of the time.

Stepping into the foyer, I stop when I see all the men in Gabriella's family standing in suits. It's like one giant *GQ* shoot. Best of all, they're unaware of how hot they are. "Hi." I wave to everyone. "Got to use the restroom," I lie, running to the bathroom in the back of the house.

I stop in my tracks, literally, when I see him walk out of the bathroom I was going to use. He looks down for a second before he looks up at me. A smirk fills his face, making a certain part of me pulse. Fucking Stone

Richards in all his fucking glory. Wearing a blue suit, as if he wears one every single day instead of sweaty hockey equipment, his brown eyes sparkle in the lights that are on in the house, along with the sun coming in through the window. He doesn't even try to hide the way he checks me out, his eyes roaming me from head to fucking toe. "Hey there, gorgeous."

"Ryleigh," I remind him, trying not to show him that he's gotten to me.

"I know your name." He stops in front of me, looking down at me, and it's just like the first time I met him a year ago. The pull to him was something I've never felt before. It was also the stupidest thing that's ever happened to me.

"Then use it." I walk around him toward the bathroom before I do something dumb like grab him by his lapels and pull his mouth down to mine. I'm about to close the bathroom door when he stops it with his hand. "What in the world?" I question as he walks into the bathroom. "What the hell are you doing?"

"Research, gorgeous," he mutters, turning me so my back is against the bathroom door as he shuts it with his left hand over my head and his right hand locking the door.

"And what research is that?" My chest rises and falls as he steps even closer to me, almost pressing his chest against mine.

"It's better if I show you." His hands grip my face. "So much better if I show you."

I make the mistake of opening my mouth to tell him

to step back. Instead, his tongue slides into my mouth as his lips crash onto mine. My body doesn't listen to my head. My head screams at him to back away, but my body arches into him. My hands grip his lapels as my eyes flutter closed. His hands move from my face to my hips, pulling me toward him, and I feel his hard cock on my stomach. I moan as my tongue rolls around his, and he moves his head to the right side, taking the kiss deeper.

We hear voices right outside the door and then the jiggle of the handle, but he doesn't let go of my mouth. His eyes fly open and so do mine. Looking into my eyes, he continues to kiss me. He moves his tongue around mine, not even caring our families are right outside this door. To make matters worse, I don't care either. I couldn't care less. Actually, if he set me on the counter and fucked me, I don't think I would mind. His tongue plays with mine as he stares into my eyes. It's the most erotic thing I think I've ever done. The voices move away from the door, and he lets go of my lips once the steps have faded away. "Fucking gorgeous," he says as if he didn't just kiss the shit out of me. As if I wasn't just going to beg him to fuck me. As if this one fucking kiss didn't rock my world. "I knew it."

As my heart hammers in my heaving chest, I ask, "What did you know?"

"Two things," he says, loosening the hold he has on my hips and cupping my ass slightly before he lets go of me. My own hands let go of his lapels as he steps away. "One, your eyes turn green when you get pissed or turned on." He holds up his index finger. "And two, your lip gloss is still shiny." His smirk fills his face, and I hate that it actually makes me even more wet.

"Well, I've learned two things also." I push away from him even though I want to pull him back. "One, you're a cocky one." I hold my own finger up. He chuckles, lifting his hand to his lips to wipe the gloss off them, but nothing is there. "And two, you suck at kissing." Once I step out the door, I look around to ensure no one is there.

I shut it at the same time I hear him laugh. "You really have to up your lying game, gorgeous."

Not one to not have the last word, I reopen the door as I see him smooth down his jacket. "Again, it's Ryleigh," I repeat before I close the door again to make sure I have the last word.

I make my way into the foyer where everyone slides into the back of the room. As Gabriella and Romeo walk down the stairs, people start to move out of the foyer toward the front door. I smile up at her, pretending I'm fine, and I didn't just have the hottest make-out session in her bathroom. Since she's gotten back together with Romeo, we've become really close. Actually, I'm close to most of her cousins also, and even went on a girls' trip with them not too long ago.

I step forward to stand next to my father and feel a hand on my left side as the touch sweeps across my lower back. The touch almost makes me shiver as I look over my shoulder to see who it is. "Sorry, gorgeous." Stone smiles at me as he walks past and follows everyone out the front door. I watch him go, not moving from the spot

I'm in. It's almost as if I have cement in my shoes.

"Are you ready?" my father says, and I turn to look at him. "You okay?"

No. I shut my mouth before the word comes out. Instead, I smile and put on my game face. Stone Richards just started a game I plan on winning—if I even decide to play. "I'm more than okay." I smooth down my dress. "Let's do this."

THREE

STONE

Six Months Later

"YO!" CHRISTOPHER YELLS from the other side of the house. "The car will be here in fifteen minutes."

"I'm putting on my jacket!" I shout back at him as I slide on my black suit jacket. I pull the cuffs from the black shirt out before slipping on my black shoes. Taking one more look at myself in the mirror, I push back my hair to the side. I spray my cologne on one side, then the other, before I walk out of the bedroom. "I'm downstairs!" I shout to Christopher's door right before he steps out wearing a black suit with a white shirt and a black bow tie.

"I'm coming," he assures me as both of our phones ping at the same time. "I hate wearing ties." He pulls at his collar. "I feel like I'm being strangled."

"Batcall," we both say at the same time, looking at each other as I take out my phone from my inside jacket pocket while Christopher holds his in his hand.

Uncle Matthew Sr.: *Holy shit, Romeo just won an Oscar.*

It's followed by a picture of Romeo on the stage talking.

"Holy shit," Christopher says, "the motherfucker did it."

"It was a great movie," I remind him, looking over at him as we walk into the kitchen. I go straight to the fridge for a water bottle, my shoulder hurting me as I reach out. "Tweaked my fucking shoulder."

Christopher laughs. "That's what happens when you try to show off."

"You hip-checked me into the boards." I point at him as I take a pull of the water.

"It was a soft tap. Don't be such a pussy." He looks back down at his phone when another ping comes in.

"What were the chances that the All-Star Game was in Vegas at the same time as the award ceremony, giving everyone three days off after?" The All-Star Game was a highlight for the fans and some of the players. They choose the best of the best to come out and play together. Out of everyone in the family, Christopher and I were the only ones who were there. Dylan, Tristan, and Xavier all opted out of going to spend time with the family. I guess if I had my own kids and stuff, I would have opted out of it also. As soon as the game was done, we hopped on a plane and headed to L.A.

"I want to say it was a coincidence, but knowing Uncle Matthew, he probably had a talk with someone." Our uncle is the biggest name in the hockey world. He was once GM for New York, but then his father-in-law gave him the team, so he's now the owner. He has his hand in many pots, and talk around the league is he is in negotiations to purchase another team, but we aren't sure which one. He has his eyes on a couple, and he mentioned even going to the West Coast.

"Car is here." Christopher looks up from his phone, his face now filled with a bit of worry.

I nod at him, heading toward the door of our rented condo. "On a scale of one to ten, how freaked do you think Gabriella will be once he tells her they're getting married tonight?"

"That depends," Christopher starts, "if she's had some wine, she might be okay. If she's nervous, I'm going to go with he doesn't stand a chance. It's a toss-up, really."

He gets in the back seat of the car and pulls up his phone to FaceTime Abigail. She answers after one ring and looks like she's rushing. "What do you want?"

"Is that any way to talk to your older brother?" he asks, pretending to be shocked.

"And your favorite cousin." I stick my head into the frame, seeing Abigail, and it looks like she's been crying. "Why are you crying?" I ask, worried.

"Oh my God, did she say no?" Christopher asks. "We're still having the party, right?"

"What is wrong with you?" I gawk at him.

"I'm hungry, and if I know my parents and also Romeo's parents, they ordered a feast tonight," he explains.

"She said yes, obviously," Abigail relays. "We are on

our way over to the house."

"Good," Christopher says. "We're on our way there also."

"See you there." She hangs up before we ever say goodbye.

I pull up my Instagram, going to check and see what I missed. There are posts from the all-star game, but then I see a post from Abigail. It's a picture of her and Tristian all dressed up, and when I swipe right, I spot her. Ryleigh. The woman who I've been secretly, and not so secretly, crushing on since I met her. I've seen her twice, and both times have been surreal. Especially the last time I saw her. My plan was to ask her out, maybe even flirt with her. What happened was so much better. Spotting her right when I came out of the bathroom was a sign I should do more. The fucking dress was a man's wet dream. Her pale skin looked like it felt like velvet if you touched it. It drove me wild. It was sexy and classy at the same time, and my cock sprang up even before I touched her. Pushing my way into the bathroom and making out with her was hands down the best thing I've ever done in my life. Fuck, did she drive me crazy. I could spend the day just fucking kissing her, and I'd be a happy man. She's wearing her black hair pulled back, and her bangs pulled to the side. Her eyes have more makeup on than I've seen her in before, and they now look a deep green. But my eyes roll down her outfit. This time, she went with a sleeveless lilac-colored dress. The straps at her shoulders look like they're a bunch of material, but my eyes go to her tits, which look like there's a trace of lace sticking out. Then they roam down to her waist, where it appears she's wearing a belt, but it's fabric. The bottom seems like it's full of material, but then it looks like lace underneath. I have no idea what it is, but I can't wait to get my hands on it.

"You've been looking at the picture for over five minutes now," Christopher observes. "Should I leave the two of you alone for a second when we get to the house?"

"Isn't she fucking gorgeous?" I turn the phone toward him, ignoring what he just said.

"Um," he says, "if I say yes, you'll punch me. If I say no, you'll punch me. So I'm not answering that."

"Fair enough." I laugh. "Also, if I see you even looking at her…"

"You think I need you on my ass?" He points at me. "And what's even funnier"—he laughs—"you think Romeo isn't going to kick your ass?" He shakes his head. "Better yet, you think she is going to want to date you?"

I think about the way she looked when I kissed her. "I think I can be very persuasive."

"Remember, no means no." He tilts his head to the side as we pull up to the house, but we're stopped by security.

"Um, guys," the driver says, "they aren't letting me in. They say you need a password."

"A password?" Christopher says. "I'm the brother of the bride."

"I don't think that's a password," I mumble to him as two guys dressed in black stand on both sides of the car.

The driver talks to one of the security guards, who

just shakes his head. I take my phone, calling Uncle Matthew, who answers after one ring. "Let me guess." I can hear him laughing. "You didn't read the invitation, so you don't know the password."

"One," I begin, "what invitation? I was told to be here at this time, and two, no." I look over at Christopher. "Did you get an invitation?"

"Since when does our family dish out invitations?" he says.

"It's Stone," Uncle Matthew shares, "and before you think it's for you, it's not."

"Stone," I tell the driver, who tells security. He nods his head and presses a button to have the black gate open.

"Have I mentioned I'm not a fan of Hollywood?" I say to Christopher.

"If you're going to marry Ryleigh, get used to it," he jokes, getting out of the car as soon as we stop.

"Let's not go that far." I side-eye him. "I have to get her to date me first, don't you think?" I get out of the car, expecting the same commotion as every family event we've attended, but instead, it's calm. "Are we at the right address?" I ask, looking around and not seeing one person I know here.

"I was thinking the same thing," Christopher replies as we walk in the front door. The spiral staircase hits you right away, along with the chandelier. The banister has what seems like a million flowers around it.

Two servers hold silver trays with glasses of champagne. "Sir," the one on my side offers, but I hold my hand up at him. I might have a beer here and there during the season, but I stay pretty clean. "Thank you."

"It's bad luck not to drink champagne at a wedding." I look to the side, seeing my mother standing with the woman of my dreams. She smirks at me before she sips the champagne from the glass in her hand.

"Is that really a fact?" Christopher asks, kissing my mother on her cheek, then turning to Ryleigh. My hands fist at my sides as I wait to see what he's going to do. He smirks at me, and I know he's going to lean in and kiss her, but instead, he just nods. "Congratulations on the big day."

"I would say thank you," she replies, "but it has nothing to do with me and everything to do with Romeo and my dad." You can see her eyes light up with pride as she says it. "I'm just happy she said yes or else this would have been an awkward reception."

"In our family," I say, kissing my mother's cheek, "once you live with a man, you've already said yes." I turn to her, and unlike Christopher, I reach out and put my hand on her waist. I can see her eyes go big as I lean down and kiss her cheek. The almost silent gasp makes me smile even more. I've got to keep her on her toes. "It would just take a bit of convincing." I move my hand from her waist, sliding it softly down to her ass, wanting to cup one of her cheeks in my hand.

"Or," Christopher adds, trying not to laugh, "he'd just drag her there."

"Would you two stop it?" My mother shakes her head. "You're scaring Ryleigh."

"Something tells me that she doesn't scare easy,"

Christopher mumbles. "Now, I'm off to find my parents and then the groom so I can, you know, give him the big talk."

"What big talk?" my mother asks him.

"The 'don't fuck with my sister or I'll break your face,'" Christopher deadpans, "and I'll bring Uncle Max with me since he's a monster."

"Good luck with that," I tell him as he walks away.

"I'm going to find your father," my mother says as if she knows I want to be alone with Ryleigh. "Just to make sure he doesn't want in on that big talk." She puts her hand on my arm. "You take care of Ryleigh."

"Oh, I will," I assure her as she walks away, then I turn back to the woman of my dreams. "I'll try at least," I mumble. She tilts her head to the side, and I see that she's tipsy. "You look gorgeous, by the way." My hand reaches out for her hip, seeing the lace ruffles up close.

"Thank you," she says, trying not to look at me. She looks off to the side as she finishes her glass of champagne.

"I've been thinking about you," I tell her honestly, and her eyebrows shoot up. "In fact, I can't get you off my mind."

"The last time I saw you was six months ago." She holds the top of the empty champagne glass by her fingertips, letting it swing back and forth. "A lot can change in six months."

"So you've been thinking about me also, then?" I put my hands in my pockets before I drag her to one of the bedrooms upstairs and mess her up.

"All day, every day," she states, "and twice on Sunday. I've sat in my office and doodled your name and hearts ever since."

I can't help but laugh at her joke. "So you've thought about going out with me?"

"Yes, I've thought of nothing else to be honest and…" She nods her head. "I've decided that it's going to happen when donkeys help pigs fly."

"So soon, then?" I ignore what she just said, taking one hand out of my pocket and putting it on the side of her neck, my thumb rubbing the vein where I can feel her heart beating.

"Oh, yeah, so soon." Her eyes stare into mine as she licks her lips, and it would take nothing to bend my head and slip my tongue into her mouth.

But it's not the time and place. Today is about Gabriella. But one thing I know, I'm not waiting another six months. "Okay, good. I'll call you," I say as I bend and kiss the corner of her lips before walking away.

FOUR

THE KNOCKING MAKES me open my eyes, but it's the biggest mistake I have ever made. The room is as bright as if someone is standing there with a spotlight straight in my face, and I'm sure everything spins. "Are you decent?" I hear my mother's voice as the door opens. I plan on answering her, but a slew of cotton balls sits on my tongue, and all I can do is groan. "Well, now." I hear her voice coming a bit closer. "Why is every single light in the room on?" I don't know what she does, but I can feel the room go from bright to dark. "Oh my God, are you still in your dress?"

"Mom." I try to swallow. "I have something in my mouth." My mother comes over to my bed and the side of the bed dips down.

"I brought you water," she says, and I open my eyes. In my head, I'm moving, but in reality, I'm still lying on my stomach. The only thing moving are my eyelids.

"Can you pour it in my mouth?" I ask her and she just

laughs as I open my mouth, but lying on my side.

She puts the glass of water down on the side table. "Do you want me to help you turn over?"

"No." I nod yes. "I think I can do it."

"You want another shot?" She winks at me and all I can do is glare at her, or in my head I'm glaring at her. In reality, one eye is closed.

"Why do you hate me?" I moan as I try to get up on my elbows, but I slip and then fall back down, face-first into the pillow. I take a deep inhale before I turn on my side. "My head is…" I try to think of the word but nothing comes to my mind because all I can do is hear a buzzing sound.

"I have this for you also." She holds up the bottle of ibuprofen for me.

"You love me." I open and close my mouth, trying to swallow down the little pieces of sand I think are in my mouth.

I scoot my butt back until I sit with my back against the headboard, and only then do I reach out to grab the water. She opens the bottle and hands me two pills, and before I put them in my mouth, I take a sip of water. "It tastes like tequila." My face scrunches up. "I don't want this." I hand the glass back to my mother and then start to rub my tongue to get the taste off it.

"It's not tequila," she snaps. "You probably still have the taste on your tongue."

I side-eye her, thinking she could be right. "Fine." I grab the pills. "I'm putting my faith in you." I place them on my tongue before taking another sip of water. "You were telling the truth!" I gasp. "Why did you let me drink so much?" I ask, and she laughs at me.

"I told you to drink water," she reminds me. "The rule of the game is one glass of booze, then one glass of water."

"There was no water anywhere," I inform her, and her eyes about fly out of her head.

"There were bottles of water everywhere." She points at me. "You were too busy being the life of the party."

"It's not my fault I'm the fun one of the bunch." I take another sip of water. I was doing whatever I could to try to stay away from Stone. So obviously, partying with his sister and cousins seemed like a better plan than sitting down at the table gawking at him all night long. "What time did we come back?"

"Your father carried you in at four."

"What?" I sit up. "We were going to watch the sunrise." I look around for my phone, the fear now setting in. "I lost my phone." I look at the side table. "Oh my God."

"Is this your phone?" my mother asks when she reaches toward the edge of the bed, next to an iPad, and pulls up my phone.

"Yes," I breathe a sigh of relief. "I just dodged a bullet."

"Whose iPad is that?" I ask, and she laughs.

"That's how you turn the lights on and off," she tells me, picking up the iPad and showing me by opening the curtains.

"Oh, I think I remember that." I recall a memory of last night, getting up to get undressed but then I must have fallen back asleep.

"I'm just happy you were in bed." She gets up off the mattress.

"When we brought you in, you went to bed on the floor." She points over to where my bag is, my clothes thrown all around it. "We asked you to get up, but you just said you were fine where you were." She shrugs. "So we just left you."

"Oh, good, you're up." My father comes into the room wearing gym shorts and a backward cap on his head, his chest is all wet. "The plane leaves in two hours." He looks at me.

"Why are you wet?" I ask.

"I went running," he tells me, and I just stare at him. "What is that smell?"

I lift my arm. "Probably me."

"Okay, let's get you up and in the shower," my mother urges. "Unless you can stay longer."

"No." I shake my head. "I have to be back in the office tomorrow." I move out of bed, but it takes me like five minutes because I have to stop twice.

"What a wedding," I declare, looking at my parents. "Thank God she said yes. Can you imagine?" I shake my head when I finally put my feet on the carpet. "What were you guys going to do?"

"She wasn't going to say no." My father is quick to say, "She loves him."

"I don't know why, but who am I to judge? In my last relationship, he was more interested in his cat cam than me standing there naked. I was doing cartwheels, and he was 'look at my cat.'" I shake my head. "He should have looked at this cat." I point at my vagina.

"La-la-la-la-la." My father puts his fingers in his ears. "There are things I don't want to know."

"Dad, I'm a single woman in my prime," I remind him. "This is when I'm supposed to make mistakes."

"Yes," my mother adds, "make the mistakes, but can we also talk about Stone?" I stop moving and look over at her.

"What?" I pretend not to know what she's talking about. "Who?"

"Oh, please." My mother rolls her eyes at me. "The man who followed you around all night, making sure you didn't fall on your face."

I put my hand to my chest, the pounding in my head moving to my rib cage. "No, he wasn't." I shake my head. "He was following Zoey around."

"Sure, if you say so." She appeases me, smiling before she walks over to my dad, grabbing his hand.

"You and Stone?" my father says, shocked. "I didn't even know you knew him."

"I don't." I hold up my hands. "I've met him twice." I avoid looking at their eyes. "Now can I shower, please?"

"I'll bring you coffee," she says, and I smile at her.

"You're the best mom in the whole world," I say. "If Dad ever hooks up with another girl, we'll put shrimp shells in the curtain rods."

"Good God," my father moans, then looks at my mother with a stern look on her face. "Why would you tell her that?"

"There is nothing wrong." She smiles up at him and

gets on her tippy-toes to kiss his lips. "We ended up together."

"Thank God for that." I hold up my hand. "And to think, I was the fastest swimmer." Throwing my other hand in the air, I spout off, "I think I'm still drunk."

"You think?" my father mocks me before he turns and walks out of the room with my mother.

I walk over to the bathroom and painfully, ever so painfully, get in the shower. I have to sit down midway just to get my bearings for a bit, and I think I even nap. Needless to say, when the car comes to pick me up two hours later, I still feel drunk.

Kissing my parents goodbye, I head to the car. I'm wearing gray sweatpants that are tight at the ankle and a white T-shirt. My hair is in a ponytail, and I stole a baseball hat from my father while sunglasses block out the light. I don't even bother conversing with the driver like I normally do. Instead, I sit with my head back and my eyes closed. When we get to the private plane, I get out and grab my purse and backpack, then walk up the four steps. "Welcome, Ms. Beckett," the flight attendant greets me.

"Hi," I mumble, trying not to sound like I'm dying, but I think I actually am. I walk over to the couch on the plane and sit down. "Is it okay if I lie down?" I ask, and she nods.

"Your father sent this," she offers, taking out a brown bag, and you can see the grease stains on it. "A double cheeseburger and fries."

"I love him." I hold out my hand to her. "He's the best

dad in the world."

I pull out my phone and I'm about to text him when I see my lock screen is a picture of Gabriella and Romeo with all of us around them. I'm standing next to Romeo, holding his arm, and Stone stands beside me, his hand on my hip, while he smiles at the camera. I have to say he has to be the hottest one in the bunch, and that's saying something. I open it and text my father.

Me: *You're the best dad in the world. I don't care what anyone else says.*

Opening the bag and grabbing the burger, I decide to go through my camera roll. I groan as soon as I see the first picture of me trying to take a selfie with someone. It's blurry, and all that's there is my shoulder. I swipe and see a bunch taken on the dance floor. I have to give it to Gabriella's family—they can party. Everyone was there, and, by that, I mean everyone; not one person from the family was missing. It was enormous and overwhelming and, at the same time, so fucking amazing. The love they have for each other is hands down something you see in movies and think it can't be real, but it is. Swiping, I see there is one with me in it, and I don't even know what move I was doing. But I was holding my dress up in my hands, and I'm squatting with my bare feet. I take a bite of the burger at the same time the plane door closes, and I see I've taken a candid snapshot of Stone.

He's standing with his cousins, Christopher—who sent the tie flying through the air the minute he sat down for dinner, we have yet to find it—Dylan, Michael, Mini Cooper; who I think is forty-five but they still call him

Mini Cooper even though he has like eight kids. The four of them are telling a story, and all of them are laughing. I think I only meant to take a picture of Stone, but I captured this one instead. The next one is the one that stops me. It's a picture of Stone and me. I vaguely remember taking it. It was the one time I let myself get close to him. He put his hands around my waist and pulled me to him. I can still feel his hand on my hip while he kissed my temple.

I turn off the phone, not wanting to read more into it. I'm not this woman who sits around waiting for her Prince Charming. That is so not me. In fact, it's the opposite of me. Growing up in Hollywood taught me a couple of life lessons, which means I learned very young that people always have two sides to them: the one they show the world, and the one they really are. I also learned everyone always has an ulterior motive for being your friend or even being around you. I was, after all, Tyler Beckett's daughter. At first, I thought I was cool—you know, all the kids pointing at you when your dad came to school. I mean, don't get me wrong, I went to a school where all the celebrity kids went, but—as you know—there is always a pecking order in Hollywood. I can count on one hand how many people I'm actually close to from my life in Hollywood. I also knew I would be going away for college as soon as I entered high school; the only question was where I would go. I busted my ass to make sure my GPA was the highest it could be because I also knew that I wanted to major in pre-law. The thrill of arguing with someone and winning got me every single time. After I took the LSAT and received a top score, I had my choice of law schools and I decided to attend Yale Law School. I want to say my last name didn't help, but I would be lying. Knowing I wanted to eventually become a district attorney, I knew that I had to go above and beyond and I exceeded those expectations. I'm currently one of the top ADAs—assistant district attorney—in my department in Chicago, and I help prosecute criminals. I'm busting my ass so I can eventually become a district attorney. I did an internship in Chicago, and it was love at first sight. I loved everything about it from the minute I landed in the city. It was like I was born to live there.

"Would you like something to drink?" the flight attendant asks, and I nod.

"Can I have a bottle of water, please?" I ask, and she returns carrying a silver tray with a bottle of water and a glass. "I don't need the glass, thank you." I grab the bottle of water, opening it and finishing half of it before I put it aside and decide to close my eyes.

The next thing I know, we're landing. I open my eyes and stretch before standing. "Your jacket and boots are waiting," the flight attendant says.

"Bye-bye, palm trees. Hello, reality," I mumble, slipping off my sneakers and putting them in my backpack before sliding my feet in my winter boots and then slipping on my big parka jacket. The door opens, and the wind gusts in. "If that doesn't say Windy City, I don't know what does."

She laughs as I walk down the stairs. I make sure one hand holds on to the railing as I head to the waiting black SUV. Something my parents arranged because if it was me, I would be flying coach and hitting up an Uber when I got back. The back door is open for me, so I climb in, then wait for my luggage to be loaded into the trunk.

My phone vibrates in my pocket, so I take it out, seeing a message from Gabriella.

Gabriella: *Thank you for being part of our special day. Also I'm so bummed I didn't see you before you left. Call me later, sister. I can say that now because I'm married to your brother.*

I laugh at the last part.

Me: *There is no one better for him than you. Actually, you might be too good for him. I hope you made him sign a prenup.*

I add a winky face before pressing send and putting my phone away when he starts to drive. I look out the window, seeing a foot of snow was somehow dumped from the time I left on Wednesday until I got back five days later. Wheeling my luggage into the front door of my apartment building is so much fun, especially with the world's largest hangover.

When I make my way into the lobby of the building, the heat hits me right away. I stomp off the snow from the bottom of my boots before heading to the elevator. The building only has four floors, and if it was up to me—and I didn't have my luggage—I would take the stairs, but I need every ounce of strength in my body to make it to my apartment.

Huffing as I unlock the big silver door, I push it open before I step in. I turn the lights on before kicking my boots off at the front door. Putting my suitcase in the corner, I decide I'll tackle that this weekend. My backpack falls on the floor with a clunk before I take off my coat and hang it on the coatrack right beside the door. I grab my telephone from the pocket before I make my way from the front door into the open-concept loft apartment. Well, it was completely open concept, but we put up walls for the bedrooms. It was an old factory building right by the water that was converted into condos. It was the only thing I accepted from my parents. According to my father, it was an investment. It was the one fight I let him win, but I drew the line there. I paid for everything else even though it irked him not to take care of me.

I'm walking to my bedroom when my phone beeps in my hand. I look down and see I've gotten an Instagram notification. But I stop in my tracks when I see it's from Stone Richards.

My fingers swipe up as the phone scans my face, and then I open the app, pressing the corner where the messages are.

I have a bunch of messages I'm ignoring, and he's at the top. It shows the green dot next to his picture, which is of him in his uniform looking straight into the camera. I press his name and see the gray text.

What is your type, and why is it me?

I can't help but snort at his cocky fucking message. I'm about to reply when the phone rings weirdly in my hand, and I see he's calling me from Instagram. What in the hell is this? I obviously accept it and put it to my ear, wondering if it works the same way as a phone call. "Hello?"

"Hey, gorgeous." His smooth voice sounds like he just woke up.

"Did you just call me on Instagram?" I ask, so confused about this.

"I did." He chuckles.

"I have so many questions." I walk over to my bed. "Number one, how can you just call someone on Instagram?"

"I'll answer all your questions." I hear the rustle of covers from his side of the phone. "One, you can't just call anyone. You need to be friends with them."

"I'm private." I climb onto my big king-size bed. I splurged big-time when it came to my sleep. I sink into the down comforter that feels like seven comforters in one. "And we aren't friends."

He laughs, and it sends shock waves through my body, landing straight in my vagina. "We became friends last night," he says, and I close my eyes, vowing to never drink again, "sort of."

"What do you mean sort of?" I should just end this conversation and be done with it, but instead, I prolong it, telling myself not to be rude.

"Well, I kind of took your phone to hold on to when you went to do some dance move or something." I lean my head back. "And I added myself."

"Wow," I reply, shocked, "so why are you calling me on Instagram instead of my phone?"

"I don't have your number," he admits, and now I'm the one howling with laughter.

"Wouldn't it have been easier to send you a text

message from my phone instead of adding me on Instagram?"

"Whoa," he says, and I can hear him walking, "that's an invasion of your privacy. If you're going to give me your number, then I'll use it." I hear the fridge door close. "This was the best option."

"I don't even think I can argue any point on that logic," I admit.

"Good," he responds, drinking something, "so are you going to give me your number?"

"No." I bite my lip, trying not to smile.

"You're going to go out with me?" He breathes out a deep breath, something that normally irritates me, but with him I get these little flutters, which now irritate me.

"No." I don't even give myself a moment to think about it.

"Okay, good." I can hear his smirk through the phone, and now my stomach flutters have moved down south. "It's a we'll see." I shake my head at his persistence. "I'll call you tomorrow, then." He doesn't even wait for me to reply before he hangs up.

I look at the phone, and it says call ended. I think about calling him back, but instead, I put my phone down. "He'll get bored soon enough," I tell myself. They always do when they realize my job comes before anyone. "Then it'll be just another memory."

FIVE

STONE

"MOVE YOUR ASS, Richards!" my coach, Darryl, yells from the other side of the rink as I hustle down the middle of the ice. "Pick it up!" I hear his words, but my whole body fucking aches. To say I'm dragging ass is the understatement of the year.

Jay, my left winger, passes me the puck from the side, and the whistle blows as soon as it touches the blade of my stick. "Offside, Richards." The coach points at my right foot that went over the blue line before I touched the puck.

I look down, seeing he's not wrong. "Motherfucker," I grumble. "Sorry, guys." I skate back over to the start of the drill we're doing this afternoon.

"Think you can not fuck this up?" James, my right winger, goads, but he's hiding a smirk. "I think I'm going to die out there," he huffs and puffs.

"You?" Jay says. "I spent five days on a beach drinking beer like it was water." He breathes out like a bull. "How does five days on a beach get you so out of shape?"

"I spent half the time on the ice, and I'm out of shape," I remind them. "It's the age."

"Fuck you," they say at the same time. "Let's fucking do this." I get down on my haunches with my hockey stick in both hands, leaning on my legs, waiting for the puck to be dropped.

"If you fuck this up," Jay declares, "you owe me five hundred dollars."

"Times two." James holds up his gloved hand with two fingers.

"I don't even know what you are betting," Gally, the second line centerman, adds on. He's in the same stance as me, but during practice, we face off against each other. "But if I have to do this again, I'm going to kick your ass, and you'll owe me, too."

I shake my head and focus on the puck in assistant coach Robby's hand. He spreads his feet to the sides, holding the puck out in the middle. I see it fall and swing into action, slapping it away from Gally and to Jay, just like the diagram the coach showed us twenty minutes ago. Part one of the play done, I skate around Gally, who I'm not sure lets me get around him or if I'm suddenly faster than I was before.

Jay passes the puck back to Benny, the defenseman, who then whips it back to Jay. I push toward the blue line, timing it, knowing Jay will send it back to me. The puck touches my blade at the right before I hustle into the zone and send it to James, who makes it past the defensive players in the zone just like the diagram shows.

Getting into my position right in front of the goalie, I block his view as the puck is passed from James to Jay to Benny, who whips it to the goalie who saves it, but I pick up the rebound once it bounces off his right leg and tip it over his left side where he isn't expecting it.

"Now, that's what I'm talking about!" the coach shouts, pointing his hockey stick at the net. "Good job, boys." He blows his whistle. "See you all tomorrow. Don't forget we head out for Chicago right after the game, and then we have a couple of days off. Try to rest up. Playoffs are coming, and we need all the points we can get." He blows the whistle twice, meaning practice is officially over.

Skating off the ice, I take off my right glove, tucking it under my left arm before unsnapping my helmet. "Well done, Stoney," Jay declares, picking up a green bottle and squirting water in his mouth as he waits for everyone else to get off the ice.

"I was not going to lose a thousand bucks." I stand on the other side of him, grabbing my own bottle and squeezing water into my mouth as I wait for the rush of people trying to get off the ice.

Once everyone but Jay and I have left the ice, we make our way down the red carpet toward the locker room. I place my stick along the outside of the wall with all the other sticks before walking in. Putting my gloves on top of the shelf with my name on it, I then add the helmet to it before taking off my jersey and tossing it in the bin in the middle of the room. I sit down and untie my skates. Sweat drips off my forehead as I finish getting undressed and head to the shower.

I shower in record time. The only thing on my mind is sliding into my bed and sleeping until tomorrow morning. The past two days, I think I've gotten maybe ten hours of sleep. We stayed up until I think seven o'clock the morning after the wedding. But I don't think I would have had it any other way. The wedding officially ended at four, but then all the cousins just went to one house, and we chilled. Laughing as we replayed parts of the wedding that were funny, we ordered six hundred dollars' worth of breakfast sandwiches and then rushed to catch the plane leaving at ten. I slept the whole five-hour flight back home, only waking when the wheels touched down. I was thankful my father had the good mind to book me a private flight back home.

Pulling up to my house, I swear I almost groan when I press the button and pull into one of the three garage doors. I park it right next to the black BMW.

I get out, pressing the button to close the door before walking to the side of the garage and entering my house through the bright-white mudroom. I kick off my running shoes before walking through the side door that leads to the kitchen.

I get one of my prepared meals out of the massive two-door stainless-steel fridge, then walk over to the oven and press the buttons to turn it on. Once it beeps, I get a tray to put it on. When I get home from practice, I usually hit my gym, but since my whole body feels broken, I'm skipping today. It'll probably be worse tomorrow, but I'll listen to my body for now. I walk past the big island in the middle of the room that leads to the family room. I go to grab the remote control to turn on the television hanging over the fireplace. When I moved in here, the house had no televisions, but I quickly rectified that. I had my cousins come over, and now every room in this house has a television.

The oven beeps at the same time as my phone makes a weird ringing sound. Pulling it out of my pocket as I walk back to the kitchen, I look down and see Ryleigh is calling me on Instagram. The smile fills my face as soon as I see her name, and then my cock stirs in my shorts.

I answer the call right away, putting her on speaker. "Hello, gorgeous."

"Did you send me chocolate?" she barks out, and I chuckle.

Opening the oven door, I put the tray in it before starting the timer for twenty minutes. "No." I laugh. "I sent you an array of chocolates. I didn't know what type of chocolate you liked, so I sent you milk chocolate, which is my favorite. I also sent you white chocolate and dark chocolate."

"Why?" she groans. "Why would you do that?"

"Because you're bitter and sweet." I pull out one of the gray-and-white cushioned stools. "And I want to take a bite out of you."

"How did you even get my address?" She ignores my comment about taking a bite out of her, but my cock suddenly is fully alert.

"I have my ways." I tap the counter with my finger. Also, Google did help. "Did you like my gift?"

"No," she huffs. "I hate chocolate."

I put my head back and laugh out loud. "You are such a beautiful liar. They had chocolate fondue at the wedding, and you told me chocolate was your weakness."

"I did not," she denies. "You can't take what a drunk woman says and use it against her."

"I didn't use it against you, gorgeous." My voice goes low. "I did it to make you smile."

"Well, it didn't." Her voice gets tight. "Goodbye." I'm about to say something when I see she hung up on me.

I send her a message instead.

Should we not exchange phone numbers?

The message shows in blue, and then I see the little writing on the bottom that says it's seen. It takes ten seconds before her message comes through.

We shouldn't even be following each other on Instagram. I should unfollow you right now.

Don't forget, gorgeous, I now know where you work.

Don't forget I know half of the police department here, so good luck showing up.

You'd bail me out.

I think you should try it and see.

Are you asking me to come see you?

Yes, I'm asking you to come see me so I can have you arrested for stalking.

Are you going to cuff me yourself?

Go away.

Call me later. 615-233-5674

Here is my number 9-1-1

I can't help but smile even bigger with her last

message. Instead of calling her back or messaging her, I call Christopher to see if he has any pointers he can give me.

I scroll down my favorites until I reach his name and press the FaceTime button. It rings three times before his face fills the screen.

He is facedown on his bed, his head leaning over the mattress. "Are you sleeping?"

"Dude," he groans and rolls to his back. "I feel like someone kicked every single bone in my body twice."

"I skipped my workout," I say because the one thing I do every single day is work out. During the off-season, I usually get in two workouts a day.

"You must be dying," he replies.

"I had practice this morning and got my ass chewed by my coach," I tell him as the timer goes off on the stove. "Jay and James said if I fucked up one more time, I would have to pay them money." He shakes his head at that. "I'm eating, and then I'm going to bed." Grabbing the oven glove, I take out the tray before grabbing a plate to put it on. "Hey, let me ask you. How do you get a girl to go out with you?"

"I usually use my words and say, 'hey, want to go out with me?'" I roll my eyes at his response.

"What if she says no, but she really means yes?" I ask, and he laughs.

"If she said no, chances are she really doesn't want to go out with you." He throws the covers off him as he gets up and walks out of his dark bedroom, the light from the windows making him squint his eyes.

"I think she does." I grab a fork and scoop a forkful of rice. "If she didn't want to go out with me, she wouldn't answer me."

"Who are you talking about?" he asks, opening his own fridge.

"Ryleigh," I say, and he just stares at me with big eyes.

"Are you insane? She's practically family. How are you going to date her? Then what?" he rapid-fires at me. "Then you have to see her at every family get-together." He shakes his head. "Why would you want to do that to yourself?"

"Well, for one, she's fucking gorgeous." I wait for him to say she isn't, and when he doesn't, I point my fork at the screen. "I'll slice under your feet."

"She's not my type," he informs me, and I almost believe him, "but go on, tell me why you want to date her."

"She's funny, she's smart, she's an amazing kisser." I stop talking when he gasps.

"You made out with her?" he asks. I didn't tell anyone because I wanted it to be just mine. "At the wedding?"

"No, sadly not at the wedding. The last time I saw her at the house, I cornered her in the bathroom, and, well, I couldn't not kiss her."

"Six months ago?" He laughs at me. "You made out with her six months ago, and now you want to date her?"

"Yeah," I say. "I'm guessing you have no advice to give me."

"I wouldn't have waited six fucking months to ask her out after I stuck my tongue in her mouth." He gawks at me while drinking.

"This was enlightening," I tell him, grabbing a couple of pieces of string beans. "I'm going to call Dad and see what he says."

"Let me know what he says about this." He shakes his head. "Six months." He hangs up on me, and I call Dad right away.

"Hey there," he answers after one ring. "What's up, kid?"

"Dad, you know I'm in my thirties, right?" I point out to him.

"Are you or are you not my kid?" he counters, and I'm not going to get into this discussion with him.

"Okay, well, I need advice, old great one," I say. "There is this girl I'm interested in."

"Go on." He smiles.

"What can I do to get her to go out with me?" I hold up my hand before he talks. "And before you say ask her, I already did."

"Well, when I wanted your mother to go out with me, I showed up at her work unannounced," he shares.

"And that was not a good idea," my mother chimes in from the background.

"Really?" My father looks over at her. "Did you not end up going out with me that night for pizza?"

"Technically, you drove me home and stayed," she states as my father shakes his head.

"She wanted me to stay."

"I almost stabbed you with a fork," she reminds him, and I can't help but bite my lip not to laugh at him as he glares at her.

"Okay, well, this is fun," I say in annoyance. "Thanks for all the advice."

"See what you did?" my father blames my mother, who snatches the phone from his hand.

"Honey." She looks at me. "Why don't you just tell her why you want to take her out."

"Just like that?" I stare at her.

"Just like that," she repeats, and I nod.

"Okay, I'll try that," I tell her. "Thanks, Mom. Love you guys." I hang up and pull up the Instagram message with her.

Hey, I'll be in your town in a couple of days, and I'd like to take you out. I can't stop thinking about you, and there is nothing I want more than to see you again. What do you say, gorgeous, go out with me?

SIX

RYLEIGH

I LOOK UP from the brief I'm reading when my phone pings with a message. When I grab the phone and see that it's Stone, I want to be annoyed, but my eyes read the message on my screen.

(Ryleigh Beckett) Stone Richards

Hey, I'll be in your town in a couple of days, and I'd like to take you out. I can't stop thinking about you, and there is nothing I want more than to see you again. What do you say, gorgeous, go out with me?

I shake my head and tap the back of my pen nervously on the brief I was reading in front of me. "That charming motherfucker," I mumble before I toss my phone to the side, not opening the message because then he'll see I've seen it.

I thought it was going to be another day in the office. But when Claudia, the receptionist, called to tell me I had a delivery, I was shocked. I never ever get deliveries unless it's food, but I didn't order anything. Instead, I was given a white box with a brown bow on it, and a white envelope tucked under with my name written in the middle of it. I literally had no idea what it was, and when I finally got back to my office and sat down, the first thing I did was untie the brown satin bow, pulling off the top of the white box. A brown paper was hiding what was underneath it, and when I saw it, I stopped moving—three rows of chocolate. Grabbing the envelope right away and pulling it open, I about fell off my damn chair.

These are only half as sweet as your lips.

Stone

I should have taken a moment to calm down before calling him, but well, I didn't. Instead of thinking it through and ignoring him, like I should have, I called him. That was a mistake, and I don't make mistakes. It was the main reason I was so good at my job. I thought calling him and telling him I didn't like his gift was a bright idea. It wasn't, especially since he knew I was lying. Instead of eating even one piece of chocolate, I got up and walked over to the communal kitchen and placed them on the table with a note: Please help yourself.

I came back in my office and didn't give him another thought until he texted me his number and I texted him back 9-1-1. I then put my phone down and focused on the case in front of me. Making notes, I tried not to think about the fact he didn't get back to me. Until now. Until his fucking message popped up, making my leg bounce.

"Hey." Kristal, another ADA, sticks her head in my door. "We still on for dinner tonight?" The two of us started here at the same time. We both came from different schools but clicked right away, especially since we were always the last ones to leave the office at night. One night, I had leftover pizza and took it over to her. She was knee-deep in a case, and I don't think she had left the office for two days at that point. The next day, she brought me a coffee, and from that day on, whenever we worked late, we usually shared dinner.

"Yes." I nod. "You still okay?"

"I'm just so over today," she answers. "It's like the most Monday Tuesday ever."

"Oh, dear." I tilt my head to the side. "Should we go now?"

"If you're free," she says. I nod, getting up and closing the file in front of me. I walk over to the brown messenger bag I took from my father's closet when I was in high school. It is so old there are little white lines in the leather from the scripts he used to put in it, back in the day. After I finish putting my files away, I walk over and slide my feet into my boots, putting my heels to the other side. I grab my big parka jacket, sliding it on and zipping it before grabbing my phone and slipping the crossbody messenger bag around my head, and walking to Kristal's office.

She's zipping up her own parka when I walk in. "Nothing says I'm sexy like wearing a parka," Kristal says breathlessly as she takes off her own parka.

"Chicago is a toss-up. We could be in spring jackets tomorrow," I say, "with rain boots, obviously."

The two of us walk out of the office and head down the street to the little bar/restaurant we like to eat at. I take off my jacket and hang it on the chair before I sit down. I push the oversized sleeves up on my cream-colored sweater and pull out the brown pub chair. As soon as I settle, the server comes over. "Good evening, ladies." He smiles at us. "My name is Steven, and I'll be your server tonight. Can I start you off with something to drink?"

"I'll have a glass of red wine." I look at Steven with a smile.

"I'll have a pinot grigio," Kristal says and he nods at us as he walks away. "I swear to God, when I'm done with this case, I'm taking a week off."

"A whole week?" I joke with her, knowing full well she'll take three days off and then die of boredom.

"Seven full days, six nights," she confirms, and I just look at her in shock. "I think I'll visit one of those places where they don't even have cell service."

"You mean jail?" I wink, and she laughs.

"That might not be such a bad idea if I wasn't afraid of being someone's bitch. Because, let's be honest, I would definitely end up being someone's bitch," she teases, smiling and tucking her bleached-blond hair behind her ear. "Just the thought—" she says but then stops when the server comes over with our wine. She waits a couple of seconds for him to walk away before she continues. "Anyway, what's up with you? How was the wedding?" She takes a sip of her wine. "Forget that, how was the freaking Oscars?" She shakes her head. "And in that freaking dress."

Taking my own sip of wine, I answer. "It was surreal that both of them won," I say, proud of the two of them.

"If either of them was going to win, I was rooting for my brother."

"So nice." She smiles. "So the wedding, umm, hello. Who were all those hot-ass men in your pictures?"

"Um." I take a sip of wine or maybe it's a gulp. "Gabriella's family is mostly hockey players."

"Ohhh." She smirks. "Sign me up for one of those." I laugh nervously. "I need all the tea."

"Well," I start, and she hits the table with her hand, her mouth open, "I might have…" I think about how to word this. "A couple of months ago, I made out with one of them."

"Excuse me?" Now her eyes go as big as her mouth that is still hanging open.

"Stone Richards," I say his name, and I get a pulse in two places, my stomach and my vagina. Not sure if I'm going to be sick of him or if I want him to fuck me.

"Please hold." She holds up her hand while she grabs her phone and pulls up Instagram. I see her fingers move across the phone and think this is a good time for me to finish my glass of wine. "Um," she hums, turning the phone around to show me. It's a picture of him on vacation, I think. His hands are in his hair, and water runs down his face. His eyes are the warmest brown I've ever seen them. "This man?"

"That would be him," I confirm, holding up my hand to catch the server's attention, who looks over at my empty glass. He nods his head and turns around. "The one and only."

"How was it?" She doesn't even bother looking up

at me as she scrolls through his Instagram, something I forced myself to ignore doing. "Damn." She turns the phone toward me, and there is a picture of Stone with his cousins Christopher, Stefano, and Matty—all of them in bathing suits, all of them shirtless, all of them top-tier boyfriend material. "Look at his body."

I can't even stop my hand from reaching out for her phone as I grab it from her. I read the caption first, *Summertime fun and mischief.* I roll my eyes at it and then make the stupid mistake of reading through the comments. The number of girls is insane, but what did I expect with half a million followers. "It's a thirst trap," I mumble, trying not to look only at Stone. I mean, I felt his hard chest under his shirt when he kissed me, but now seeing it, I'm definitely getting tingles elsewhere.

"I don't know what that is, but someone sign me up for that trap," Kristal muses as I hand her back her phone. "How was the kiss?" She again just trolls his Instagram while I get another glass of wine, drinking half of it before I speak.

"It was a kiss, and I was surprised," I admit. "Nothing spectacular," I lie because, well, what else was I supposed to do, tell her it was the best kiss I've ever had? Fuck no. No one needs to know that. Tell her that it was a kiss I still thought about occasionally? I definitely don't need to say that. Tell her I was a bit disappointed when he didn't try to kiss me at the wedding? Not one person needs to know that.

So instead, I avoid talking about him and change the subject to talk about work. We each order a burger, and

I have two more glasses of wine, and by the time I get home, I'm a little tipsy.

I kick off my boots and dump my bags at the door before walking straight to my bathroom. After I undress, I take a shower, then slide into bed wearing a tank top and panties. I grab my phone and see his Instagram message is still there ready to be read.

Instead of answering his message, I decide to snap a picture of half my face and my naked shoulder as I look up. **Hmmmm, let me think about it for a second**, I type as I press send to the picture and the message.

I can see that he's just read it, and my heart speeds up as I turn in the bed, waiting for him to answer. I wonder where he is tonight, if he's home by himself. When was the last time he had sex? Just random thoughts I want to ask him, but know I would rather die than actually ask him these things.

I'm expecting him to answer, but instead, I see a voice message has come through. I hover my finger over the Play button, and then his voice fills my room. It sounds like it's heavy with sleep. "Damn, gorgeous, I've never been more jealous of a bed than I am right now." He chuckles, and my chest contracts. "What I wouldn't give to be able to kiss you right now. I'm also thinking of other things we could be doing right now."

I think about not answering him, but the pull to him is too great. Instead, I press the microphone button and talk into my phone. "Well, I don't know what you would be doing right now," I say softly, "but in about five seconds, I'll be doing that to myself. Have a great night, Stone."

I toss my phone to the side and reach for the vibrator in my drawer, and I may or may not picture him using it on me.

SEVEN

STONE

THE SOFT ALARM bells start slowly but then build up to a blaring sound. I wait until I can't stand it anymore before I roll over and turn it off. I check my notifications first, then my email, and finally, I open Instagram since I can't fucking text her.

The last thing on the chat thread was her voice last night, and I replay it. Her voice comes out soft, and the minute I hear it, my cock gets hard. "Well, I don't know what you would be doing right now, but in about five seconds, I'll be doing that to myself. Have a great night, Stone." Fuck, even hearing it the morning after I'm ready to stroke my cock. But before I jump into the shower, I send her a message.

Just wanted to say good morning, gorgeous, and let you know I'm already looking forward to talking to you later.

I send her the message and toss my phone to the side before I slide out of bed. I turn the shower on to get warm before I step in. My cock is already in my hand, her face in my head, and her voice in my ears. It takes me less than three minutes before I moan out her name. Last time it took me less than this morning. She drives me to the point where I feel like I'm a kid again.

I step out of the shower, grab a pair of boxers, and slip on shorts. I feel just a little more human today than I did yesterday, that's for sure. It's a game day, which means we have a practice at ten, so I'm heading over to the gym before practice. I toss my covers over and grab my phone, looking down to see if she messaged me back. I'm not surprised she hasn't since it's six thirty in the morning.

I walk through the almost-dark house, the sun trying to come out, but it's fighting the clouds. I walk out of the mudroom door to the backyard and over to the pool house I converted into a home gym. I press the code to get into the black doors. As soon as I step inside, I hit the lights and television before jumping on the bike. I go through my game day workout, sticking to light weights and the bike. Two hours later, I walk back into the house to make myself a protein shake before heading to the rink, where I have breakfast.

The phone beeps as soon as I take a sip of my protein shake, showing me Ryleigh has left me a message. I really need her to give me her fucking number.

You are mighty sure of yourself in the morning. I'll be sure not to answer any calls today. Thanks for the heads-up.

Instead of answering her message, I decide to call her

instead. Putting the phone on speaker as I walk through the house, I head to my bedroom to grab myself a T-shirt before I head out. It rings four times and then tells me the call has ended.

The old Ryleigh can't come to the phone right now. Why? 'Cause she's dead. Goodbye.

You can't use T Swift as your answering machine.

Did you not read above??? Also, I did not take you for a Swifty.

If you give me a chance, I have more in me that can blow your mind.

I can blow my own mind, thank you very much. Don't you have like skates to put on or like someone to go beat up?

I'm headed to practice now. We have a game tonight, then I'm flying into your city.

I'll alert the presses and tell them to keep their wives and children inside.

I don't think I've ever had a woman make me laugh as much as she does.

I have a game on Friday. Would you like to come and cheer me on?

I can't, I have to watch the paint dry in my apartment. Maybe next time.

I'm staying a couple of extra days. Would you like to go out with me?

No.

I shake my head, making a plan for myself as I get into my truck and head to the rink. I arrive at the same time as a couple of the guys and make a beeline for the kitchen. I stock up on eggs and bacon before we skate. Since it's a game day, everyone takes it easy on the ice, and I take another shower before going home. I pack my away bag before taking a nap. Another thing I do on game day is take a two-hour nap.

Dressing in a blue suit and grabbing my bag, I make my way over to the rink, my head focused on the game. It's game time. I have one goal and one goal only, winning the game. We end up winning in the last minutes of the game. Everyone showers and rushes to get ready to head to the plane. The bus is waiting for us, and three hours after we finish our game, we touch down in Chicago.

It's cold as balls when we arrive, the wind blowing through all of us. I set my alarm for nine o'clock even though I'll probably be up before then. Crashing as soon as I close my eyes, shockingly enough, I sleep until the alarm wakes me up. I open my eyes to the dark hotel room before shutting off the alarm.

I have to be at practice at one, so I have four hours to set my plan in motion. I slide on a pair of jeans and a T-shirt before I slip a blue knit turtleneck on top. I snag my boots before I grab the jacket and beanie. I grab the stuff from my luggage, then walk out the door. The whole floor is for us, and no one is up so far. Getting into the elevator, I open the Uber app and type in the address I'm going to. By the time I get to the lobby, he's outside.

I expect the wind to hit me right away, but it's not that bad today. The sun is actually out, and it feels warm. I take off the hat and tuck it in my pocket when I get in the car. The driver starts small talk, but I'm so nervous all I can do is look out the window until we get to the brown building. "Thank you," I say, shutting the door and looking at the glass doors, wondering if I'll even be able to get to her.

I pull open the door, heading to the lobby. The man looks up from the desk in the middle of the area. "Can I help you?"

"I'm here to deliver something to Ryleigh Beckett on the seventh floor." I hold up the white bag in my hand with tissue paper sticking out.

"I need your ID," he says. I reach in my back pocket, taking out my black Louis Vuitton wallet. Pulling out my Nashville license, I hand it to him, and he turns to the side, scanning it before handing it back to me. "Sign in on that." He points at the clipboard. "Then empty your pockets." He points at the white circle bin. "And go through that." He gestures to the metal detector. I nod at him, taking my phone, hat, and wallet out of my pockets and putting them into the white bin before someone else comes over to me, pointing at the bag in my hand. My pulse starts to pick up even though I have nothing to hide. The thought I could be strip-searched never even crossed my mind. I'm just a guy who wants to ask a girl out. She better fucking say yes.

"Need to look in the bag," he states, and I hand him the gift bag. My heart palpitates as if I'm actually carrying stuff I shouldn't be even though it's just a fucking shirt. He moves the tissue paper around and squishes the bag before passing it to the guy waiting on the other side of the metal detector. I walk through it, saying a silent prayer that it doesn't somehow beep for whatever reason. My palms are fucking sweaty as I wait for the guy to give me the go-ahead. It takes maybe five seconds, which feels like a million years, and he points to the right. "Elevators are that way."

"Thank you." I grab my stuff in a rush, not even bothering to tuck my hat back in my pocket. Instead, I wait until I'm in the elevator before I start putting my wallet back in my pants and then my hat away. My phone is in my hand, with my finger tapping the back of it. I step out on the seventh floor and look at the girl sitting behind a brown desk. "Hi, I'm looking for Ryleigh Beckett."

She smiles at me. "Who can I say is here?"

"Stone," I say my name, and she raises her eyebrows. I'm not sure if it's because she doesn't believe me or she knows who I am.

She picks up the black phone and punches some numbers in and waits. "Hey," she says, her voice going low as if I won't hear her while I'm right in front of her, "there is a Stone here to see you?" She looks at me, then tries to hide her smile. "Standing in the reception area right now." She tries to keep a straight face. "Um," she says, and I can just imagine what Ryleigh is saying. "Correct." She hangs up the phone.

"Should I just go and surprise her?" I say, pointing to the side where I think the offices are. Her eyes go even bigger, and she shakes her head. "She likes me," I insist. "She's just not sure of it."

"If you say so," she mumbles. I hear the sound of heels clicking and I can't help the smile that fills my face. I look over and see her walking down the hallway wearing wide-legged red pants with a black belt and a long-sleeved black shirt. Her hair is piled on her head in a bun, leaving me access to bite and kiss her neck.

I'm waiting for her to look up and see me, and when she does, the glare she gives me would make any other man run the other way. Lucky for me, I grew up in a family where glares were given with love. I wait for her to stop in front of me before I say, "gorgeous." I put one hand on her hip and lean in to kiss her cheek.

"What are you doing here?" She folds her arms over her chest before looking at the receptionist, who watches the scene unfold in front of her like we're some soap opera. "Ugh, come with me." She turns back toward her office.

"I'll follow you anywhere, gorgeous," I say to her receding back.

"Are you checking out my ass?" she hisses.

"You bet," I admit, "I'm deciding which side I'm going to bite first." Her face gets pink, and instead of answering me, she turns into the doorway, stopping to hold the door and wait for me to be clear before she shuts it behind me.

I walk into her office and see her desk with two computer screens on it. Her jacket hangs in the corner with her boots right under. "What the hell do you think you're doing?" she snaps.

"I came to give you a present." I lift the white bag in my hand. "It looked a lot prettier before the guy downstairs fucked it up."

"You can't just show up here, Stone," she huffs as she walks to meet me in the middle of her office, cocking her hip to the side. "You do realize that I work in a government building and not just a regular office. There are protocols. You can't just walk in here."

"Oh, I know," I grit out. "I was basically fingerprinted to get in. I had to give them my ID. I was praying there would be no beeping when I walked through the metal detector." I look down at her. "But it was all worth it."

"This might actually work in my favor when I tell them you're stalking me," she muses, and I can see her anger dissipate just a bit. Her eyes are getting lighter. "You're now on every single security camera there is." She puts her hands on her hips. "Easier for them to shoot you now. Thank you for that." She smiles, and I close the distance between us.

She doesn't move from where she stands, but I can see her chest heaving. "It's good to see you, gorgeous," I say softly, dropping the bag in my hand so I can grab her face. "I missed you."

"I find that—" she says, but then stops because my lips are on hers, and my tongue slides into her mouth. I close my eyes as her tongue rolls with mine, making the whole thing I just went through worth it. Being in the same room with her makes it all worth it. She steps into me, putting her hands on my hips. I could kiss her all day long and be happy.

"Hmmm," I mumble when I let her lips go so I can look at her. Her eyes open. "I like this top, makes it easy to do this." I bend my head and bite the side of her neck before sucking it.

"Don't you dare give me a hickey, Stone." She pushes me away from her. "Now, what the hell are you doing here?"

"Well, I came to kiss you." I kiss her lips again. "To give you this." I hold up the white bag. "And to ask you to dinner."

"I already said no." She shakes her head, and I bend to kiss the side of her lips.

"I know, which is why I came to persuade you." I trail kisses along her neck. "It's just a dinner, gorgeous."

"Ryleigh," she hisses out, and when I look up, I can see her eyes are closed as she enjoys my kisses on her neck. I wrap an arm around her waist before my hand slides to her ass, pulling her toward me. She shrieks when I palm her ass and squeeze. "Good God, you aren't going to take no for an answer, are you?"

"No," I answer her honestly as I nip her ear. "Dinner. Me and you tonight."

"Ugh," she puffs, and I take a second to look at her, staring into her eyes.

"Have dinner with me, gorgeous," I invite softly. She pushes me away from her, straightening her pants even though they don't need to be straightened. "It's just dinner."

"If I say yes, will you leave me alone?" she asks, and I can see I'm wearing her down.

"For today anyway," I answer, making her roll her eyes at me.

"Fine, I'll go out to dinner with you."

EIGHT

Ryleigh

WHAT ARE YOU doing? my head screams as soon as I utter the words I said I would never say. "I'll go out to dinner with you."

"Really?" he says, the smile on his face beaming. "Shit, I have to be at practice in two hours, or I would kidnap you right now."

I can't help but laugh. "You know this is a government building, and they literally will shoot you." I shake my head, ignoring how good it is to see him. "You need to go, and I'll call you about tonight."

"What time do you finish?" he asks. "I'm done at five. I can come and get you."

"Absolutely not," I snap. "I will meet you there." I see he's about to argue with me, so I change the subject. "What's in the bag?"

"Something for you." He holds up the bag by the handle, swinging it side to side on his finger.

"Well, at least it's not a box," I mumble, taking the

bag from him.

"I should have put it in a box. The guy literally took the bag and crushed it between his two hands." He imitates the guy downstairs.

"Again, it's a government building," I point out. "I work with criminals."

He just gawks at me. "Is that safe?"

"As safe as putting on skates and skating on ice, hoping you don't lose a glove and have someone skate over your hand." I move the tissue to the side, seeing the white thing inside and pulling it out. "What the?" I throw the bag down and hold the heavy shirt in my hand. "Is this a jersey?" I ask, turning it to see that it's his number nineteen with his name, Richards.

"It's for you to wear to the game tomorrow," he announces, and I just look at him.

"I said yes to tonight," I remind him. "I never said anything about tomorrow."

"I know." He smirks. "I'm going to persuade you tonight with my charm." He kisses my lips again, just like that. Like he's okay to do it. Like I've watched my father do to my mother countless times. Like Romeo does to Gabriella. I don't like it. I kind of always thought it was stupid, and now it's happening to me. I'm not that woman. "So will you text me where you want to go?"

"Yes," I confirm to him, trying to think if I can ghost him, but chances are he'll show up again tomorrow. Might as well just get this out of the way so he can go back to wherever it is he came from. "Now, you have to go. I have a hearing to get ready for," I lie to him. The next case I have to appear in court for is in about three weeks, but he doesn't have to know that.

"Will you walk me out?" he asks, and I roll my lips. "So the girl can see you like me."

"I don't," I quickly correct him. "I'm tolerating you. There is a difference."

"Okay, gorgeous." He turns and waits for me at the door, as if I just didn't tell him I don't really like him.

"Oh my God." I throw my hands up, tossing the jersey on the chair before walking toward the door, standing away from him in case he wants to kiss me again.

I wait for him to open the door before I step out into the hallway. I walk side by side with him, putting my hands in my pockets to make sure he doesn't try to hold my hand. "There," I say once we get to the lobby and in front of the elevator, "happy?"

"Yes," he answers, pressing the button to go down. The doors open right away as if they were waiting for him. "You'll call me?" He keeps his finger on the button instead of getting into the elevator.

"I told you I would."

"Okay, I'll talk to you later, then," he says with a sly smile. "You look gorgeous, by the way." I literally take an inhale of breath because it feels like it's getting harder to breathe. He bends his head and kisses my lips before getting into the elevator. "Bye." He holds up his hand before the doors close.

"I like him," Claudia says, and I whip my head around to look at her, my lips still tingling from the kiss.

"Good, you can go out with him, then." I avoid

looking at her and also avoid thinking about how it felt when she said she liked him. "He's free tonight, if you want."

"If I didn't have my husband and child at home." She snaps her fingers. "I would so take you up on that."

"Good to know," I mumble before I tell her to fuck off and walk back to my office. The shirt on the chair stares at me. "I'm not going to the game," I tell myself to make sure my brain informs other parts of my body.

I'm about to sit back down when my phone rings, and I look down, seeing he's calling me through Instagram. "I said I would call you," I snap into the phone.

I hear him chuckle, and I swear my pussy contracts. "I just want to make sure because I really don't want to go through a cavity search to come and see you again." This time, I'm the one who chuckles. "When I walked out, I think the guy didn't stop watching me until I was outside of the building."

"Again." I sit down in my chair. "A government office. Not to alarm you, but they probably are doing a spot check on you. As soon as your face is entered in the system, they do all sorts of background checks." I can't help but fuck with him.

"gorgeous," he says, "don't make me come back up there." I hear a car door shut. "I will if I have to but—"

"Stone, I will meet you tonight at seven," I assure him. "You can meet me at thirty-one thirty-one Clarke Street. They have the best sangria. I will be there at six fifty-seven to make sure I'm not late."

"Okay, gorgeous, have a good day at work because I

know my day will be better now that I got to taste you." I put my head back; this fucking guy with his pickup lines.

"How many times has that worked on your dates?" I ask, and I want to kick myself for asking him because it. Does. Not. Matter.

"Don't know, it's the first time I've ever said it, so I'm banking on one."

I ignore his words, telling myself he's obviously lying. No way would he not have game with that face, that body, that confidence. "Bye, Stone." I hang up on him, and the rest of the day I bury myself with my latest brief, getting ahead of the game.

I rush out of the office at five thirty, shoving the jersey in my bag, along with the iPad. "I'll see you Monday," I tell Claudia, who just waves her fingers at me. Friday is a work-from-home day unless I have to be in the office, but luckily, I can work from home tomorrow.

"Good luck with Stone." She smirks at me as she gets up to leave. "I'll expect details Monday."

"I can tell you right now," I say as the elevator doors open, "nothing will happen."

I step into the elevator before she calls me a liar. Rushing home, I hop into the shower and then go into my closet. "What do you wear to say I don't care that you are here, and I don't want to fuck you?" I ask the rack of clothes, letting the towel drop and slipping on a pair of my lacy silk panties before pulling out my black jeans that I know work wonders for my ass. I walk over and grab a white bra with black embroidery and lace edging before I slip on a long-sleeved white button-down shirt, leaving the first two buttons open so you can see the lacy bra underneath it. I pull the sleeves up to my elbows and slide on my black booties.

My phone buzzes, telling me it's six thirty, so I rush to grab a leather jacket before I put my phone in my pocket and hurry down to the waiting car. I pull up his Instagram, going to his name.

I'm in the car on my way.

He answers right away.

Same. My ETA is twenty minutes. I can't stop thinking about your lips.

"Good God," I mumble to myself, putting my phone away before I tell him what I'd like him to do with his lips.

Instead, I look out the window at the people walking together. My finger taps my leg as we make our way down to the restaurant. I've chosen this place because it's got a nice vibe with the low lighting. Plus, the food is good, and their sangria is life. He stops at the curb, and I get out, thanking him. Looking around, I spot Stone waiting for me. A beanie on his head, as his head is down on his phone. "Hey," I greet, walking to him, and the smile fills his face.

"Hi," he replies breathlessly, or maybe I'm the one who is breathless. He's wearing blue jeans with a white button-down shirt and a blue sweater over it. The collar of the shirt and the hem stick out of the sweater. A bomber jacket finishes the look with his white sneakers. "You look—"

"I know," I say, "gorgeous." Not giving him a chance

to say the word beautiful again. He wraps his arm around my waist and kisses me on the cheek, making my pulse speed up.

"I was going to say good enough to eat," he whispers in my ear, and now I know why he kisses my cheek. The words send shivers through me. "Shall we go in?"

He pulls open the door for me to step in, and the heat hits me right away. The hostess stands there waiting for us. "Can I help you?"

"Table for two." I look at her as I take the packed restaurant in.

"Do you have a reservation?" the hostess asks me as she looks down at her iPad.

"No," I say.

At the same time, Stone says, "Yes, under Richards." I look up at him, shocked.

"How did you…?" I ask him as the hostess takes two menus and tells us to follow her.

"I wasn't going to give you an excuse to bail on me, so I made sure," he explains, putting his hand on my lower back, pushing me to walk, while my head is still blown that he took time out to come and make sure we got a table.

My feet move before my brain can even register it because it's going around and around with the fact he searched the restaurant by the address and then made a fucking reservation. A. Reservation.

"Here you are," she says when she gets to a table in the corner, "as requested." I look at the square table with four chairs.

I look over at Stone, who just smiles at her, then looks at me. "Grab a seat," he urges me and doesn't move until I've taken off my coat and sat down on the seat in the corner. He shrugs off his jacket and then pulls the beanie off, putting his hat in his jacket pocket before placing it on the chair facing me, where I'm expecting him to sit, but nope, not Stone. He pulls out the chair next to me and sits beside me.

"Why are you sitting there"—I point at where he's sitting—"instead of sitting across from me?"

"Because if I sit in front of you," he starts, reaching over to grab my chair and pulling it to him, "I won't be able to do this." He bends his head, and I'm expecting a kiss on the lips, but instead, he kisses me right behind my ear.

All of the words in the whole entire dictionary are stuck in my throat. There is not one word, not one vowel, not one syllable that comes out of my mouth. "How about you not do that?" I suggest when I'm finally able to speak.

"What fun would that be?" He puts his arm around the back of my chair and rubs his thumb up and down on my shoulder, the feeling like a feather through the silk top. "How was your day?"

"Spoke with Homeland Security about you," I deadpan with a straight face, "that was fun." His mouth hangs open. "Relax, I'm kidding."

The server approaches us, and I order a pitcher of sangria while Stone orders a sparkling water. "How was your day?" I ask, trying not to sound nervous or that being this close to him is making me sweat.

"It was good," he says. "Not as great as right now that I'm with you." He smirks at me and winks. "Always better when I get to be with you."

The server comes back, putting down two wineglasses and filling them up with sangria before giving Stone a glass of sparkling water, telling us he'll give us a minute to look over the menu. "Shall we toast?" I ask, anxious to busy my hands before I reach over and massage his impressive package in those jeans.

"We should," he replies, grabbing his sparkling water and not the glass of sangria. "Here is to the best first date ever. But the second-best day ever."

"That makes no sense," I say to him, holding up my glass and clinking it with him. "What was the first-best day ever?" I bring the glass to my lips, taking a sip, not expecting what comes out of his mouth.

"The first time I kissed you was the best day ever." He takes a sip of his water. "This is the best date ever."

"Pretty sure of yourself," I mumble to him, and he just chuckles. "How the hell did you make reservations?" I finally ask him, drinking the rest of the sangria in my glass.

I will admit, Stone really pushes me out of my comfort zone. He says things I'm never expecting him to say. He kisses me when I least expect it, so it's no surprise when he tells me, "After practice, I came by here to make sure I spoke with the manager and got a reservation. I wanted a quiet table where I could sit next to you and be able to touch you." My mouth hangs open, literally catching flies as they say. He reaches for the pitcher and pours me another glass. I reach forward to take a sip, but I finish the glass instead. "Cat got your tongue?" he asks, then doesn't give me a chance to answer. "I'd rather do other things with your tongue, to be honest."

"Is that so?" I finally say, this I can do. The flirty, sexy talk I can do. It's the caring little things he does that I can't do. I don't want to do.

"That is," he confirms, taking another sip of his water. The server comes over, and Stone reaches for the menus, ordering pretty much one of everything.

"So tell me, gorgeous." His head gets closer to me as he whispers in my ear, "Did you have fun with yourself the other night?"

I throw my head back and laugh, giving him the opportunity to kiss my neck. "I always have fun with myself." I pretend I don't still feel his lips on my neck. "Don't you have fun with yourself?"

"What did you think about?" he asks with a smirk. "Was it me?"

"It was not," I deny quickly right before I drink another glass of sangria.

"You're a beautiful liar," he tells me softly, then leans in to whisper in my ear, "Just so you know, whatever you thought about me doing to you, it's going to be even better in real life." He nips my ear.

"Is that so?" I ask him as some of the food comes to the table, and I want to tell them to take the food and go away.

"That is so." He picks up the conversation when the

server leaves. "I've been thinking about nothing else since I kissed you six months ago."

The meal goes by way too quickly. He changes the topic from sex to the wedding. We laugh about the pieces I can't remember, and when it's time to leave, I secretly wish the night wasn't ending.

We walk out, and he looks at me. "What's your address?" he asks, and I gasp.

"I haven't even given you my phone number. What makes you think I'm going to tell you where I live?" I giggle, the effects of finishing the pitcher of sangria making me tipsy.

"Fine, why don't you order the Uber," he says, "and then I'll grab a cab from your place."

"Okay," I agree, pretty much thinking he's going to spend the night. Figuring that once we have sex, this chase will be over, so I might as well make him remember this date.

We get into the Uber, and he sits way too close to me. I look up at him, the heat from his arm around me pulling me close to him seeping into me. "You," I tell him, then go to whisper in his ear, "naked." I bite his jaw. "With your hands in my hair." I look at him and see his eyes are darker, so dark they look black. His jaw is clenching. "That's what I was thinking about."

His mouth crashes onto mine, his tongue mixing with mine as I pull him to me. His hand reaches over me and grabs my ass. The kiss is everything I've thought about since the last time he kissed me in my office. It's hungry and full of need. I throw my leg over his and feel his cock through his pants, and if we were in a private car, I would massage his dick through the fabric.

The car stops, and he lets go of my lips. "Is this you?" He looks out the window at my building.

"It is." I smile at him as he gets out of the car and holds his hand out for me. I slip my hand into his and laugh. "Big hands, you know what that means." I giggle when he walks to the door, opening it. I walk in, turning to look at him and walking backward, watching him follow me. My eyes go from his eyes to his package, where those jeans leave little to the imagination. I can see the outline of his cock, and it's making my mouth water.

I push the elevator button, and the door opens. He steps in beside me as I press the button to my floor. My hands itch to touch him, my body tingling to be touched. The anticipation to get him naked and ride his cock is stronger than I've ever had before. We get off, and he follows me as I take my key out and put it in the door. He stops my hands, turning me around, my back to the closed door. "Gorgeous," he says in a whisper. "Fuck," he groans before he bends his head and takes my mouth in another scorching kiss. My tongue fights with his, trying to get the upper hand, trying to get the kiss deeper. He pushes me harder into the door, and my hands grab his jacket to take it off.

He steps away from me as if someone just caught us making out. "You're drunk," he says, and I don't know if he's asking me or telling me.

"I'm not drunk. I'm happy." I smile at him and reach for his sweater to pull him to me. "Tipsy."

"At the wedding," he starts softly, "I wanted to kiss you all night but didn't because you were drunk, and I wanted to make sure you wouldn't forget." He kisses me now, his tongue sliding into mine for a second before he stops again, making me groan. "When I'm going to get you naked for me and be balls deep inside you..." He grabs my hips to pull me to him, lifting me off my boots and lacing my pussy directly on his cock. "When I sink into you for the first time, you will not be drunk. You won't have one drop of alcohol in you. You'll know who is fucking you, and you won't regret it in the morning."

"Trust me," I assure him, "I'll have no regrets in the morning about fucking you tonight." I move my hips, feeling his ridge down my core. "And when you're balls deep inside me, I'll be calling your name."

"Gorgeous." He puts me down. "When I'm balls deep inside you, it'll be after I make you come with my fingers and then my mouth. Just thinking about it makes my mouth water."

"Stone." I put my head back and literally have to cross my legs. "I'm begging you now to take me inside and fuck me."

"Lock up," he urges me, kissing me once more on the lips. He turns and walks away from me. "Thank you for the best date ever." He doesn't wait for the elevator. Instead, he walks over to the stairs and disappears.

I just stare at the door, wondering if this is him playing a trick on me. I pull out my phone, stumbling to get the Instagram thread when I call his actual phone number. He picks up after one ring. "Hello."

"You just fucking left me here," I blurt into the phone.

"Gorgeous," he says softly, "are you inside?"

"No." I shake my head before I turn and unlock the door, finally stepping inside. "I can't believe you just left me." I leave out he left me here panting and needing an orgasm. Leaving out I'm so horny and hot for him I want him to do all the things to me. I want to sit on his face. I want to suck his cock. I want him to be over me, thrusting into me.

"Do you want me to come back?" he asks.

"Yes," I snap, and he laughs.

"Ryleigh," he says, "walking away from you killed me."

"Good," I finally say. "I hope you get blue balls."

"Trust me, I have them. I've never been in so much pain before in my life."

"I find that very hard to believe. Anyway, I have to let you go. I have another date with a very special friend." I don't even wait for him to answer me before I put the phone on the bed and open my side table. "Hello, my old friend."

NINE

STONE

I PLACE MY head against the steel door, close my eyes, and listen to her on the other side of the phone. She threw her phone to the side but didn't hang up. "Hello, my old friend," she says right before I hear the buzzing sound, and I look at the phone. The need to listen to her is stronger than I am. She moans a little, and then I open my eyes and press the red button, hanging my head. I tuck the phone in my back pocket before I jog down the stairs to the lobby.

Pushing the door open, I enter the bright lobby with my hands fisting by my sides. Walking away from her was probably the stupidest thing I've ever done, but I wasn't going to go there with her the first time when she's been drinking. No, when I get there with her, and I'm going to get there with her, she'll be sober and not freak out the next day. Fingers crossed at least.

The ride back to my hotel is brutal, but not any more brutal than my hard-on that has yet to fully go down since I kissed her against her door. I have no choice but to fist my cock, though my cock wished it was her. My head has only visions of her, and my lips groan out her name when I finally come.

The alarm rings at ten the following morning, and I'm shocked I slept the whole way through. Grabbing my phone right away, I FaceTime her now that I have her number. She picks up after four rings. "How did you get my number?" Her hair is piled on her head, and I can see she's wearing a white T-shirt, and from the background, I also see she's at home. I can only laugh at her as I turn on my side. "You called me last night."

She opens her mouth and then closes it. "I—" she starts to say but then quickly stops talking when I cut her off in asking her.

"How is your old friend?" I try my best not to smile or laugh but fail miserably, especially after her face gets a little bit pink.

"He's better than ever." She rolls her eyes. "He's never ever let me down, that's for sure."

"Good to know." My cock gets hard thinking that when I get her there, I'll be torturing her with her old friend, and that will be one time he lets her down. "I have plans for us tonight."

"Good," she huffs. "Have fun with that, I'm busy."

I shake my head. "If you have a chance, take a nap after work."

"Oh, good God, so full of yourself and your stamina."

"Gorgeous." I chuckle. "I have the game tonight, and we have dinner reservations at ten thirty, and then we are going out."

"Going out?" She repeats my words. "Where are we going?"

"It's a surprise," I tell her. "Do you want to come to the game?"

"Absolutely not," she snaps.

"Okay, I won't push it this time," I concede, already knowing what I have planned for her tonight might make or break us. "But next time."

"Next time." She shakes her head. "Like there's going to be a next time."

"Gorgeous, there will be so many next times. There will be a time when you aren't even going to remember what it's like not to have me there."

"I remember now, and it was blissful." She smirks at me. "And fulfilling."

"We shall see." I get up from the bed, tossing the covers off me. "I'll be at your place to pick you up. Dress comfy."

"Stone," she warns, "if you give me one more order." Her jaw gets tight.

"Have an amazing day. I'll call you after practice."

"Or not," she retorts, hanging up on me, leaving me with my phone in my hand.

I get dressed in my tracksuit and grab a coffee in the lobby before heading to the bus to go to the rink. Practice is smooth, and right after that, I hit up the gym to do my cardio while my phone beeps, telling me everything is set for tonight. I am so hyped up for the date I don't even nap properly. I'm even the first one on the bus, waiting to get the game over. Instead of calling her, I send her a text.

Me: *Can't wait to see you tonight.*

She responds right away, and I can't help but smile.

Gorgeous: *I can.*

I put the phone away once I get to the arena and get into the zone. The game is hard-hitting, both teams vying for points to make it into the playoffs. Both teams doing what needs to be done to end up on top. After three periods, we're tied at one and going into overtime. "I'll give five hundred dollars"—I look at the bench—"to whoever scores in the next two minutes."

"I'll double it," Jay says, panting next to me as the coach calls my name to get on the ice with James and Freddy, our defensemen.

"I can't wait to get the fuck out of this cold," James whines as I skate over to the middle of the ice.

"Let's just get this over with," Freddy says, "I want that five hundred dollars."

"It's yours, big boy." I nod at him as I take my position in the middle of the ice. The crowd is on their feet as the announcer screams overtime. It's almost deafening as I skate in a circle before squatting down, ready to win the face-off.

The referee drops the puck in the middle, and we smack sticks before I toss the puck to the back where Freddy is. Jay and I skate our way with him to the blue line. He passes the puck to Jay, who quickly makes the pass to me, and I lift my stick, but instead of shooting it at the net, I pass it quickly back to Freddy. He slap shoots it at the goalie, who isn't ready for it since his eyes are on me. It flies to the back of the net as the red light goes off.

"Someone owes me five hundred bucks," Freddy gloats when I skate over to him and hit my helmet with his.

"With pleasure," I say as the rest of the team joins us before we skate off the ice on the other side.

"Bus leaves in one hour!" someone shouts as we walk into the room. I quickly undress and make it to the shower, slipping on my jeans and sweater before I slide my jacket on. I pack my suit in my backpack before walking out to the garage, where a car waits for me.

I take my phone out of my pocket and call her. "You were serious," she answers me instead of saying hello.

"I'm always serious when it comes to you." I laugh. "I'll be at your place in about fifteen minutes."

"We're really going out to dinner?" she asks, and I hear her running around on her end.

"Yes, and then…" I almost slip the secret, but I don't. "See you soon." I hang up the phone before she tells me she's not coming.

When I get to her place, I take the elevator up to her floor. Knocking on her door, I hear the sounds of running with heels on. I smile when I hear the locks open on the big door. "I can't even with you," she huffs, and I can see her trying not to smile. She's wearing black pants with a red sweater and a black scarf wrapped around her neck.

"Hi, gorgeous," I greet her, stepping in and grabbing her face while I kick the door shut with my foot right before I kiss her lips. Her hands go to my hips, and I'm surprised she's not pushing me away. I kiss her softly, but it's her, so my tongue slides into her mouth as she presses up against me. I let her go before my thumbs rub her cheeks. "We better go before—"

"Yes, before I have to whip out the old friend." She walks over to the coatrack and pulls her black leather jacket off the hook. Then she snatches her purse before slipping it over her head to wear it across her body.

"The car is waiting," I tell her, grabbing her hand to drag her out the door instead of pulling her to her bed.

"The car?" she repeats. "Aren't you fancy-schmancy?" she says as we step into the elevator. I walk to one side, and she faces me on the other side. "Where are you taking me?"

"To a small place, then someplace else." I wink at her as she looks at me. "Have I told you how fucking gorgeous you are?"

"You have." She nods. "But it's nothing I haven't heard before." She pushes off the side of the elevator when the doors open.

I watch her ass for a second, and she stops walking, looking over her shoulder. "What are you doing?"

"Enjoying the view." I walk out of the elevator.

"You could have enjoyed the view up close and personal last night." She turns back around and walks toward the door. The driver sees me and opens the back door to the car, and she gets in, scooting across to the other side so I can get in.

She rubs her hands together. "It's a little chilly," she observes.

"I can warm you up." Putting my arm around her shoulders, I pull her to me.

"Yeah, warm me up." She rolls her eyes. "And then leave me high and dry."

I don't bother answering her and just kiss the side of her forehead. My heart pounds in my chest, wondering if maybe I should have told her about the surprise instead of just going with it. We pull up to the little restaurant that looks like it's closed, but I know it's staying open for me. I knock on the window and then see the woman hold up her hand and come over to unlock the door. "Welcome, Mr. Richards," she says, holding the door open for us and then closing it as soon as we step in. "Choose a table, and we'll get started."

"Go ahead." I gesture for Ryleigh to pick a table.

She walks in and looks around. "Are we the only ones here?"

"We are," I tell her as she pulls out a chair at a table for two.

"Did you shut down the whole place?" she asks as she takes off her jacket and then her scarf. I see her red sweater is cut down to her belly button in a V and shows me she's wearing a black satin bra underneath.

"You forgot half your shirt." I point at her as she sits down and laughs, making my jeans become very fucking tight.

"You're lucky it's cold out, or I wouldn't even wear the sweater." She puts her elbows on the table and clasps her hands together. "Now, what are we having?"

"Menu is set." I shrug my jacket off. "Only because

we have to be someplace in an hour."

"Really?" She raises her eyebrows at me.

"I'm Maria," the woman says, coming out from the swinging door, wiping her hands on an apron that used to be white but is now covered in sauce. "Can I get you something to drink?"

"I'll have a water," Ryleigh answers, then turns to me. "No excuses now, Stone."

"I'll have the same," I reply, smirking at her. Maria leaves, and I look back at her. "So you really want to have sex with me, then?"

"I really want to have sex. You just happen to be the lucky suitor."

"Is that so?" I ask. "If I was anyone else, you would have sex with them?" I watch her eyes narrow at me. "That's what I thought. Because the one thing for sure I've learned about you, gorgeous, is that you don't need a man, but you want me."

"It's a wonder your big-ass head fits through any doorways," she huffs, and I don't have a chance to answer her because Maria comes back with four plates.

"Little bit for you to try," she says, "meatballs, calamari, arancini and caprese salad."

"Thank you. What would you like to try first?" I ask Ryleigh as Maria walks away.

"I like balls in my mouth," she announces, picking up a meatball, "especially when they are slapping against my chin."

"I'll keep that in mind when I'm holding your head and fucking your face, making you gag." Her eyes change in the blink of a second, and if I wasn't looking right into them, I wouldn't see it. "Now eat up. You will need your strength."

"Promises, promises," she mutters, taking a bite of the food. "So did you win or lose?"

"I'm sitting across the table from the woman who has been driving me to the brink of jumping off the cliff of the Grand Canyon." I smile at her. "I'm winning."

She rolls her eyes at me, and Maria comes back, placing four pasta dishes in front of us. The two of us seem to be too nervous to eat. "So now that you have me here, what are you going to do with me?"

I pick up the glass of water in front of me. "There are a lot of things I want to do with you, but I also want to get to know you." I take a sip of water. "What made you want to go to law school?"

"According to my parents"—she folds her arms on the table in front of her—"I started to argue with them when I was eighteen months old." The smile on her face makes her even more beautiful, if that's even possible. "Then, when I was three, everything became a dispute. But in reality, when you grow up in Hollywood, I made up a game to sniff out the bullshit people would feed you. Sort of like Instagram vs. reality." I don't interrupt because she's getting comfortable. "Then I did a mock trial for the first time in high school for a debate team, and I just fell in love." Her eyes light up.

"Do you work long hours?" I ask, and she nods, picking up her fork to put a piece of meatball in her mouth.

"About twelve hours a day, depending on the case. Might be more."

"When do you let your hair down?" She just looks at me. "When do you take you time?"

"I'm here now, aren't I?" She smirks but continues, "I knew a long time ago that if I wanted to be a district attorney, I had to give up certain things."

"All work and no play—" I start to say, and she holds up her hands.

"Makes me a happy person," she finishes, and then, like the lawyer she is, she turns the tables on me. "Why hockey?"

"Well, considering my grandfather holds most of the records, and my father played hockey, I was on skates before I even took my first step. There is a picture at my parents' house of me on skates. I must have been around eleven months old, and my grandfather holds me under my arms while I move my feet."

"It's like you're a product of your environment," she points out.

"Yes," I agree with her, "and, apparently, I was really good at hockey. But that's because I was always on the ice. My older cousin Cooper was my idol growing up. He was the coolest kid I knew, so I wanted to be like him." I grab a piece of meatball myself. "Then the rest is history." She looks at me and is about to say something when Maria comes to ask if we need anything else. The rest of the conversation is about the wedding and the parts she remembers. I fill in the details she thinks she remembers but doesn't. We get up at the end of the meal, and she doesn't bother putting the scarf on. "It's cold out."

"I'm hot," she says, tying it around the chain of her purse.

"That you are," I mumble as we walk out. The car isn't there, but it's a black minibus this time.

"What's going on?" she asks as we approach the black van with the tinted windows. A woman comes stepping down the stairs of the little bus with a smile on her face, wearing all black.

"Hello, you two," she greets us. "I'm Brianna, and I'll be your tour guide for this evening."

"Tour guide?" Ryleigh repeats softly.

"If you want to head on in," Brianna invites, "we'll start the tour."

"After you." I motion to the bus as she goes up two steps where the driver sits, then up the one step to where the seats are. There are about five rows of seats, two on each side. "Take a seat."

She steps into the second row of seats, and I sit next to her as Brianna gets on the bus, but we can't even see her. "Hello." Her voice comes on in the speakers of the bus. "Can you all hear me?" she asks and then laughs. "I mean, can you guys hear me?"

"Yes," we both say at the same time. I look over at Ryleigh, who is staring at me, probably wondering what is going on.

"Good," she says as the bus starts to move. "I'm very excited to show you the dark side to Chicago. The side they don't tell you about. The side they keep under cover.

For the next three hours, I will show you places you've probably walked by before and had no idea what they were."

"Oh my God," Ryleigh whispers, leaning over, "is this a ghost tour?"

I chuckle. "It's not a ghost tour." I turn toward her. "Do you like ghosts?"

"I mean, not to live with me," she says, "but you know."

The city zooms by us. "Now, if you see this alley over here." She slows down in the almost vacant street, and we both look out the window at the empty alleyway that has four or five dumpsters all against the walls. "There have been over fifty movies filmed here."

"This is like a murder show," Ryleigh states, and I can't help but bite my lip not to laugh.

"All of them filmed in the middle of the night, all of them ending as soon as the sun comes up. Can anyone guess what movies they were?"

"*Nightmare on Elm Street*!" Ryleigh shouts out like we are on *Family Feud*.

"Close," Brianna says, "it was called *Wet Dreams on Elm Street*."

"*Wet Dreams*?" Ryleigh repeats softly, and I watch her face.

"This also has two loft apartments that rent by the hour," Brianna continues, "and you can add a videographer if you want to film something intimate." The bus starts moving. "For the next three hours, we will visit a dominatrix sex dungeon. We will also have a little demonstration on dildos and vibrators before ending the night at the ultra-secret sex club."

Ryleigh's head whips to me. "Is this a sex tour?"

TEN

MY HEAD SPINS while I listen to Brianna say what we will be doing for the next three hours. My head whips to Stone, who sits there wearing a cocky grin, his hands folded in front of him. "Is this a sex tour?"

"Yes," he confirms. "A private one, obviously." He leans in. "We aren't allowed to take photos either."

I open my mouth, thinking words would come out of it, but I'm literally too stunned to speak. "You brought me on a sex tour?" I have to ask him again because the shock of it has not settled in yet.

"I did," he says as if it's just another day in the office. "I'm really looking forward to the dildo demonstration." I bite on the inside of my cheek to stop from laughing. "If we see your old friend there, can you point him out?" He leans in and nips at my jaw. "I want to see what I'm up against."

"He's ten inches long and the size of my arm," I snap, "so you lose."

Brianna stops the bus. "First stop is the underground dominatrix dungeon." She gets up from her seat. "I will ask you at this time to please leave all your phones in this box." She holds up a blue and white box. "There will be no photography. The places I'm taking you are discreet and not available to the public." Stone gets up and holds out his hand for me. "If you could also leave your purse on the bus," Brianna says, "and if you can, your jackets as well. It'll be easier when we pass security."

"Pass security?" I don't know if I'm asking her or telling myself. But my hands move to take off my purse from around my body, and then I shrug off my jacket. I look over at Stone, who takes my jacket and places it in the seats across the row from us. I should have known something was up when I saw the blacked-out bus.

"If you can follow me," Brianna urges, taking off her headset and placing it on the dash. I follow her down the steps into the cold of the night, shivering once, but I'm not sure if it's because I'm cold or turned on. I look up at the brown building that looks like an office building, and a man about six foot seven opens the side door for us. "This building has four different floors for your pleasure." I step in but then feel the heat from the room and also because Stone slides his hand into mine.

The man comes over to us and eyes us up and down. "No phones, no videotaping, no touching of anything or anyone." His voice is gruff, and I know I would not fuck with him, so I just nod.

Brianna claps her hands together. "This is one of my favorite places to visit," she says with a twinkle in her eyes. "Each floor has four different playrooms. The top floor is one large playroom rented out for events."

"Imagine having your wedding here?" I joke, and Brianna looks over her shoulder.

"I know a friend who did it with her swinging friends." I look at Stone, who nods his head. "We will be only seeing two rooms this time. There will be Melinda, who likes to be called Goddess." She looks at me as we walk down the brown hallway, stopping at the first door. She knocks on it once before it's opened by the most beautiful woman I've ever seen. She's wearing a latex one-piece outfit that is open all the way down the front, pulled together like the top of a shoe. She wears a leather collar with a round silver ring in the middle of it. Garters hold up fishnet stockings with thigh-high latex boots, and she holds a small little whip in her hand. "Goddess," Brianna says to her.

"Welcome," she purrs, "to my playroom." She moves her wrist so the whip in her hand moves against her leg.

"Thank you for having us," I respond as if I'm visiting someone's house. I step into the darkened room that is painted black. Stone steps beside me but holds me in front of him, his hand wrapping around me from behind as he places his palm on my stomach. I look around the room, seeing many things that intrigue me. One wall has a mirror hanging on it with a table in front of it, and a brown wooden bed is in the middle of the room with four poles at each end with rings.

"Goddess." Brianna looks at me and almost hisses.

"Goddess," I repeat, not trying to offend anyone.

She walks over to me. "Isn't she a sight for sore eyes?"

"She's also mine and off-limits," Stone retorts as soon as she gives me the up and down, "Goddess."

I look over my shoulder at him as I wiggle my ass against him. "Interesting," she murmurs as she walks away from us and toward the desk, where she starts explaining how she likes to train her subs by having them open for her. She goes through the many whips she has hanging on the wall and then points at the bed. "Imagine if you held someone else's pleasure in your hand." She walks over to the bed, stepping up on the platform at the head before she turns to sit down on it. "That you can control what they feel." She spreads her legs. "It's the ultimate power."

"I bet," Stone mumbles, and I roll my lips when she looks at him and winks.

"You should try it sometime." She sticks her tits out. "If you want, I can help train her."

"I think she's good," Stone says for me, "but I'll let you know if we change our mind."

She smirks as Brianna says, "Thank you, Goddess," before turning to us. "Now, let's go to the other room."

She opens the door, and we step out. "Does that turn you on?" I look up at Stone, who looks at me.

"Not really. I mean, pleasing you turns me on. Taking you to the edge and then stopping just to tease you again." He puts my hand on his cock, which is harder than hard, rubbing it up and down and then releasing my hand. I want to literally get down on my knees and take him in my mouth. "That makes me harder than anything."

"This is Lady Louise's playroom," Brianna tosses over her shoulder before she knocks twice on the red door. "This one is more of a pain chamber."

The door opens, and I grab Stone's hand in mine when we step inside, squeezing it. Paddles of all shapes and sizes hang on the wall. There is an empty spot in the middle of the room with a wooden beam hanging and clips or what look like hooks. "This is a no." I lean into Stone. Lady Louise comes in wearing a latex bikini, also in black, except her nipples are out of the top with clamps on them, then have a chain that runs down her stomach and is in her bikini bottom. I'm about to run out the minute she starts talking, but instead, I listen politely until it's time to go.

I follow Brianna out of the room and toward the bus, sliding into the inside seat and waiting for Stone. "Hope that warmed you up," Brianna says. "The next place we're heading to will be a dildo demonstration."

Stone turns to me. "So I take it, it's a no for the bondage."

"Let's just say, if you are going to flog me, you better make sure I can't flog you back over the head." My eyes go into a glare. "I can see the appeal, but I'm going with you smacking my ass."

"Good to know," he notes before he bends his head to kiss me, his tongue sliding into my mouth. I'm getting hot from just kissing him when the bus stops.

"Ready to see your old friend?" Stone asks, and I laugh.

"I might be ready to meet a couple of new ones." I

wink at him before I stand and walk out with him.

"Careful of your step," Brianna warns me as we walk down the steps into a shop with a black door. The sign on the door says Closed, but she turns the handle and opens the door.

She turns on the lights, and I'm shocked. A huge chandelier hangs in the middle of the room with steps to the side that go up five flights of stairs. Mirrors are on all four walls, making it seem bigger. "There are five floors. The first floor is vibrators and dildos. Second floor is strap-on and anal toys. Third floor is kinks, fourth floor is for couples, and the fifth floor is for men."

"Well, then," I say, looking around at all the displayed vibrators, "shall we get started?"

"We shall," a woman states, walking in with long blondish-white hair, wearing a kimono. "I'm Debbie, and I'll be your teacher." She claps her hands together, and each finger has a ring on it.

"Shall we start over here?" She points at the glass display case. "Now, I'm sure we all know dildos are sex toys meant to be inserted in your vagina, anus, or in the mouth. There are also the double-sided ones, but that's for later," she says, looking down at the five vibrators before her. "As you can see, most of them are shaped like the best organ a man can have. His dick."

"Hear! Hear!" I cheer, knocking my hip to Stone's, who just laughs.

"Take this one," Debbie says, pulling out a beige-looking penis with a pink cock head and a suction cup at the end, right under the balls. "Looks like the real thing."

I look over at Stone, whose eyebrows pinch together. "It's called the Lovehoney Lifelike lover." She fists it in her hand. "It is almost lifelike with the veins and ridges, which help for G-spot stimulation. Plus, it has a suction cup that can stick to mirrors, headboards, and even shower walls. I would rate this a ten out of ten."

"I'll take one to go, please." I hold my hand up, making Debbie laugh and Stone glare at me.

She then takes a pink one out, and I smile at her. "Stone, say hello to my little friend." I clap my hands and laugh. "This baby has gotten me off in less than seventeen seconds."

"Five for me," Debbie shares, "at high speed. My eyes roll to the back of my head."

"Made me squirt," Brianna admits. "Best orgasm of my life."

"I guess we can skip that one," Stone declares, and I wrap my hand around his waist.

"Size doesn't matter, honey. It's what you do with it," I tell him. "It's where it hits. It's okay, you'll get there in time."

"I have no problem getting there," Stone retorts. "None whatsoever."

"The next one is my new favorite," Debbie confesses, taking out a purple one that looks like it's a two-for-one. "It's best used with couples since it comes with a remote." She holds up the remote. "You insert this into you, and the front piece works the clitoris. There are nine intense vibrating modes and nine thrilling vibrating modes. Wore this out with my husband, and I was leaking for days." She smiles so big. "It's best to be used by couples who have some experience with toys."

"You can add this one to the bag," Stone says, and I look at him with my mouth open. "We'll work up to it. Don't worry, you'll be okay." He pats my hand, and I have to say I have to rub my knees together. I'm so worked up right now.

"You won't be sorry, honey," Debbie assures me.

We spend an hour going from floor to floor. Stone remains at my side, placing soft touches here and there, from my back to my hip to pulling me to him. I'm ready to combust. We leave with a white bag with assorted lubes and massage oils. He also wanted to get edible underwear for me. "It'll be a snack." He winks at me, making Debbie laugh as she bags the two dildos.

The bus ride to the last place is torture, with Stone kissing me and then sucking on my neck. I'm practically panting when we get to the club. Brianna gets out, and a Black man dressed all in black with an earpiece smiles at her. She grips his jacket and pulls his mouth down to hers. "Say hello to Vince," she introduces when she steps away from him. "He's my lover."

"Nice to meet you, Vince," Stone greets, nodding at him.

"Welcome to the club," he says, opening the door. "Please step in." We both step into the dark entranceway.

A woman sitting behind a booth looks up at us and smiles, then beams when she sees Brianna. "They're with me.

"Okay, you two." Brianna turns to us. "This is an elite

sex club, which means there are rules. You need to wear a bracelet," she states, pointing at the chart beside the booth. "Please let me know which color you want."

"Red," Stone announces immediately, not even giving me a chance. I look and see that red means no contact. Yellow means maybe you should ask. Green is yes, let's go. Orange is group, and pink is whatever, wherever.

"Red it is," I confirm to Brianna, who grabs two red bracelets from the girl. "Make sure this can be seen."

"Pull up your sleeves," Stone grinds out between clenched teeth, "and don't move from my side."

"You sure are bossy," I sass, putting the bracelet on.

"Would you like masks?" Brianna asks.

"I would," I say, pointing at myself, and she hands me a black mask that I put around my head. "He needs one also." I point at Stone, who just smirks at me. They hand him one with ears, and when he puts it on, he looks even sexier, which is annoying as fuck.

"This is where I stop," Brianna says, "down those stairs are the stairs to heaven or hell, depending. You can watch or interact; the decision is all yours."

I look up at him. "Lead the way," I say, "since you brought me here."

He slides his hand into mine as he walks down the steps slowly, the heat rising as soon as we get halfway down. The soft lights come up the black stairs, and when we get to the bottom, we step into a red room. The bar at the back of the room has bartenders going back and forth. A couple of men on the stools look over at me as they talk to each other. Soft music fills the room, along with soft lighting. Just enough for you to see what is going on but not bright enough to be a spotlight. The red velvet walls add a bit of richness to it. I've never been to a sex club before, but I think this might be the classiest.

Stone pulls me to a high-top table in the corner. He puts his back against the wall and pulls me in front of him. So far, it looks like a regular bar until I look to the right and spot a long bench. "Oh my," I gasp. A woman sitting down wears a slinky dress with spaghetti straps. One of the straps fell, and her breast is out. She has a man on each side of her, and her spread legs are propped on each of their legs. She's making out with one man, who's fingering her while the other man plays with her nipple. The man stops kissing her, pulls his fingers out of her, and the other man takes his place. She turns her head to kiss the other man, the three of them in their own world, not caring if people watch them.

There is a group of six men, all sitting around a table, with three women sitting on three of the men's laps. All are dressed, but the women sit with their backs to the men, and you can see them moving up and down. "Time," someone at the table says, and the women get off the men and move on to the next man beside them.

"They are all having sex." I look up at Stone, who grips my hips.

My eyes scan the room as I see a woman in the middle of two men on the dance floor. Her legs are wrapped around the man in front of her, but her arms are wrapped around the man behind her as she devours his mouth. Her skirt is rolled around her waist, and the only thing you can see is the cocks out of their zippers as she takes them both. The ecstasy is all over her face as they work her together.

Stone moves his hands from my hips to my side, softly rubbing my torso up and down. "Which one are you watching now?" he whispers in my ear before sucking it into his mouth, and I can feel his cock on my back.

"Which one are you watching?" I wrap my arm around his neck, just like the woman on the dance floor, my nipples ready to be rolled.

"Over there." He motions with his head to the right side.

A woman sits on the bench with another woman in front of her, her shirt is pulled open and her legs are spread wide. The woman sitting behind her rolls her nipples in each hand as she whispers something in her ear. They look at each other right before the woman behind her leans down to kiss her. "She's ready!" she shouts when she slides her tongue out of the woman's mouth. "Who wants to play?"

One of the men gets up from a stool at the bar and walks over to them. "Hey, baby," he says softly to the woman sitting in the back, bending to kiss her. They make out with each other as the woman in front opens his pants, takes out his cock, and sucks it into the back of her mouth for a second before the man steps away and bends his head to lick and finger fuck the woman.

"Stone." I close my eyes and push back on him. He grabs my hand and pulls me toward the door. "Wait." He jogs up the steps, taking off his mask at the booth, and then ripping mine off me before he pushes the door open.

"No more," he declares to me as we step outside, and Brianna opens the door to the bus.

"Home," Stone orders, and she doesn't bother answering him.

I get into the seat and look over at him. "Why did you just drag me out of that place?"

"You looked like you were about to come," he explains softly to me, pulling up the armrest between us, "and there is no way in fuck anyone is going to watch you get off but me." He pulls me to him.

"I was," I admit to him, throwing a leg over his. "I was so close."

"How close?" He leans in to suck my neck. "How wet are you?" His hand roams up my leg toward where I need him the most. "Did you soak through your pants?" he asks me right before he cups my pussy through them. "Just a bit," he observes, and I know he's not lying because I can feel it. "Fuck, you're beautiful." His hand goes to the top of my pants, moving my sweater up. "So beautiful," he murmurs, sliding his hand inside my pants, and I'm not telling him to stop. His hand slides under my lace panties as I wait for his fingers to touch me. He glides right into my slit and thrusts two fingers into me. His mouth covers mine when I'm going to moan out, swallowing it. He doesn't say anything to me. All he does is slide his tongue into my mouth while he finger fucks me. It doesn't take much before I grip his wrist, making sure he doesn't stop before I close my knees and ride his hand. My pussy convulses around his fingers, and we don't even, or at least I don't even, notice the bus has stopped until he pulls his fingers out of me. I slowly open my eyes. In a daze, I look to my right and see my apartment building before I look over and see him stick his fingers into his mouth, cleaning them. "I can't wait to fucking feast on you."

ELEVEN

STONE

"IF YOU DON'T put your mouth where you say you are going to put your mouth, I'm going to hurt you," she warns me softly, pulling her leg off mine before grabbing her purse and putting it around her. She doesn't even bother with her jacket.

"Tonight is a whole different game. You're sober." She has to know that walking away from her last night was not easy.

"No, I'm drunk," she says, sitting up, the smirk on her face sexy as fucking hell, "on dick."

I laugh, getting up from my seat to grab the bag that contains the vibrators and my backpack, my cock straining against the zipper of my jeans. Tonight has been the longest foreplay of my life. From the sex dungeons to the dildos I plan on using on her—tonight, tomorrow, and the day after—to the sex club, all I want is to sink balls deep into her.

"Thank you so much, Brianna," Ryleigh says, looking

over her shoulder at me. "We had a great time."

"It sounds like you did." She doesn't even try to hide the smile on her face. "I'll see you both soon."

Ryleigh looks over her shoulder, her eyes twinkling. "We just might."

I just nod at Brianna as we walk down the steps and out of the bus. "Like fuck we are." There is no fucking way we are going back to that sex club ever again. If she wants to watch people have sex, I'll hang mirrors all around the house. That is how.

"Oh, please," Ryleigh counters, "don't tell me you didn't enjoy watching."

"It's like porn, just in real life." I pull open the door, waiting for her to step in.

"You could say that," Ryleigh mumbles as she walks in front of me and presses the button to the elevator. She waits for me to get in before she presses the floor number and then comes over to me. "Which one was your favorite?" she asks as she rubs my covered cock with the palm of her hand. My eyes narrow in on her eyes, watching her hand rub me. "Did you see that girl with two guys?"

"It's never going to happen, gorgeous," I deny right away. "The only dick you get is mine and mine alone. You want to use one of the toys as the other one, let's try it, but it's my dick and my dick alone that is going to make you come and come and come." I lean down to slide my tongue into her mouth, right before the door of the elevator opens and she turns around to step out, pulling her keys from her purse.

"Never say never, Stone." She unlocks the door, and I stand here.

"You sure about this, Ryleigh?" I say, and she looks at me, shocked I used her name. She takes off her bag and dumps it to the side of her.

Then she throws her jacket to the side, where it lands on her purse, before kicking off her shoes. Crisscrossing her arms in front of her, she pulls her sweater over her head, leaving her in her bra and black pants. Her tits are the perfect size for my hands. Her nipples pebble, and my hands tingle to graze them with my fingers. "There are a couple of things I'm sure of." She puts her thumbs in the sides of her pants and pulls them all the way down before she kicks them off sideways with all her discarded clothes. She peels her socks off next and then stands there in the middle of her entranceway wearing a black bra and black lace panties. "If you don't get in here"—she points to the side of her—"and fuck me like you said you could fuck me, I'm going to—" She stops talking because I'm inside her apartment in two steps. I toss my bag to the side along with the vibrator bag that goes kerplunk on the floor. One arm wraps around her waist, picking her up off her feet. Her legs wrap around my waist while her arms slide around my neck, and she smashes her lips onto me.

The kiss is full of hunger, her tongue fighting with mine for a couple of seconds before she moves her hands from around my neck to shrug the jacket off my shoulders. I let it fall off one arm before I switch arms around her waist, but she's locked so tight around my waist she can't fall off. "Bedroom or couch?" I ask as I let go of her lips. The sound of us panting fills the silent room.

The only light in the place comes from the outside. "Bedroom," she pants out, pointing backward before she sucks my neck and then moves the kisses up to my ear, sucking in the lobe. "You know, I'm sucking your cock the minute you put me down." I groan as my cock twitches in my pants. "The whole time we were watching, all I wanted to do was suck your cock. Get down on my knees and take you to the back of my throat."

I walk through the kitchen and living room to the door in the corner. My hands palm her ass, squeezing it as I get to the foot of her bed. "You want me standing up or lying down to take my cock?"

She pushes off my neck and looks at me, smiling. "Decisions, decisions."

"If I stand, I want you on your hands and knees so I can play with your ass." She tilts her head to the side. "If I'm lying down, I want you sitting on my face."

She throws her head back and laughs. "You know, either of those ends with me coming."

"So which is it going to be?" I ask.

She untangles herself from my waist before she reaches for my sweater. "First things first, you are way overdressed." Lifting it, I help her pull it over my head.

"Damn." She rubs her hands over my chest. "You hide the package well."

I chuckle. "Glad you approve." I lean down and kiss her clavicle, my hand moving to unclasp her bra strap.

She lets her bra fall forward, and I bend my head, taking one nipple in my mouth and sucking it in.

Her hands go to the button of my jeans as I move over to the other breast. The sound of the zipper going down echoes in the quiet room. Her hand slides into the front as she cups my cock. "Packing in more ways than one."

"Get on the bed." My voice is thick as she places one knee on the bed and then the other. I pull my pants down to my ankles, kicking off the shoes, jeans, and socks all in record time.

I get on the bed on my knees, meeting her in the middle of her king-size bed. Her hand roams up my chest as she leans in to kiss me. I turn on my back, taking her with me, her legs going over me and straddling me. She sits smack-dab on my covered cock, and I can feel her wetness through my boxers. Her hand rubs my chest as my hands come up to pinch her nipples, and her head goes back. She moves her hips back and forth as I roll them between my fingers. Then squeezing them tightly, she bites her lips as she watches my fingers slowly roll the nubs. She leans forward, putting one hand on my cheek while she slides her tongue into my mouth, twirling it once before moving down from my lips to my chest, her tongue leading a trail straight down to my cock.

She moves the boxers down my hips, and my cock springs free. I lift my hips to help her shed the boxers, and she throws them over her shoulder somewhere. My eyes on hers, she grabs my cock at the base and then licks it from my balls all the way to the tip. Her tongue comes out to lick the precum away before she moves back down to the base, repeating it again, her eyes never leaving mine. She comes up, flicking her tongue on the head of my cock before she kisses it. My head falls back for a second as I take in the heat of her tongue. I lift my head again and see her watching me as she sucks the head into her mouth, swallowing half of me before pulling up again, her hands now fisting the base of my cock. "Gorgeous," I call her name through clenched teeth, "turn that ass around and sit on my face." She wiggles her ass from side to side. "So I can taste that ripe pussy."

"You don't have to ask me twice." She lets go of my cock to throw her leg over me, her ass pointing in my face. "Let me take off—" She doesn't finish because my hands tear through her lace thong. "Did you just…?"

"Sorry." I curl up. "Can't talk," I mutter, sucking her pussy in my mouth, "eating." I roll back down, taking her with me. She sits up straight for a second, my tongue fucking her pussy while my hand moves to the front to play with her clit. "Ride my face, baby," I mumble before getting back to eating her. She moves her hips up and down before she falls face-first and puts my cock in her mouth. I hold her ass cheeks in my hands while I lick from her clit to her opening before sucking her lips into my mouth. All she does is moan, and the vibrations run through my cock. I lick her up and down twice more before adding two fingers inside her.

"Yes!" She lets go of my cock to moan before taking it back in her mouth. My fingers move at the same speed as her hand on me. She's come already, so she's primed for another one, and I can feel it on my fingers as her juice runs down my hand. "Right there," she moans, and I curl my fingers, rubbing her soft G-spot. She wiggles her ass in my face, and I lift my hand, slapping it down on her softly once before rubbing it in a circle. Her pussy pulses over my fingers when I do it again.

"Yes!" She lets go of my cock, but her hand moves up and down, her head resting on my thigh. "I think I'm going to…" She doesn't have to tell me because she's moaning out my name, my fingers moving in and out of her as I slide one inside her ass. "Oh, fuck!" she yelps as I move three fingers into her at the same time. "Yes," she breathes out, her hand not working my cock, but I don't even care because all I want to do is make her come over and over again.

"Right fucking there," she groans between clenched teeth, and I move even faster. "Oh my God." She shakes on top of me, and I move my head, taking her clit into my mouth and sucking in while she comes on my fingers. "Oh my God," she repeats over and over again as she moves her hips from side to side, trying to get away from me as her orgasm subsides. However, I'm going for another one. She's fucking sensitive because she's trying to close her knees, but I want one more.

"One more, gorgeous," I demand frantically, sucking her clit while fingering her over and over again. Her panting and moaning fill the room, and her hand finds my cock.

"If I go again, I want you to come in my mouth."

"Deal," I agree between clenched teeth. After this

whole night, it takes her two more sucks of my cock before she's coming on my fingers, and I'm releasing down her throat.

TWELVE

RYLEIGH

I SUCK HIS cock to the back of my throat, taking everything he has to give me, swallowing every last drop before letting his cock go with a plop out of my mouth. My legs give out, and I'm sure he's suffocating, but all I can feel is his tongue still licking me. His fingers are gone from my pussy and my ass, something that is brand new for me. I didn't know if I would like it, but then again, I don't think I've ever had back-to-back orgasms like that.

"Do you want to ride, or do you want me to fuck you?" he asks before licking again.

"I think I'm dead," I answer him honestly, and he chuckles before moving away and getting off the bed. I turn on my back to watch his ass and, fuck, did I win the jackpot with him. His cock is bigger than I've had in a while, but the girth, fuck, my jaw was sore after two minutes of taking him in my mouth.

He comes back, tossing condoms on the bedside

table. I put my hand under my head to watch him, my legs open only because I don't think I can close them. He puts one knee on the bed, tearing the condom pack in his hand before pulling the condom out and tossing the foil wrapper to the side. "I've never actually watched a man sheathe himself before." My mouth says the words my head is thinking. His eyes find mine for a second before my eyes move back down to his hand holding the base of his cock as he rolls the latex down to the base.

"Do you know how fucking sexy you look right now?" He moves between my legs.

"Nipples red and tight." He moves his fingers to pinch them before rolling them. "Legs spread with your pussy wet and pink." He rubs his fingers through my folds. "Clit nice and tight, ready to be played with." I think he's going to rub it, but instead, he flicks it right before he slaps his hard cock on it. "Your pussy is waiting for my cock, isn't it?" he questions, and I think I could come just from him talking about it. "I want you to watch your pussy swallow my cock."

"Yes," I say because instead of that, all I want to do is beg him to fuck me.

"I'm going to give it to you nice and slow." He slides the tip of his cock in an inch before pulling out. My hands go to his hips to pull him into me. "Want you nice and fucking soaked when I slap my balls against your ass." He pushes another inch into me, and I groan. "Your pussy is like fucking heaven." He pulls out before feeding a bit more into me. "Look at how well you take my cock," he praises. I look down between us, seeing half of his cock fit into me, and I've never felt fuller in my life. "That's a good girl." I look into his eyes. "Your nipples need me." He slips half his cock into me before leaning down and biting one nipple. My hips move up, and he stops. "This isn't how this is going to work," he informs me, and I glare at him. "I'm going to fuck you the way I want to fuck you." He pulls out to the tip. "Then your pussy will suck the cum right out of me."

"Stone," I moan, moving my head from side to side, "please."

"What do you want, gorgeous?" he asks me softly, like he's not making me want to pull out my hair. He pushes his cock into me halfway again.

"I want you to fuck me, goddammit," I bite out between clenched teeth.

"I am," he assures me, sliding out, and this time stopping at the tip of his cock, moving his hand right onto my pelvic bone, "but there are so many other places I want to touch." He moves his thumb down to my pussy, sliding it in with his cock and then moving it up to my clit. "Like right here," he says, moving my clit in circles. "She needs attention too." He moves three-quarters in now, and my legs grip his hips, and he stops. "No." He shakes his head. "I need you to bend those knees and pull them back so I can go so deep you'll feel like I'm in your throat."

"Yes!" I grab my knees, pulling them back. "Is this what you want?" I ask. "I'm open for you."

"Almost." He looks between us as he slides his cock

into me twice but stops where he was before, his thumb moving my clit around and around. I swear I'm about to come again, which makes no sense since he hasn't even pounded into me. "Your pussy." He looks down, and I can feel the wetness dripping down my ass to my bed. "It's strangling me." He pushes more into me, and I close my eyes, trying to breathe instead of coming, but I can't help it. He bends to take a nipple in his mouth, sucking while his thumb moves my clit side to side. He finally slams into me. I swear to God, I see stars. My eyes roll to the back of my head, and I come on his cock after one fucking thrust. "That's my greedy girl," he says, pulling out and then pistoning back into me again, his balls slapping my ass. "Coming on my cock." He slams back into me now. "For the next three days, my cock is going to be in your pussy or your mouth." He slams into me over and over again. "It's going to be where you'll be begging me to either stop fucking you or to fuck you again."

"Both," I mumble as my toes curl, and my stomach tightens.

"Your pussy is begging for me to come," he growls between clenched teeth as he puts his hands on the sides of my head. "I want you to come with me." I shake my head, not sure I can. "If you don't come with me, the next time I eat your pussy, I won't make you come on my face." He slams into me over and over again, and my hand comes up to hold his arm. "That's my girl, I feel it." He doesn't let up. "Hurry, I'm there." And just like that, my body listens to him, and we come at the same time.

His cock twitches inside me, pushing as he buries it to the hilt. "Fuck." He buries his face in my neck as my legs wrap around his hips, and my arms stay dead on the side of me. "That was—" he says, catching his breath, and I don't even notice I'm still panting, "that was fucking incredible."

"It was all right," I lie. His head comes out from my neck, and he just smirks at me, pulling his cock out and then slamming it back in, before rotating his hip on my sensitive clit. "Okay, fine, fine, it was incredible."

"That's what I thought," he says as he pulls out of me. "I have to get rid of the condom." He looks down at my pussy. "But, fuck, I want to taste you again." He bends his head, sucking me into his mouth.

"Go get rid of the condom." I push his head away from me, and he smirks. "The bathroom is over there." I point at the side door where my bathroom is.

I watch him walk into the bathroom before I put my head back and exhale. I hear the toilet flush and then the water turn on. I'm about to get off the bed to go clean myself when he walks out of the bathroom, turning the light off, not giving me a chance to check him out with the lights on.

He walks to the side of the bed. "Open," he urges, and I look at him confused. "Open your legs for me, gorgeous." I don't know why I do what he says, but I do, and there, in the middle of my bed, he leans over and cleans me. He swipes the warm cloth over me a couple of times before he tosses the rag to the side. "I want to fuck you again, but I need a catnap before." My head is still spinning from him taking care of me after sex, so I don't know what to say or do. "You okay sleeping naked, or do you want a shirt?"

"I'm—" I start to stumble with my words. "I'm okay like this," I lie to him. I hate sleeping naked, but I also want to feel his skin on mine again.

"Which side do you sleep on?" he asks, walking to his clothes. He pulls his shirt from the pile and comes back to the bed.

"In the middle," I admit, and he laughs as he pulls the comforter from the bed before putting his knee on it.

"Lift your arms," he says, and again, I do what he tells me. He slides the T-shirt over my head, and I smell him all around me. "Let's sleep a bit."

"I said that I'm okay sleeping naked." I protest having his shirt on me, but I'm also not doing anything to take it off.

"Yeah, and I have always said you are a gorgeous liar." He slides under the covers before wrapping his arm around my waist. "Now, get your ass under the covers so we can rest," he mumbles, and I slide under the covers with him.

I turn in his arms, my face in his chest. "Why do you get to sleep naked?" I ask as my legs tangle with his.

"Because I sleep naked." He kisses my head.

"You're annoying," I mumble, tucking myself into his side.

"You're gorgeous and amazing," he continues, "and you have the best—"

I put my hand in front of his mouth. "If you're fishing

for compliments, it won't happen."

He laughs, and my head moves with his chest. "All you need is for your head to be bigger than it already is if I tell you it was the best sex of my life."

"You don't have to tell me," he replies, and I slap his chest. "If it wasn't, then we'll practice and practice to get there."

"Is that so?" I ask, my eyes getting heavy.

"I have three days off," he states, his hand rubbing my arm, "and I plan to spend the majority of it wrapped up in you."

"What if I had plans?" My eyes get even heavier, so I just leave them closed.

"You do have plans. With me." His lips kiss my forehead before I drift off to sleep just as the sun rises, and he's one day closer to leaving. I push away the thought, instead telling myself he's a player, and I need to keep my guard up. At the same time, my heart slowly drifts off to sleep in the most content way.

THIRTEEN

STONE

"What time is the car going to be here?" Ryleigh asks as I turn off the shower and step out. She's standing at the sink with her hair wrapped in a towel and wearing the white shirt of mine she put on two days ago to sleep in.

"Four," I tell her, grabbing a white plush towel from the basket next to the shower, wrapping it around my waist, and moving to stand behind her.

I grab her hips in my hands and bend to kiss behind her ear, making her tremble in my arms. "Which still leaves us with two hours to…"

"Eat and have you packed." She picks up her toothbrush, putting toothpaste on it before turning on the water and putting it in her mouth.

"I could eat." I look at her in the mirror as my hand cups her pussy, knowing she's not wearing anything under the white shirt.

"You just ate that," she reminds me of when I set her down on her shower bench and spread her legs while I devoured her. I'm literally addicted to her. It's shocking to think about it, but even more when I admit it to myself.

"I did," I mumble as I trail kisses from behind her ear to the back of her neck to the other side of her ear, "but I thought I would get one last meal before I go."

"You thought wrong." She bends to rinse her mouth and then her toothbrush. "We need food."

"I need you," I tell her as she turns in my arms and puts her head back for me to bend and kiss her lips. I grab her hips, pulling her to me so she can feel my hard-on, and she laughs.

"Does your dick ever go down?" She giggles as I pick her up and put her on the counter.

"It does, but only when you aren't around." I start to take off my towel when the doorbell rings.

"That would be the food." She puts her hands on my chest, and my heart speeds up. "You have one hour and forty-five minutes before the car arrives."

"I can be late," I deflect as she softly pushes me away from her. "It's a private plane."

She shakes her head and moves to walk out of the bathroom. "If you answer the door like that, I'm going to smack your ass, and not in a good way."

She stops and looks over her shoulder at me. "I'm going to ignore what you just said." She grabs her robe from a hook. "And try not to put rat poison in your food." Tying her robe around her waist, she walks away from me.

I make my way over to my bag, grabbing a pair of boxers before sliding them on and then my track pants and another white T-shirt. I pick up the towel and walk back toward the bathroom, past the bed that looks crooked. I stop at the night table with four empty condom wrappers from last night. I grab them in my hand, then hang the towel and toss them in the garbage.

"Are you coming?" Ryleigh shouts from the kitchen.

"All over your face!" I shout back at her and listen to her laugh out loud, which makes my chest get tight and my cock twitch.

She stands at the island where I ate her out last night, right before I fucked her brains out, or at least that's what she told me. "I got you a double cheeseburger, loaded." She points at the container. "And a loaded baked potato."

"What did you get?" I pull out the stool and sit down, grabbing the food.

"The same but a single and not a double." She sits down next to me, and I look over at her as she eats.

"So what are your plans this week?" I ask, trying not to overthink anything.

"I have work." She takes a bite of her burger. "Then I plan on icing my vagina and taking lots of baths." She looks over at me, and I wink at her.

"What about next weekend?" I ask, instead of saying what I really want to say. *How about you come and stay with me next weekend?*

"Not sure yet," she mumbles as she eats. I wonder if she'll ask me about my travel schedule, but she skates around it. We both finish eating two minutes before my phone alerts me that the driver's waiting downstairs.

"I'm going to go get my bag," I mutter, walking back

into her room and shoving my stuff in the bag before I return and see Ryleigh cleaning up the counter.

"Did you get everything?" she asks, her voice a bit cheerier than I want it to be.

"I did," I confirm, walking to the door and sliding my boots on before grabbing my jacket. Picking up my backpack and tossing it over my shoulder, I look up to see her standing there.

"Thank you for coming to see me," she says, getting on her tippy-toes and wrapping her arms around my neck, "and for all those awesome orgasms."

I smile and laugh at the same time. "You are more than welcome." I kiss her lips. "But I think the orgasms were mutual." I stare into her eyes, trying to prolong the inevitable goodbye. I lean down and slide my tongue into her mouth. Of course, it goes from zero to a hundred in two seconds with her.

"You have to go," she whispers when we let the kiss stop.

"I'll call you," I declare softly, not ready to let her go but also knowing I need to leave.

"Okay," she gives in. "Let me know you got home safe."

"Will do." I kiss her one last time before walking out her door. She follows me to the elevator, and I step in to press the L button, holding up my hand. "Be good," I urge as the door closes, and all I can see is her holding up her hand.

The driver opens the door for me as I toss my bag on the seat and then get in. When I get there, the plane is waiting for me, and I jog up the four steps into the plane. I toss my bag into one of the chairs and sit down in the one facing the front when my phone rings. I stupidly think it's her, but instead, it's Christopher.

"Hello," I answer right away, putting the phone to my ear while they close the plane doors.

"Hey," he huffs, and I know he's working out on the bike. It's when he usually calls me. "What's up?"

"Nothing much, on my way home," I tell him as the plane moves, and I look out the window, hating I'm putting so much space between us.

"On your way home from where?" he asks, and I exhale.

"I spent the weekend in Chicago." I don't know if I want to tell him anything, but I also know I need to talk to someone.

"You spent the weekend in Chicago? Why the hell would you do that?"

"I was with Ryleigh," I finally admit.

"Shut the fuck up," he fires back right away. "You spent the whole weekend with her?" He doesn't wait for me to answer. "Or you were in town and had dinner with her?"

"We played Chicago and then had a couple of days off, so I stayed with her."

He laughs. "Romeo is going to kick your ass." He mentions Ryleigh's brother and his brother-in-law.

"Well, he needs to get used to it." I look out and see we've already taken off.

"Is that so?" I can hear the humor in his voice.

"That is so," I tell him. "I'm not going to lie. I'm fucking obsessed with her." Fuck, saying the words feel good. "She's like all that and then some."

"Jesus, how good is she in bed?" I clench my fist.

"None of your fucking business," I say tightly. "All you need to know is this isn't just a fling."

"Stone," he says, "you live in Nashville."

"I'm aware." I pretend I'm not irritated with that fact.

"She's in Chicago and has a really important job." I'm annoyed he even knows this much about her.

"Again, I'm aware, but thanks for letting me know."

"I'm not the bad guy," he reminds me softly. "I'm just pointing out the obvious; long-distance relationships suck balls."

"When is the last time you were in a long-distance relationship?" I counter him, and he groans.

"I would think spending all weekend with Ryleigh would have you in a better mood." I put my head back and close my eyes.

"I'm sorry. It's just we're figuring it out," I tell him. "We just haven't spoken about it."

"You spent the whole weekend with her and didn't have the conversation about what happens after you leave?" He laughs the whole time. "You are so dumb."

"Thanks, appreciate the talk."

"Anytime. Let me know how it works out for you when you do bring up the, 'hey, are we dating even though I live in Nashville and you live in Chicago?'"

"How's your girlfriend?" I snap.

"Well, considering I haven't met her yet, I'm going to

say she's miserable without me." He gulps some water. "That's just my guess."

"You're a dork." I laugh. "She's probably living her best life without you."

"Maybe," he laughs, "or maybe not. Anyway, I'm hitting the shower. We leave in two hours for Vegas."

"Again?" I laugh as he groans.

"The last time this season, thank fuck. Unless it's the playoffs, but so far looks like it'll be Calgary."

"So far we don't even qualify for the playoffs," I inform him. "Be safe," I say before I hang up with him.

It takes an hour and thirty minutes from wheels up to wheels down, and when I'm walking into my house, I have this tightness in my chest I can't get rid of. I don't even bother turning on the lights before walking upstairs to my bedroom. When I call her, she sounds like she's sleeping, so I tell her I'll call her tomorrow. Going to bed without her isn't fun at all.

The next day is a game day, and we text a couple of times, but I'm busy, and she's preparing for a trial, so it's just short texts here and there. Even when I get home that night, I know it's too late to call her, so I text her instead. I'm surprised when she answers me back, so I call her.

"Hey," she says, and her voice sounds tired.

"Why are you still up?" I ask her softly instead of telling her how much I miss her.

"Reading my brief and making notes," she says. "I'm going to go to bed in about ten minutes."

"Okay, gorgeous," I reply, waiting for her to tell me she misses me or she saw the game, but she doesn't say anything. "Sleep tight. Try not to miss me," I joke.

"I'll try my hardest." She laughs before hanging up.

The next day is the same thing—just little conversations here and there—so by Wednesday, I'm ready to kill someone, anyone.

When she calls me after seven, I'm just getting home from my second workout of the day. We've played two games since I left her, and both games have resulted in us getting our asses handed to us.

"Hey, gorgeous," I answer after one ring.

"What did you send me?" she asks, and I press the FaceTime button for the first time since I left her on Sunday. I kept waiting for her to do it, but I'm done.

Her face comes onto the screen, and it's even more beautiful than in my memories. "What did you send me?" Her eyes go big as she looks at me.

"Just something that reminded me of you." I smirk at her as I walk upstairs to my bedroom. "Why?"

"Did you send me this lingerie?" She picks up something black and sheer.

"It better be me and not someone else," I snap, and she smirks. "Did you get the other present?"

"Oh, you mean the vibrator?" Her voice rises.

"The one you weren't sure about buying," I remind her.

"Yes, yes, I did." She picks up the pink vibrator she debated getting but then stops. It has a G-spot stimulator, and I can't wait to see what she does with it. "I'm not going to lie. I'm very excited to try a new little friend."

I laugh as I fall onto my bed. "How many times have

your friends visited since I've been gone?"

"No friends have visited, but," she confesses, "I did masturbate this morning before getting out of bed."

"You did what?" I gasp.

"Are you telling me you haven't come since Sunday?" she asks, and I just look at her as she laughs. "That's what I thought. Even though you fucked me a gazillion times."

"What are you doing now?" I ask softly.

"I just got home from work, and I was going to take a shower. Why?"

"Change into the lingerie and call me back," I tell her, and her eyes go big.

"Or," she counters, walking over to her bedroom, "I get naked now with you on the phone and show you how this little toy works."

"That's even better than what I was thinking," I admit.

"Umm," she hums, putting her phone down on the bed and all I see is her head. "I want to see your cock too, so get that monster out."

"You think my cock is a monster?"

"Obviously, that's the only thing you got from everything I've said." She picks up the phone, and I see she isn't wearing a top.

She gets onto the bed. "I need to prop the phone up." I don't know if she's telling me or herself. But she turns, and I see her bare back before she grabs a couple of pillows and props the phone on them, then moves back, and I see her naked. Her legs spread and show me what I've been missing since Sunday. "I want to see some dick, Stone," she demands. I pull off my shirt, and she literally moans as I see her fingers working between her legs.

I put the phone at the end of the bed with pillows behind it like she did. Getting on my knees, I pull my track pants down for her to watch my cock spring out. Her head goes back as she moans. "Did you miss me?"

"Yes," she pants, "did I ever miss you."

"Where is the toy?" I ask, and she holds it up with the hand that isn't playing with herself. "Are you wet?"

"Yes." Her nipples are so tight all I want to do is bite them. "Put it in you," I direct her, and she rubs the tip of the vibrator up and down her slit before she slips it in. "Nice and slow," I say as I grip the base of my cock. "Make sure the flicker is at your clit," I tell her of the little piece at the top of the vibrator that moves like a tongue.

"It is," she confirms, rolling one of her nipples between her fingers.

"Turn on the flicker first." She presses the button, and her hips lift off the bed.

"Oh," she breathes out. "I was not expecting that."

"What does it feel like?" I watch her face, my cock hard in my hand.

"Like you licking me." Her breathing is now coming in spurts.

"Turn on the G-spot," I order her, and she presses the button. Her head falls back against the pillows while her free hand comes up to squeeze her tit.

"Tell me what it feels like." The noises she's making

push me closer and closer and closer to the edge, so I slow my strokes.

"It feels like—" she says as she closes her knees.

"Keep those legs open so I can see that juicy pink pussy," I command her.

"It's too much." She moves her hips, and I know she's close.

"Put it on higher," I order, and she shakes her head side to side. "Be a good girl and show me my pussy." Her legs open wide, but she bends her legs at the knees. "That's my good girl. You know what you need?" She doesn't answer because she's focusing on the feeling rushing over her. "My cock in your mouth."

"Yes," she agrees breathlessly.

I stroke my cock faster, knowing she's almost there. "Me standing over you. Fucking your face." Her hips move faster as she chases the orgasm. "My hand pulling your hair while I make you choke on my cock."

"Yes, yes!" she pants. "Oh, God, yes."

"You want to choke on my cock, gorgeous?" She moans. "Nothing is more beautiful than when you take my cock." She pulls her legs back. "In your pussy." My balls get tight, and I know I'm going to come any second. "In your mouth, coming right down your throat." I watch as she comes all over that fucking toy, wishing it was my cock as I come all over my hand.

FOURTEEN

RYLEIGH

THE ALARM GOES off, and I roll over in my bed to grab it from under the pillow beside me. After I press snooze and turn back over, the smell of Stone fills my nose, making me bury my face deeper into the pillow. I pull the comforter closer to me and curl up in a ball before my phone rings, but it's not my alarm. "Hello." I put the phone to my ear without checking who it is.

"Morning, gorgeous," Stone greets me, and he sounds like he's awake.

"Why are you so chipper?" I turn on my back and blink once and then twice before my eyes get used to the sunlight streaming through the windows. His laughter makes my stomach flutter.

"I wish I was there to bring you coffee," he says.

"You and me both." I finally toss the covers off me and throw my legs over the side of the bed to get up. "You and me both," I repeat when I hear a car door slam on his side of the phone.

"Where the hell are you going at the ass crack of dawn?" I ask and then want to kick myself for asking. I've been very, very good about not asking him any questions. Not that I didn't want to know what he was doing every day, but because I don't want him to think I am more involved than I am. Did I want to call him every morning to ask him how his night was? Yes. Did I do it? Absolutely fucking not. Did I want to FaceTime him when I had a second during the day to see how he was doing and what he was doing? Again, the answer is yes. But did I do it? I would rather walk on coals with no shoes for seven days than do what I wanted to do.

"I have a game tomorrow, so today is a two-workout day. I'm going in before on-ice training starts so I can do some weightlifting."

"That sounds like a lot of work." I walk to the kitchen and start my coffee, looking down at the white shirt I've been wearing to bed every night since we were together.

"It's not that bad. What are you doing this weekend?"

"I have dinner with a couple of friends," I tell him, tapping the counter with my finger as I watch the coffee pour into my cup. "Why?"

"I was going to ask you to come and visit me." I close my eyes.

Say no, my head yells, *say no*. "It's really short notice—" I start to say.

"Yeah, that's what I thought." His voice sounds dejected. "Anyway, I'm at the rink." I know he's lying to me because I know it takes him thirty minutes to get there from the last conversation we had. "Have a great day, gorgeous."

My chest contracts. "You too, Stone," I reply. He hangs up on me, and I look down at the phone.

"Going there would be a huge mistake," I tell myself. "There is no reason for you to go there." I grab the cup of coffee since it's finished brewing. "I mean, technically, you can work at home for the next week since you have to get ready for trial." I pour the milk in my coffee. "What would he say if I showed up there?" I take a sip of the coffee. "I mean, he did come and see you for the weekend." I counter my argument. "But he was already in town for work, so it's not like he went out of his way to come see you." I take a deep inhale as I assess this argument. "But he could have gone home. Instead, he stayed with you for three days and gave you the best sex of your life." I pinch my eyebrows together. "It wasn't my entire life," I scoff as if I don't know the truth. "Either way, it would be a bad idea to show up at his place for the weekend."

I lean back against the counter, the coffee in both hands as I argue with myself over the fact I want to go visit Stone for the weekend. "Or you show up to get him out of your system and worst case is you stay the weekend, having amazing sex and a tremendous number of orgasms." I shake my head. "It's a bad, bad idea," I finally say and walk into my bedroom to get ready for work.

The whole time the lingering thought about going to surprise him is in the back of my mind. Even when I get to the office and slide on my shoes, I'm talking myself out of it. When I sit down and turn on my computer to search flights to Nashville, I tell myself it's a bad fucking idea. I buy the ticket, just in case I want to use it. Worst case, I can cancel, and it's no big deal. I also go online and look for hockey tickets, but I'm so out of my league it's not even funny. So I pick up the phone and dial the one person I know who I can ask. It's also the one person I don't want to tell, but I have no choice. "Well, well, well," Gabriella answers right away. "Look who it is."

I laugh, turning in my chair and looking out my window at the skyline. "It's your favorite sister-in-law," I tell her, and she snorts.

"Considering you are my only one, I agree," she retorts. "What's going on? It feels like I haven't spoken to you in forever."

"Not much, busy preparing for a case, same old same old…" I trail off. "I have to ask you something but I need you to promise me you won't tell anyone, and then you won't judge me."

"Uh-oh," she mumbles, "am I going to need bail money?"

"No, nothing like that." I smile, happy I know she would have my back. "Hypothetically—" I start.

"I love hypothetical questions." Her voice pitches high. "They are always my favorite."

"Good to know." I take a second to think how to word this question, but there really is no way to sugarcoat any of this. "Let's say I would want to go to Nashville and watch a hockey game. What tickets should I get?"

"Watch a hockey game," she repeats, "in Nashville."

"Correct." I ignore the thumping of my heart and the way my palms are getting even more sweaty than humanly possible.

"Why would you want to do that, Ryleigh?" Her voice is questioning.

"Hypothetically, of course," I start, "I would be going to visit a friend."

"A friend," she huffs. "Does this friend have a name?"

"Okay, knock it off," I finally snap. "You know damn well he has a name."

"Oh, I know he has a name, but you were doing all your lawyer cross-examining questions, and I decided to play along." I roll my eyes. "Now, I have to ask, are you insane?" Her voice pitches high. "You have to be insane because, well, I don't really know why, I just know this is a very bad idea."

"Is it really? He was here last weekend, and we enjoyed spending time together."

"He was there last weekend?" she repeats, her voice in disbelief. "And you enjoyed spending time together?"

I exhale. "What tickets do I get if I wanted to surprise him?"

"Surprise him," she groans. "Listen, as someone who went to surprise a man, that did not work out for anyone." My stomach feels like it's going to vomit all over the floor. "Why don't you give him a heads-up?"

"No." I shake my head. "I haven't decided whether I'm going." *Oh, you're going,* my head screams.

"Ugh, fine," she finally concedes. "I think I can get you tickets."

"No!" I shout at her. "You'll have to call your family, and this is a do-not-get-family-involved situation, so I just need you to tell me where I should sit."

"You can sit anywhere, really. What you want to do is show up before the game and go down to the glass so he can see that you are there," she instructs me, "but don't make a sign."

"Don't make a sign?" I question the statement. "What the hell does that mean?"

"People write signs and stand around the glass like 'You're My Favorite Player' or 'Rock, Paper, Scissors for a Stick.'" I'm amazed at this.

"I could make a sign that says, 'You Banged Me so Good I Came Back for More.'" I laugh while Gabriella groans.

"I don't tell you how good your brother is in bed." I close my eyes and fake vomit. "So it's a two-way street." I agree. "So no sign."

"That I can do," I assure her. "So like what time should I get there?"

"You should get there as soon as the doors open so you can get a good place at the glass. I would stand next to the kids since the players usually go where the kids are," she informs me. "Maybe I'll come and meet you for the game."

"No!" I shout. "I haven't decided whether I'm going."

"Oh, you're going. You knew you were going before you called me, or else you wouldn't have called me."

"I have to go," I deflect instead of saying she's right. "Wish me luck. And don't forget you promised not to tell anyone," I remind her before I hang up and buy a ticket to the hockey game.

That night when he calls, I'm so nervous he's going to guess I'm coming that I rush off the phone with him, and when he calls me in the morning, I lie and tell him I'll be in court all morning long. My flight lands at four o'clock, and I check into the closest hotel I could find next to the venue. I don't know if he's going to invite me to his house or not, and I wasn't going to be stranded in Nashville without a place to sleep.

I toss my crossover bag on the bed before opening my carry-on luggage. I take a quick shower before I slide on my black jeans with a black turtleneck and a black vest. "It looks like I'm going to a funeral," I tell my reflection when I put on a bit of mascara before grabbing my white sneakers and black purse. I walk out and set the GPS to the venue, my heart's beating so fucking fast it's making it feel like it's going to explode in my chest. I wasn't even this nervous when I was in court for the first time.

I walk up to the door, seeing all the yellow jerseys along the way, a chunk of them with his name on them, and I can't help but smile. Pulling out my phone and scanning the ticket, I walk toward the section Gabriella texted me to go to. I walk into the arena and see the lights are mostly off. Walking down the concrete steps toward the glass, I stand here with my phone in my hand and text Gabriella a picture of the ice.

Me: *Am I at the right spot?*

She answers me right away.

Gabriella: *Yes, they are going to skate out and*

practice where you are. I'm so nervous for you.

I laugh.

Me: *I'm not nervous at all. Worst case, I order room service and go home tomorrow. Best case, I have the best sex of my life.*

Gabriella: *I just threw up in my mouth thinking of my cousin having sex with you.*

Me: *It can't be worse than listening to you at your bachelorette party describe my brother's penis. In detail, down to the tip.*

Gabriella: *Touché.*

I stand here with the phone in my hand, rethinking everything I've done in the past two days. Who am I even? Working from home is nothing for a Friday, but then I took Monday off, in case I was here until then. I haven't taken a day off since I started, and now, here I am taking a day off to spend it with Stone, who doesn't even know I'm coming. What if he has someone he invited to the game since I told him I couldn't come? The thought makes my hand shake and my mouth run dry.

I'm about to turn around and walk away when I look around and see the glass is now packed with people waiting for them to come on the ice. I look around, wondering if I should just go back to the hotel room and maybe text him. Then he can decide if he wants to come to me or not.

The crowd cheers as the lights come on full blast, and I see black pucks being tossed on the ice. I look at the ice and beside me I see a teenage boy wearing Stone's jersey and hat. I can see the players skate onto the ice, and my eyes look from one to the other. Then I spot him, laughing with someone he is talking to on the other side of the rink.

I swear my heart stops in my chest as his head turns, and he looks over to this side of the rink. I don't even know if he'll recognize me or not. But the minute I see him scan the crowd and his eyes go past mine, then whip back and go big, as the smile that was on his face is now gone. His mouth hangs open, and he shakes his head before skating over to my side of the rink. The kid next to me goes crazy and slaps the glass, calling his name, but his eyes are on mine, and I can't help but smile at him. All the nerves from the last two days leave my body.

He stops in front of me. "What are you doing here?" he shouts, and the kid next to me calls his name.

I motion my head to the kid next to me. He bends over and picks up a puck before tossing it over the glass and then looks back at me. The smile fills his face and his eyes are light golden brown, and all I want to do is kiss his lips. "Surprise!" I shout, shrugging, and he just shakes his head before he looks around and then holds up a finger, turning and skating away to the bench. I look at the kid beside me, who is freaking out he got a puck from Stone, and I'm stupidly proud that I'm with him. Well, not with him, but that I know him sort of.

I don't have time to think about whatever it is that has my mind playing tricks on me because Stone comes back over. "Someone is going to come over and take care of you," he says, and I look at him confused. He looks around again and sees a blonde with two kids who is not too far from me. He motions with his head to follow him, and I roll my eyes, but I follow him from my side of the glass as he skates over to the blonde.

"Katie." He knocks the glass for the woman who is with two kids. The kids wear little jerseys with the number of their father because they have Daddy on the back of the jerseys. "She's with me."

"Oh my God, I have a ticket!" I shout, hoping he can hear me, and Katie just laughs.

The horn blows, and I look at him. "I have to go, but stay with Katie," he says, smiling at me. "Katie, take care of her for me."

"Sure thing," Katie agrees, smiling at him and then turning to me. "I'm Katie, Jay's wife." She puts her hand out for me.

Taking her hand in mine, I shake it. "Hi, Katie, I'm Ryleigh. I have a ticket for the game, so you don't have to worry about me."

She smirks at me. "It's okay. They each have seats in the box." She points up. "Unless his family is in town, the seats are always empty, so you might as well use it."

I'm about to decline her when a man comes toward us wearing a suit. "Hey, Katie," he says to the girl and kisses her on the cheek. "And you must be Stone's girl." He looks at me, shocking me by giving me that title. "Let me show you to your seat."

FIFTEEN

STONE

"DID YOU GET her?" I ask Glenn, the public relations guy, when he walks back into the room. I stop myself from going back out there, knowing there is no way I can until it's time to get on the ice when the game is starting.

"She's sitting with Katie," he tells me as if I'm not dying over here.

"Can you get her after the game and make sure you bring her down here?" I ask him quietly, and he smirks.

"Is Stone Richards smitten?" he asks, and I'm the one who smirks at him.

"Did you not see her?" I ask, and he smiles. I'm not sure I will admit that I think I'm past being smitten.

"Oh, I did." The words earn him a glare from me. "Relax, I'm happily married with two point five kids, three dogs, a cat, and now a fucking bird," he says, looking at me, but continues to talk. "Why did I get a bird when I have a cat, you ask?"

"Um, I don't think I—" I start to say, but he holds up

his hand to stop me from talking, and I have no idea what to do.

"I'll tell you why. My daughter fell while she was walking into the house and not looking where she was going because she still had my phone in her hand and was watching a video. She stumbled up the stairs and ended up bumping under her chin. Did you know that's the thinnest skin on the body? Well, now you know." He puts his hands in his pockets. "Well, needless to say, she needed four stitches, and it was obviously my fault that she fell since I didn't take the phone from her. The only thing that would make her feel better was a fucking bird." He looks to the right. "The cat is about to run away from home."

"That's a lot to unload." I slap his shoulder. "Now, if you will excuse me, I have a game to win and a girl to get to."

"Yeah." He shakes his head. "Good luck with that."

"Thanks," I reply, turning and grabbing my stick to head out and wait for our time to get on the ice. I'm bouncing on my skates, wishing I could just go up and talk to her for a second. When I stood on the ice and looked over, spotting her, I thought my eyes were playing tricks on me until I looked back and saw her fucking smile. I swear to everything, it was like the earth shifted. I second-guessed everything about her not being into me, but then she went out of her way to fly here and surprise me.

The crowd cheers as we skate onto the ice, but I look up to where I know the seats are. She's sitting there looking at the ice and clapping with everyone else. She smiles at me, and my heart speeds up, but I have to lock it away for the next sixty-plus minutes. The only time I look up at her is when I skate on the ice at the beginning of the periods. Luckily for us, we win four to two. At the end of the third period, I rush like a madman to get out of my equipment just to get to her.

I shower, putting on my suit—but not the tie—before going into the family room where the wives or girlfriends all hang out waiting for the men to be finished. I pull open the door and spot her sitting on the couch with her phone in her hand while a couple of conversations happen around her.

I walk in, and a couple of the kids call my name, so she looks up from her phone. I high-five the kids as I make my way over to her. She stands up and tucks away the phone in her purse. My arm wraps around her waist, pulling her to me. "Hi, gorgeous," I greet her breathlessly before I kiss her lips softly. Totally not how I want to kiss her, but too many kids and families are here for me to slide my tongue into her mouth.

"Hi," she says, wiping my lips with her thumb to get the lip gloss off my lips.

The smile fills her face, and my cock gets hard. "Shall we get out of here?" I ask, and she nods her head.

"Lead the way." She looks over at Katie. "Thank you so much for being so kind."

"You are more than welcome." Katie smiles at her.

I slide my hand in hers as I pull her out of the room. I step into the long hallway, looking at people walking around. The equipment people grab and sort through things. I see a couple of the players doing media interviews, when I look over and see her side-eye me with a smirk. "What are you smirking about?"

"Nothing," she denies, looking down at her feet and then looking over at me. "Just, you are really sexy in a suit."

"You've seen me in a suit before." I walk toward the door that leads to the garage.

"Yes," she agrees as I open the door with my hand and hold the top of it. I wait for her to walk through it, but I'm not willing to give up holding her hand. "But now that I've seen what's under the suit, it's sort of even sexier." My cock wakes up, knowing that not only is she here but I'm touching her. I walk over to the passenger side of the truck. "I mean, you are obviously sexier naked," she continues talking, pushing me to the brink.

Instead of opening her door for her, I'm pressing her against it. I put my hands on top of the truck, framing her head. Her hands come up to my chest. "I missed you," I finally say what I've wanted to say the last fucking week. I stopped myself every single time, trying not to push her, but maybe her showing up here means she missed me too. I lean down and rub my nose with hers. "So fucking much." I close the distance and finally kiss her the way I want to kiss her. My tongue slides into her mouth, and we groan. One hand moves from beside her head to around her waist. She moves one of her hands from my chest to the back of my neck. I turn my head to the side, deepening the kiss, and then I hear laughter from the side of me.

"Hey, Richards." I turn my head, letting go of her and seeing Kenny, one of my teammates. "Media is coming out." He motions with his head to the side door.

I nod at him. "Thanks, buddy," I say, opening the passenger door. I wait for her to get in before I lean in and kiss her lips. "I'm so fucking happy you're here. It's like the Tooth Fairy and Santa Claus came on the same day."

She laughs, and I lean in to kiss behind her ear. "I mean, if you added in the Easter Bunny, I would think you were really, really fucking happy I'm here."

"All holidays," I tell her, closing the door and getting into the driver's seat. "If I knew you were coming, I would have used the car and not the pickup." I start the truck, and I can't help but grab her hand in mine. "I can't believe you're here." I kiss her hand before pulling out of the garage.

"So where are we going?" She turns in her seat but only to look at me.

"My house," I say like *duh.*

"But I have a hotel room," she replies, and I look over at her, shocked.

"What do you mean you have a hotel room?"

"Well, I was speaking to Gabriella," she says, and I groan right away, "and, well, she said it was a bad idea to surprise you."

"Never listen to her," I grit with clenched teeth, "never ever."

She laughs. "Noted."

"Now, let's go get your bag and then get you naked." I pull away from the curb.

"Well, we can always sleep over at the hotel and get naked there," she mumbles, and all I do is growl.

"No, I want you in my bed," I inform her, and she tells me what hotel she's staying at. She runs into the hotel. In a matter of four minutes, she's out and back in the truck, tossing her bag into the small back seat.

"There," she huffs as she puts her seat belt on, "happy now?"

"No." I shake my head, leaning over to grab her face in my hands and kiss her. And because it's her and because I haven't kissed her in a week, it goes from a peck on the lips to intense tongue. A horn honking makes her pull away from me and laugh. "I'll be happier when we're home."

I turn in my seat and head toward my house. "Are you hungry?" I ask her.

"For dick," she deadpans without missing a beat, and if I was drinking water, I would have choked. "Is that on the menu?" My hands grip the steering wheel while my dick fights to get out of my pants. "If so, I'd like one of those, please." It's her turn to lean over, and this time, she bites my earlobe.

"So tell me, Stone." Her breath makes me shiver. "Is your dick on the menu?" She takes her hand and palms my cock. "Hmm," she moans, "it looks like he's ready." She trails her tongue down the side of my neck. "Is he ready to be eaten?" I'm gripping the steering wheel so tight I'm surprised it doesn't shatter in my hands. "You want to know a secret?" she whispers in my ear. "I play with myself, thinking about your cock down my throat." I literally count to ten in my head. "One night, I was using that vibrator you got for me," she purrs, "and then I took another one to suck on it and pretended it was your dick."

"Ryleigh," I growl between clenched teeth, biting down so hard that my teeth grind together.

"Yes," she replies as if she hasn't teased me to the point of no return.

She moves away from me, and I sigh in relief, but I should have known better. She takes off her jacket and tosses it in the back before she kicks off her shoes. "What are you doing?" I ask, but my head already knows what she's doing. I'm just not sure I can handle it. I speed up even more to get home. I know I'm about five minutes from home, and every minute will feel like an eternity.

"I'm really hot," she purrs out, and the next thing I know, she's lifting her hips off the seat and wiggles herself from side to side. "Like so hot I'm melting." She kicks her pants off, and all I can see is her bare legs. I look around to make sure we are away from anyone who can see in the truck and want to kick myself for not getting tinted windows. "Are you hot?" She turns in the seat, putting her back to the door as she throws one of her long legs in my lap while she keeps one foot on the floor. "I'm so hot, it's like I'm dripping wet," she states as I turn the corner to enter the gated community I live in.

I stop the car when I get to the gate, rolling the window down to enter the code when I hear her moan.

I look over and almost come in my pants. She's got two fingers inside her while her shirt is pushed up and her bra is pushed down, showing me her tits. "Stone," she moans my name as she looks into my eyes. I roll the window up at the same time I lean over the middle console and slide my finger in with hers. "Yes," she pants out.

"Move your fingers with mine," I direct her as I drive down the street, moving my fingers in and out of her slow at first, both our fingers working her. "How many times did you make yourself come thinking about me?"

"Five," she pants, "maybe seven."

"Did you say my name when you came?" My fingers move faster, knowing she's almost there.

"Yes," she admits, "every time."

"Is that so?" I ask, and she nods her head, not able to say words when my thumb rolls her clit at the same time I bury my fingers to my knuckles.

I turn onto my street. "I thought about you too, about coming down your throat." I pull into the driveway and press the button for the garage. "About coming inside you, fuck, you have no idea what it feels like."

"Tell me," she whispers as we both play with her.

"You feel like fucking heaven." I put the truck in park and my seat belt flies off me. She sits up, my fingers sliding out of her as she takes her own seat belt off. We both lunge for each other. I pick her up and pull her over the center console and onto me, my hands on her hips as she slams her mouth down on mine. Her tongue fights with mine with a vengeance. Her hands move down to my belt, frantically getting it undone and then getting me out of my boxers. It takes her a matter of ten seconds before she slams down on me. The heat from her pussy shoots straight through me. One knee is on the side of my hip as she moves her left knee to the center console, opening herself up for me as she moves her hips in a circle. "I lied," I tell her, panting as she puts one hand on my chest and another on my shoulder as she moves up and down on my cock, her eyes closed, her mouth open. "This is fucking heaven." My hands move to her ass, helping her move up and down on my cock. "Your pussy," I say, watching the ecstasy fill her face, "that's my fucking heaven."

"I'm going to come," she cries, and I can feel her pussy get tighter with each rise and fall.

"Is my girl going to suck the cum out of my cock?" I ask her as she nods her head, her forehead on mine, her mouth open as my tongue slides into her mouth. "Take my cum, take it all."

"Give it to me," she moans as she kisses me. "I want it all," she croaks out before she comes with a shudder, slamming herself down on me, and I follow, coming with her.

SIXTEEN

RYLEIGH

I COLLAPSE IN his arms, and all I can feel is them fold me in closer to him, and my hands crush his chest. He leans down to kiss the top of my head. "Now, that is a welcome home." I can't help but laugh with my ear on his chest as I listen to his heart beating.

"Um." I sit up on his softening cock and try not to freak out. "I just…" I look down at us conjoined. "Condom." My eyes go big now.

"Are you?" He stumbles with his words. "Are you on, like protection—" he says and then quickly adds, "I don't care if you are or aren't, whatever happens."

I gasp at the same time that I slap his shoulder. "Whatever happens, my fucking ass. I have my whole life ahead of me. You think I have time for a child?" I huff. "Are you?" Now I'm the one stuttering. "You know?" I avoid looking into his eyes. "Disease-free?"

I lift my eyes to his, and he serves me with a very intense glare. "I've never had sex without a condom," he bites out, and I roll my eyes at him before I turn to get off him. His hands grip my hips, pulling me back down on him. "I've never, not once, had sex without a condom. Now to answer your question, I'm disease-free since I get tested monthly with work."

"You don't have to go that far." I try to make it a funny situation. "You could just say you're clean."

"I don't know what to do with you." His hands move from my hips to my face. "But I think the first thing we have to do is clean you up." His soft voice makes my stomach flip up and down. Especially because the last time he went out of his way to clean me, I tried to pretend it didn't mean anything. It was the first time, I think, someone other than my parents had taken care of me.

"You know, I can take care of myself," I inform him as I avoid his eyes and pull off him.

"Trust me, I know that," he replies, tucking himself in. "But when you're with me, taking care of you is my job." The minute the words are out of his mouth, the only thing I can say is this fucking man. He has a way with his words that leaves you breathless and swooning. I hate every second of it.

I put my panties back on and grab my jeans, looking out the back to see if he closed the garage door. Seeing it closed, I pick them up along with my boots. "Can I use the bathroom?"

"No," he says and then silently laughs. "Come on, let me show you my home." He reaches back and grabs my bag and jacket as I get out of the truck. The cool air hits my bare ass as I tiptoe to the front of the truck, looking over at the car he mentioned before. "Give me that." He holds out his hands to take my jeans and boots.

"I can carry that," I tell him but he just walks up the steps toward the door to the house. I follow him up the stairs, stepping into his white-and-black mudroom. He has about six or seven pairs of sneakers all lined up along the wall with jackets that are hanging.

He dumps my boots beside his shoes and then looks over at me. "Come on, gorgeous." He motions with his head. "This is my kitchen," he says of the white-and-gray kitchen.

"Can we do the tour maybe when I'm not, I don't know…" I motion to my vagina area.

"To the bedroom it is." He takes one of my hands and pulls me through the house. I have enough time to see the family pictures hanging on the walls as we walk up the stairs toward the bedroom down the long hallway.

He walks in and turns on the lights to the massive room with its own sitting area. The big king-size bed in the middle of the room is against a dark gray wall. The covers on the bed are white with the same color throw pillows. The side tables are a gray also, but an almost gray blue. He walks to the side where the sitting area faces a wall of windows, and I see that it leads to a balcony with furniture. He walks to the corner of the room, and I walk through a hallway that has a closet on each side. I see his clothes in one and nothing in the other one. My mind suddenly wonders if there was ever anything in the other one, while I tell myself it's none of my business.

I walk into the white bathroom, with a long vanity against the wall that is a light gray and a white counter. The two sinks have enough space between them to have a cream-colored vase with blue-gray fake flowers. Two mirrors are in front of each sink, with lights on each side of the mirror.

"Do you want to take a shower?" he asks, pointing at the shower with glass doors, right next to a big white bathtub that has a black side table next to it with a little tree. "Or a bath?"

"Actually, a shower would be great."

"Yesss," he exclaims cheerfully, "I was hoping you would say that." He walks over to the shower, opens the glass door, and starts the water. "I'll be right in to join you."

"What makes you think I want you to join me?" I stand in the middle of his bathroom. "Maybe I want time to myself."

"Well then, I guess you might be shit out of luck." He shrugs off his jacket and tosses it on the little bench beside the table I didn't see. "You came to surprise me, which means I get to spend the whole weekend with you by my side." He kisses me behind the ear. "And I have to say, gorgeous"—he smiles big—"I couldn't be fucking happier." He winks at me before walking out of the bathroom and, like, because I'm me, I follow him. He walks into the empty closet and puts my bag down.

"What are you doing?" I ask as he opens my bag.

"I'm putting your stuff away," he states, grabbing my stuff and placing it on the built-in shelves. "Why aren't you in the shower?"

"I'm only here for two days." I try to get my head to stop spinning. "I can just live out of my bag."

"But this way you'll feel more comfortable." He places everything on the shelf and then grabs my toiletries bag, walking past me again and toward the bathroom, where he puts it next to the sink. He pulls his shirt out of his pants and unbuttons it, and then all I can do is stare at him as he takes his shirt off. My mouth waters to taste him, and my hands tingle to touch him. He kicks off his shoes and tosses them to the side where his shirt lies. His pants and boxers follow, leaving him like a Greek god in front of me. "You coming?" He motions with his head toward the shower, where he opens the door and steps in. The water cascades around him as he tilts his head back and then runs his hands through his hair. His eyes shine as he smirks at me. "I'm going to take all the hot water and all you'll be left with is the cold."

I snap out of it and peel my sweater off myself, tossing it with his clothes before I add my bra and panties to the pile of discarded clothing. "You won't finish the hot water in two minutes."

"No, but first, I have to eat you." He pulls me into him, the warm water falling around us. "Then you have to suck my cock." He bends to take a nipple into his mouth. "And then I have to fuck you against the wall." I close my eyes, and he's not wrong. By the time we get out of the shower, it feels like I'm taking the polar plunge.

"IT'S A SURPRISE," he says, sliding his feet inside his white sneakers.

"The last time you told me this, you took me on a sex tour." I grab my boots.

He snags one of his black jackets and slips it over his white T-shirt. "Don't even fucking lie." He points at me. "You loved that tour." I smile at him because I really did love that tour. "Now get your sexy ass into my car." He smacks my ass, walking into the garage.

I grab my vest and slide it onto my gray sweater before putting on my boots and walking into the garage to meet him. He stands with his phone in his hands, typing something while he waits for me by the passenger door. "The car today?"

"Umm, we might have to take the truck," he replies, reading something from his phone.

"Do you even know where we're going?" I ask him as he shuts the car door and walks over to the truck. I watch his ass as he walks away from me, and it's crazy how sexy he is, and he doesn't even have to try. Literally wearing baggy jeans with a T-shirt and to me he's the hottest man I've ever met.

"I know where we're going. It's sort of off the beaten path."

"Great," I say, getting into the truck, "the woods where you can kill me and no one will know." I shake my head. "I'll have you know my parents had me chipped when I was younger."

I expect him to be shocked, but he just laughs. "Me too." He lifts his arm. "I think it's right in there or in the neck, we aren't sure yet." I can't help but laugh at him as he leans in and kisses my lips before shutting the door and walking around the truck to his side.

He puts the address in the GPS before he pulls out of the driveway, and I can see his house in the light now. It's white bricks with black doors and windows, the inside is even more gorgeous. It's a big house for just one person, but it feels so homey it's crazy. I look out the window at the houses around him as we drive out of his gated community and get farther and farther away from civilization. "I wasn't kidding when I said I was chipped," I state as we pass by the trees, seeing into the forest.

We pull off the main highway onto a gravel road. I look around as he rubs his thumb over mine. My hand was pulled into his as soon as he got into the truck. "You have reached your destination," the GPS says.

I look around to see a white van with a man standing beside it. The van looks like it's seen better days. "If this is sex trafficking, you literally are going to get maybe a goat for me."

Stone laughs as he shuts off the truck and then opens his door. "Let's go, gorgeous." I raise my hand to open the door and step out. I look at Stone, who walks over to the man and shakes his hand. The two of them talk as he points over at me.

"This is it," I say, taking a big inhale. "Whatever he said to you, my family will pay you double," I joke with the man who just laughs. "I'm Ryleigh."

"Brett." He shakes my hand. "Let's go." He turns on

his boot and heads to the front of his van and it's then I see the big round orange flag, I think it is, in the middle of the vast field.

"What is this?" I ask Stone as I walk beside him.

"This is the surprise." He puts his arm around my shoulder, pulling me to him. The nerves fill my stomach as we get closer and then stop when Brett starts something and fire comes out of it.

"What the fuck?" I yelp, feeling the heat from the flames. I put my hand in front of my face, but as the heat blows again, I see the flag start to lift off the ground, taking a basket with it. "Oh my God," I gasp, "is that a hot air balloon?" The orange balloon fills with air as Brett opens the wicker basket. "I can't." I don't know what to say as Stone walks me over, and I step inside it. Stone steps in behind me, putting his hand on my hip.

I look at Brett, who steps in and pulls on something. "Are you two ready?"

I look over at Stone, who just stares at me with his brown eyes that keep changing every time I look at him. His hair is pushed back from his face. "I don't know, gorgeous." The softness of his voice makes my whole body tingle. "Are you ready?" I don't answer him because I don't know if I'll ever be ready for whatever Stone Richards throws my way.

SEVENTEEN

STONE

I WATCH HER eyes light up as the basket slowly moves off the ground. "Oh my." She holds on to the side of the basket. I stand behind her, holding on to her hips to let her know I'm right here and nothing will happen to her. She laughs excitedly as we move higher and higher above the ground. She turns, and her smile is infectious. Without a shadow of a doubt, I will do whatever it is in my power to make her smile like that every time I'm with her.

"I wanted a way to show you the city without being—" I stop talking when she looks at me and her hair blows into her face. My hand comes up from holding the basket to tuck it behind her ear. "Interrupted." I move my position from behind her to halfway on the side of her, my hand still on her hip.

"Thank you for this," she says, looking back out to the view. "After the sex tour." She bumps her shoulder into my chest. "Nothing can cross off that sex tour."

"Hey." I laugh. "That means I'm always going to

be number one." I shrug my shoulders. "That's all that matters."

"It's so pretty." She looks at the view of the lake. The trees are getting fuller now that spring is right around the corner.

"You know what I don't see?"

"What?" She looks at me.

"Snow," I deadpan. Her head goes back, and her laughter echoes in the balloon.

"It's nice to have four seasons." She looks back in front of her.

"You know who says that?" I wait a second before I answer my question. "People who have to deal with snow. I grew up in New York and then moved to Canada. Trust me, I don't like one thing about the snow. I mean, the only thing I like in the winter is outdoor skating."

"See." She points at me. "If there is no snow, you can't go skate outside."

"They did the winter classic in Dallas last year," I inform her. "Texas, where it gets to one hundred and twenty-eight million degrees in the summer."

She's about to argue with me like she normally does—because there can never be a day when she doesn't tell me I'm wrong about something—when Brett starts talking about where we are. I don't really pay attention to him. Instead, my eyes are all on her. Her reaction to everything is priceless. I wish I could film it and watch it over and over again.

"Can you take a picture of us?" I ask Brett, handing him my phone. I move Ryleigh in front of me, putting my hand over her shoulder, and she reaches up to put her hand in mine. I wrap my other hand around her waist, pulling her into me as we smile for the camera.

He hands me back the phone, and I look at the pictures he took. "I like this one." I show her.

"Can you send them to me?" she asks.

"I can since I now have your phone number." I wink at her, sending her the pictures.

For three hours, we coast over Nashville side by side, both of us pointing out things and asking Brett about them. It's one of my favorite days, best I've ever had. Getting home and cooking side by side is something I've never done with anyone before, but also something I want to do all the time now. But only with her.

She sleeps in my T-shirt after I fuck the ever-loving shit out of her, wanting to touch her every single second, not thinking about the fact she's going to leave.

The following morning, I wake up to find the bed next to me empty when she comes out of the bathroom wearing a shirt that goes to her mid-thigh and falls off her shoulder. "Good morning," I mumble and hold out my hand to her, telling her to come to me.

She laughs at me. "Good morning to you." She stands by the bed instead of coming to lie down beside me. I move over to her side of the bed and kiss her leg while my hand roams up the back of her thigh and under her shirt to find her ass bare. "Come to bed."

"No," she replies, "I need coffee and to eat. My flight is at one." The dreaded words I hate to hear.

"Fine," I huff, "then we can come back to bed." I get

out of bed. "Go get the coffee started so we can speed this up." I slap her ass, making her laugh.

I walk into the bathroom seeing her stuff is all over her side of the sink, and when I go into my closet, I look into hers and see she's already packed her shit. I push down the burning in my stomach as I walk down the stairs and hear her in the kitchen. She's standing at the counter with a bowl in front of her and her coffee already done.

I walk straight to her. The need to touch her is on a whole different level. I kiss her bare shoulder and wish this could be us every morning. I wish we would go to bed together every night I wasn't on the road. I wish we could eat dinner together and watch television together. I kiss the top of her head before I move her hair to the side, giving me access to her neck, where I bite and then suck it in softly. She moves her shoulder up to her ear, giggling before looking over at me. The smile softly leaves when my head closes the distance as I kiss her forehead, then her lips, and then go back down to kiss the top of her shoulder while my hand comes up and cups her tit. I move the shirt down, letting one breast come out. I roll her nipple between my fingers while I kiss her. She turns in my arms as I pull the shirt off the other breast before bending to take a nipple into my mouth. As I savor her, her hand goes to the back of my head as I move from one nipple to the next. She puts her hand on my chest while I come up and take her mouth. My tongue mixes with hers as I push her back to the counter. I frame her in with my hand while I kiss her and then stop to get on my knees in front of her. I suck her nipples again while my hands caress her ass. I let go of her lips to bite her nipple and then suck it in before burying my hand in her hair and pulling her head down to mine. Her hand goes to the back of my head, gripping my head as we kiss each other.

I move my hands to her hips, lifting her onto the counter in front of me. "Time for breakfast," I announce as she places one foot on the counter, opening herself up to me. I open her lips for me with two fingers before I lean in and lick her up and down.

"So good," she purrs, and I eat like I'll never eat her again. I lick up and down until I get to her clit and then suck in. "Stone." When she says my name, it shoots straight to my cock. "Oh, God," she moans when my tongue and finger enter her at the same time.

"Stone," I say, smirking at her. "It's not God making you come. It's me." I slide another finger into her before attacking her clit, sucking it and then biting it.

The sound of her panting fills the kitchen. "I need more," she tells me, and I know what she needs. I know her body inside and out even though we've only been with each other for a week.

"What do you need?" I look up at her as she watches my finger fuck her pussy.

"Your cock. I need it one more time." I pull my finger out of her, licking it clean before I stand between her legs. Her hands go into my boxers and pull out my cock which is oozing precum. She rubs the cum into the head of my cock before she places it at her entrance. I slide into her. "That's it," she pants.

I fuck her slowly as I wrap an arm around her shoulder before I kiss her again. Our tongues move in the same rhythm as my cock fucks her. I let her lips go before my hands grab her tits, rolling the nipples before squeezing them in my hands and then fucking her. I pick up speed, and the thrusts get shorter and shorter. Neither of us says anything. Both of us are scared, I think, of the words that will come out of our mouths if we do talk. So here on my kitchen counter, I fuck her while I tell her with my eyes I'm obsessed with her. I tell her I want her to stay. I tell her I hate that she's leaving me. She wraps her legs around me and closes her eyes, and her head hangs back as she convulses all over my cock. I plant myself inside her and come in her before I bury my face in her neck, smelling her, hoping time freezes so she is here longer.

She slowly rubs her hand up my back, and I close my eyes, memorizing how it feels. I slide out of her. "I'll be back." I kiss the middle of her chest. "Don't move."

I walk over to the guest bathroom and grab a rag from under the sink. Wetting it, I clean myself before grabbing another one and walking out to see her still sitting on the counter. "Good girl," I praise, taking the rag and cleaning her with it. "You can get down now."

"Thanks for your permission." She hops down off the counter but avoids looking at me. She pulls her shirt up before walking back over to the bowl and making herself a parfait of yogurt and fruit like she did yesterday. "Do you want me to make you one?" she asks, and I shake my head.

"No. I'm going to make myself eggs and bacon." I

pull the pan out to make the eggs.

"Yeah, that's what you said yesterday, and you ate half my bowl." She laughs as she washes some blackberries and pops one into her mouth before taking another. I grab her wrist, pulling it to my mouth and eating it.

She laughs, and just like that, our time is up. I carry her bag with me to the car to drive to the airport. "You can't come in with me." She looks over at me. "People might spot us together and take a picture."

"So?" I ask, and she looks out the window as I pull out of the driveway. I grip the steering wheel, pushing the anger back down. I wait until I'm out of the development before I ask her, "When am I going to see you again?" My finger taps the wheel nervously.

"I'm not sure," she replies, and I can feel her pulling away. "I have a pretty big trial coming up, and I have to focus on that."

I don't say another word because all I want to do is call her out on the bullshit she just said. I take my time driving to the airport, taking the longest route I know, and when I get there, I pull up to the curb. The last thing I want to do is piss her off after this weekend. "Thank you for coming to surprise me this weekend." The tightness fills my chest. "Is it okay if I get out of the truck and get your bag?"

She looks around a couple of times, checking to see if a lot of people are there. "Do you think you'll be recognized?"

"No idea," I bite out, "but I don't care if I am."

"You might not care, but the last thing we need is

pictures coming out and then—" I cut her off.

"And then you have to tell everyone you came to see me," I fill in for her, and she shakes her head.

"You forget I grew up with cameras in my face every time my father stepped foot outside," she snaps. "So yeah, I like to be private."

"Well, then we shouldn't chance it." My heart pounds so hard in my chest. "I would hate for you to be put in that situation." I lean over and kiss her lips one last time before she leaves, knowing she's going to fight this until her last breath. "Thank you again for this weekend," I whisper before I kiss her again.

"Thank you." She puts her hand in mine on the center console. "I have to go, or I'll miss my flight."

Good, I want to say, but instead, I just nod. She reaches for the door handle and steps outside. She shuts the door and opens the back door, where she grabs her bag. "Will you call and let me know you got home safe?" I ask.

"I will," she agrees softly before she closes the door. I watch her walk into the airport with her bag beside her and her head down, feeling like this is a breakup, but what she doesn't know is I'm not going anywhere. She can push me away all she wants. It just means I have to show her I'm the man she deserves.

I watch her until I can't see her anymore, and I'm about to drive away when my phone beeps. I pull it out of the cupholder and see my screen saver is the one we took in the balloon. My arm around her shoulders and her arm around my waist. Her name's in the middle of my screen.

Gorgeous: *Thank you for everything.*

EIGHTEEN

RYLEIGH

I PRESS SEND on the text and then take a deep breath, putting my phone in my pocket before I walk over to security. I go through the motions of security before heading over to the gate, ignoring the weight of my phone in my pocket. Ignoring the fact that walking out of his car and into the airport without turning around and going back to him was killing me. Forget the fact I wanted him to walk me into the fucking airport so I could spend extra time with him.

What good would it have done if he walked me inside and to security? I ask myself as I stop for a latte. Me hugging him and spending every single second with him. So he could see how it is tearing me up inside? No, that wouldn't do anyone any good.

I sit at the gate, waiting for my flight to be called. Looking out the window at the planes, I wonder if I really have to leave. Maybe I could stay an extra day? And then what? Drag the goodbye out even more? No.

I get up when I hear them announce the last call for the flight, walking in and storing my bag in the overhead bin before sitting in my first-class seat. I tuck my purse under the seat in front of me before I take my phone out of my pocket.

I look down at the screen, seeing he texted me.

Stone: *Gorgeous, it's me who should be thanking you for the amazing weekend. Text me when you land.*

I turn the Airplane Mode on before I tuck the phone into the pocket of the seat in front of me. I look out the window as the captain comes on to tell us how the flight will go, but all I can do is stare out my window, sort of in a state of shock. All I want to do is kick myself in my ass. What is wrong with you? He's a guy. When have you ever thought about a guy for more than two days? Never. Not once. I have never in my life put a man before anything. They were always, and I mean always, a second thought. If I had a date, okay, but if not, it wasn't that big of a deal. But now I've been with this fucking man for what… two weeks, and he's all I fucking think about. It's insane. It's preposterous. It's ridiculous. I'm a thirty-year-old woman who has her dream job, looking to climb the ladder even more, and I'm sitting here on a plane semi-heartbroken because the man I like lives fucking far from me.

I close the window shade and grab my bag as soon as we are airborne, pulling up the brief I should be thinking about instead of Stone motherfucking Richards. I shut it all down like I'm used to and focus on the brief I'm working on, making notes in the sidebar. I'm so out of it

I only look up when the plane bumps when we land.

I tuck my iPad back into my bag, springing up when the seat belt sign goes off. I'm the second one off the plane as I make my way down the escalator and toward the Uber line, pulling out my phone before heading outside. I wait for it to finally get service, ignoring the text messages that come in, and just order the Uber. I look down at the map as if my life depends on it. Ignoring the way my hand shakes when I get into the car with my bag, I even go so far as to have a conversation with the Uber driver not to touch my phone. Usually, it's a hello and a thank you. Now it feels like I'm giving him a job interview with the number of questions I'm asking him.

Even when I pull up to my apartment building, I get out of the car begrudgingly and grunt goodbye to the driver. I look around, seeing all the snow has melted while I was gone, which should make me happy. Then I hear Stone's voice in my head, *"You know who says that? People who have to deal with snow."*

I sniffle back the sting that comes to my nose, pretending it's because it's cold outside. I pant when I wheel my suitcase into my apartment that feels stuffy and still. I dump my bag on the counter before walking over to open the window in the living room just a touch and see the moon shining high in the sky.

My phone beeps from the front door, and I debate going to it, but my feet have a mind of their own. Pulling the phone from my pocket in the vest, I see that it's Stone.

Stone: *Hey, gorgeous, just making sure you are okay.*

I put my head back and breathe out through my nose,

then look back down at the text message. I make the mistake of scrolling back up to where he sent me the pictures of the two of us in the hot air balloon, the smile on his face making his eyes crinkle in the corners. "I miss him," I admit to the empty room, "but it's only normal since I've just left him. Tomorrow, I'll be fine."

I don't call him back, but I do text him to let him know I'm okay. The last thing I need is him freaking out and calling Romeo.

Me: *Just got into my place. Traffic was backed up. Headed to bed. Talk tomorrow.*

"This is the right thing to do." I turn the phone to Do Not Disturb before grabbing my bag and heading to my bedroom. I unpack the bag, tossing everything in the wash but the white T-shirt I slept in at his house, which I accidentally packed in my suitcase. I undress, thinking about taking a shower, but knowing that when I do, I won't be able to smell him on me anymore.

I get into bed, hoping I fall asleep right away, but it takes forever. I rush out of the door the next day, arriving at the office ten minutes late, which I never do.

I walk into my office and see a brown bag on my desk. I toss my bag and shrug off the long cashmere jacket I took out to match my outfit this morning. I slip my heels on before walking behind my desk and seeing my name written on the brown bag. The top of the bag has staples, so I open the bag and pick up the white paper, opening it.

It's a good thing my chair is there because I sit down, regardless of whether I want to.

Good morning, gorgeous.

**Wish I was there stealing your fruit and yogurt.
Have the best day.**

S.

I put the paper down to the side and grab the bowl in the bag. Taking it out, I see it's a yogurt parfait like I made for myself at his house. "Fucking shit," I blurt, putting the bowl down while I pick up the note again.

Pushing away from my desk, I go to my phone and pull up his name.

Me: *Got the fruit bowl. Wish you were here so I could feed it to you.*

I delete the whole thing before starting again.

Me: *Morning. Thank you for the fruit bowl. Heading into a meeting. I'll call you later.*

My hand wants to pick up the phone to call him, but instead, I put the phone down. "This is what is going to happen," I tell myself. "Today, you talk to him once." I open the fruit bowl and grab a strawberry. "Then tomorrow, you text him but tell him how busy you are and miss his call, but also text him back. You aren't going to be that rude bitch. Then the day after that, you call him, hoping he doesn't pick up." I grab a raspberry. "Then, by the end of the week, it's one text a day, and you'll have both moved on." I nod. "Good talk," I say to myself as I finish the fruit bowl.

I busy myself with work, and by the time I really look up, it's past seven. I kick off my shoes and grab my stuff to get out of here. In the car, on the way home, I pull out my phone and see he's tried to call me once four hours ago and then right after a text came in.

Stone: *Headed to the rink, have a game tonight. I'll text you after. I hope you had a good day. Talk later.*

I text him quickly, knowing he's probably on the ice.

Me: *Just left work. On my way home, might grab something to eat or not. I'm exhausted. Hope you won the game. Sleep well.*

Do I feel a tightness in my chest when I send him the text? Yes. Do I want to throw up? Yes. Do I want to do nothing but go to him? Also yes. Will I do anything about it? No. This is the way it has to be.

I get into bed, smelling him all around me and holding my pillow as I drift off to sleep. When I wake up the next day, I grab my phone, and when I don't see a text from him, I can't help the sadness that comes. *This is what you wanted*, I remind myself. This is why you can't get involved with him. Look at how much you miss him, and it's only been a week. Imagine if this went on longer. No way.

So I get out of bed and take off his shirt, bringing it to my nose one time before I get dressed. I get to work without incident, and when I finally sit at my desk to start my day, a knock on the door has me looking up.

"These came for you," Claudia says, holding the crystal vase filled with pink roses in her hands.

"Oh my." I get up to walk to her, taking the vase from her. "Thank you." I turn to put them on my desk while she walks out the door.

My name is on the white card sticking out of the top. My hands shake as I pluck it off the transparent fork that holds it. Turning it over in my hand, my heart beats so freaking fast and loud it's echoing in my ears.

Pulling out the card, I already know they are from Stone. I can feel it in my bones. What I'm not prepared for is the note.

Thank you for being you.

Missing you.

Stone

At that moment, here in my office, I shed a tear for a man for the first time in my whole life.

NINETEEN

STONE

I LOOK DOWN at my phone as I walk into practice and see the last thing she sent me two days ago.

Gorgeous: *Just left work. On my way home, might grab something to eat or not. I'm exhausted. Hope you won the game. Sleep well.*

My chest tightens with each step as I head into the locker room.

"Hey," I greet, putting the phone away, seeing most of the guys here. We have practice today from ten to about one, then we are off until tomorrow night.

A couple of them look up at me and nod, and a couple wave, but everyone is either talking to someone or just doing their thing. And with the way I'm feeling, I don't really want to talk to anyone. The last two days have had me in a whirlwind of emotion. I knew the minute she was leaving she would pull away from me. I knew it. I felt it, yet I wasn't ready for it. I also knew I have absolutely not one single fucking clue what to do about it. Which made the past two days even worse.

I slip out of my tracksuit and into my gear, then go onto the ice. I'm thankful for the three hours I'm being pushed on the ice because my mind kind of shuts down. The minute I get off the ice and into the locker room, undressing—I grab my phone—thinking she might have texted me something, anything, but I don't have any new messages.

Tossing my phone back into my locker, I go to the shower and then head out. I'm pulling into my garage when my phone rings, making my heart speed up because I have this stupid hope it's her. I look at the screen and see my father FaceTiming me.

I take a huge inhale and press the green button. His face fills the screen. "Hey," he starts with a big smile and then stops. "What's wrong with you?"

I should have known he would see that something is wrong with me. I don't know why I'm surprised. "Nothing really."

"Nothing really." He leans back in his chair, and I see he's at home in the kitchen. "What does that even mean?"

"It means that something is bothering me," I admit to him, "and I don't know if I want to talk about it."

"Talking about it is better than letting it fester inside you." He crosses his arms in front of him. "Are you okay?" The worry is written all over his face.

"I'm fine," I snap, "it's just that…" I think about how to word this, but is there even a way to discuss this in a roundabout way so he doesn't know who I'm talking about.

"I met this girl," I start, not giving him Ryleigh's name.

"Oh," he says, his mouth staying open, making me wait to see if he has more to add. "That's good, right?"

"It's amazing," I confirm, "but—"

He groans. "Nothing good comes with a but. Trust me, I know. You know who uses buts all the time? Your uncles Matthew and Max. We have this tee time, but it's at five o'clock in the morning." I chuckle at his tone. "We have this amazing vacation spot, but we have to take five planes and then fourteen hours on a bus." He shakes his head. "Let's buy four horses each, but where are we going to put them?"

"Yeah, it's sort of like that." I tap the steering wheel with my finger nervously. "I met this amazing, smart, beautiful woman, but she lives in Chicago."

"Chicago." His tone is weird as if I said she lived on the moon.

"And we've seen each other a couple of times. I was there for a game, and we hooked up." His eyebrows pinch together. "Then she flew out here last weekend to surprise me."

"Did she catch you with someone else?" he asks, but then his jaw gets tight. "Stone Cooper Richards." He uses my full name. "What the hell is wrong with you?"

"Whoa." I laugh. "Full name must mean business." He glares at me. "Anyway, she didn't find me with anyone else because there isn't anyone else. There is just her." I smile when I think about her, because I'm fucking obsessed with her. "So she came down here to surprise me, and it was amazing. It was great. But then, when she left, it was weird."

"How so?" His voice is softer, the tightness gone.

"She didn't want me to go in the airport with her. She hasn't called me since she got back home. She's sending me all these texts with reasons she can't talk on the phone." I close my eyes. "I fucking hate it."

"Well," he says, "I know how much of a pain in the ass long distance is. When I started dating your mother, she was in New York, and I was in Dallas." He grimaces. "Worst time of my life."

"Good talk, Dad." My voice comes out defeated.

"Have you spoken to her about how you feel?" he asks.

"Not exactly." My heart races. "I didn't want to be too needy."

"How is that working out for you?" he asks, and it's my turn to glare at him. "I'm not the one you should be glaring at." He points at the phone. "You should be glaring at yourself."

"Dad," I snap, "I think I'm falling in love with this woman, and she won't even call me back."

"And who is to blame for that?" He tilts his head to the side. "You, that's who. She came down to see you, so obviously she must like you a little bit. No one gets on a plane to surprise someone if they don't like you. Now, when she was there instead of using your," he whispers and points down to his dick area, "you should have taken a couple of minutes to talk about how you feel."

"And what if she told me she didn't feel like that?"

My chest gets even tighter. "What if I did all that, and it was all for nothing?"

"But—" he starts, and all I can do is roll my eyes. "Don't you roll your eyes at me," he orders. "But what if you did all that, and it wasn't all for nothing? What if she's waiting for you to say something, and you said nothing, so she thought she was nothing to you?" All I can do is stare at him, wondering if this is why, when my mother comes into the room wearing her workout stuff.

"Hello." Her eyes light up when she sees me on the phone, then turns to my father. "Hello."

"Hey, sweetness," he says her nickname, which he always uses unless he's pissed, then it's full-on Zara Richards even though her maiden name is Stone. "How was Pilates?"

"Hard," she huffs and then turns to me. "What's wrong with you? Why do you look so tired?"

"Oh, here we go." I look out the window, knowing I'm not even going to get a word in because my father is going to spill the beans for me anyway. They always tell each other everything.

"Stone met a woman who lives in Chicago, and he's smitten with her," he starts, and I cringe at the word smitten.

"I like her," I cut in. "Who uses smitten?"

"Anyway, he likes her." My father continues talking. "He went to see her, she surprised him this weekend, and now she's not answering his calls."

"Were you mean to her?" my mother asks me in a tone that means the answer better be the one she wants to hear.

"Of course I wasn't mean to her. Really, Mom?"

"It's just a question." She holds up her hands. "Did you tell her how you felt?"

"Nope," my father answers for me, and my mother laughs.

"Typical. Your father did the same with me." She smiles into the camera while my father gasps out loud.

"I did not." She puts one hand on his chest like she just wounded him.

"You were going to break up with me," she reminds him, and I have to bite my lip not to laugh. "Remember that after I got drunk. Waited for me to wake up in the morning and you were going to break up with me."

"Okay, okay, okay." My father puts up his two hands. "This is about Stone."

"Wait a second," my mother says, holding one finger up on her hand. "Ryleigh lives in Chicago."

"Oh," my father starts. "My." His eyes go big. "God."

"Are you seeing Ryleigh?" my mother gasps.

"I'm not seeing anyone because she won't answer the fucking phone or the text messages or anything." The frustration finally pours out of me.

"So sort of a situationship," my mother reasons, both of us just looking at her like she has two heads. "You know, like before you are in a relationship, but you are talking, so it's like a situation." She looks at us. "Zoey told me about it."

"Is Zoey in a situationship?" my father asks. "Because I really hope not."

"Can we focus on our son, please?" my mother scolds, so she cannot tell him Zoey is one thousand percent in this whole situationship. "What have you told Ryleigh?"

"Nothing." I take a deep breath. "I didn't want to come on too strong."

"You have to tell her." My mother's voice rises.

"Mom, she's not answering my phone calls." I clench my teeth.

"Then go to her." She shakes her head. "I swear, the bunch of you are so strong and macho and then dumb and stupid, all at the same time." She looks at my father. "I'm going to have a shirt made that says that."

"Do you think I should go to her?" I ask them, and even my father looks at me like it's the stupidest question I've ever asked him in my life. "Fuck, I don't even know if there are flights I can get on." I tap the steering wheel.

"You live in Nashville." My mother slaps the counter in front of her. "There is a private airport. Jesus, Stone."

"I have to go," I tell them both. "I'll call you later." I pull out of the garage. "Maybe tomorrow after I talk to her."

"Don't fuck this up," my father warns quickly, then turns to my mother. "If this doesn't work out, do you know how awkward it's going to be when we see her parents?"

"I'm still on the phone!" I shout. "Thanks for the vote of confidence, though." I hang up the phone, then pull up the number to the private planes I booked last year when I had to fly back home quickly. Three hours later, I'm touching down in Chicago and suddenly wishing I wore a sweater under my track jacket. A black SUV waits for me when I arrive. I had forwarded them the address I was going to so all I have to do is sit in the back seat.

I arrive at her place and thank the driver, and only when I'm standing at her door does it sink in that this could be it. I raise my hand to knock on the door before looking at my phone to see it's almost five o'clock, so she might not even be home. I raise my hand again to knock, this time twice before I hear, "I'm coming," from behind the door.

I put my hands on each side of the doorjamb. My head hangs for a second before she opens the door and literally gasps. "Stone," she says, and I want to grab her around her waist and kiss the ever-loving shit out of her. She's standing there in yoga pants and my white fucking T-shirt.

"Hi," I say, my hands dropping from the doorjamb. "I figured if I showed up, it would be harder for you to ignore me."

"I wasn't ignoring you," she denies breathlessly, but I can tell how she avoids looking at me that she was.

"Okay, well, I'm here because we need to talk." I think about what my father said, and I figure this is it. "Can I come in?"

"Oh." She shakes her head and moves aside. "Of course you can." I walk in, and she closes the door behind her. "I'm just a little shocked you're here." I don't move from in front of her door, waiting for her to lead the way to wherever she wants to have this conversation. "How did you get here?"

"Plane." I smirk at her. "Then a car."

"I know that, but don't you have work?" We both walk toward her living room.

"I have to be back at the rink tomorrow night for a game," I tell her, and I see she was on her couch, her iPad beside a throw cover and her laptop on the coffee table. The vase of pink flowers is right in the middle.

"Do you want something to drink?" The two of us act like we haven't licked every single part of the other person.

"No." I shake my head. "I'm good." We just stand here. "I missed you," I finally blurt out. She looks like she's going to say something, but I hold up my hand. "Just let me get this out, and then I'll go," I say, knowing I'll probably be leaving here with a broken fucking heart. "This thing between us, I know it started like this cat-and-mouse game." I smile at her and see she's wringing her hands in front of her. "The first time I kissed you, I honestly thought it was a dream. Not that I didn't remember it, but because there was no way one kiss could have set me on fire like that."

"Well, I did help," she tries to joke, and I can see she's just as nervous as I am.

"I want you, Ryleigh." I just cut to the chase. "I don't just want a fling with you or a couple of nights. I want to be connected to you. I want us to talk on the phone and laugh and joke. I want to get on your nerves."

"You already do that," she teases.

"I don't want you running away from me. I don't want you giving me bullshit excuses on why you can't take two minutes out of your day to talk to me." I step closer to her as she puts her head down. "I want to date you, Ryleigh. I want you to give us a chance. Being with you in my house, here, wherever it is, I want it to be with you."

"I don't know if I can," she finally says, looking up at me, and I can tell in her eyes, she's about to break my heart.

TWENTY

RYLEIGH

MY HEART FEELS like it's beating out of my chest. My stomach feels like it's in my throat. My hands are shaking so much I have to hold them together. "I don't know if I can," I answer him honestly. "Stone," I say his name because I want to make sure he's really here, and it's not just my imagination dreaming that he's here.

"What don't you think you can do?" he bites out. "You don't think you can call me once or twice a day? You don't think you can text me a good morning?"

"It's not just that, Stone, and you know it." I start to talk, and the sting in my nose starts. "Do you know what I did today?"

"How would I know what you did for the last three days?" He flaps his hands to the sides. "You wouldn't talk to me."

"Oh my God." I put my hands on my head.

"Don't you oh my God me, Ryleigh," he snaps, and even I have to admit if the roles were reversed and he ignored me the way I did him, I would probably set a couple of his things on fire. Starting with his house and moving down to his hockey equipment.

"It's not as easy as you think it is," I say softly.

"Because you won't let it be." I listen to his words, taking them all in, waiting before I finally speak.

"It's not that simple." That's the bottom line to all this. It's harder than we both want to admit it is going to be.

"Why not?"

I finally say and the tears that I've pushed away the whole day come on full force. "Do you know what I did today? I'll tell you what I did. I stayed fucking home from work because I was afraid you would send me something that would make me miss you. That you would do something thoughtful for me, and I would break down at work." My voice goes loud. "Do you know how hard it is to be a woman in my position?" I throw my hands up. "The obstacles I've had to face because I'm a woman? Now I was behaving like some fucking lovesick fool at work." The annoyance is clear in my voice. "In college, one of my best friends was like me. We were both driven, both on the same path. We had the same goal, same plan, same everything. Then you know what she did? She fell in love." My eyes open wider, hoping he gets it. "Then slowly she started letting balls drop to the floor. Started hanging out with him more than she should. I saw with my own eyes how much having to worry about an extra person can be." I huff. "It's just all too much."

"God forbid you show feelings, Ryleigh." His own annoyance reflects in his voice. "I'm not asking you to sit at your desk and doodle my name."

He shouts at me, and it makes me snap, "I'm scared, goddammit." The tears seep out of me. "I'm scared that I don't know how to do this. The first boyfriend I ever had was more interested in going to the Oscar party than the fact he was actually with me. So after that, I said fuck that. I've had hookups and bad one-night stands, but I've never ever had a boyfriend after that." He's about to say something, so I hold up my hand. "And it's not because I didn't have options. It was because I had one goal in life, and I couldn't be sidetracked by some boy." I wipe the tears away angrily. "I'm an independent woman who will not have to depend on any man. I don't have time for the games. I don't have time to think about you all day and not focus on work. I don't have time for the hurt feelings when I forget certain things. I am selfish!" I shout. "There, are you happy? In the courtroom, I'm a shark. I know what needs to be done, but this is so out of my comfort zone."

"Why can't you do both?" he asks me the question I've been asking myself all day long.

"Because I can't," I tell him. "I just can't."

"Your mother is a successful journalist with a husband and two kids." His voice is soft. "My mother has an entire business and still has my father, plus me and my sister. Are you saying they aren't independent women? Heck, all my aunts have something going on."

I cut him off. "What if I forget to call you, and you wait for my call all night?"

"Well, for one, I would be worried that something

happened to you," he answers softly, and it's like he just kicked me in the stomach.

"What if I miss one of your important games because I have to be in court or something?" I'm pulling at the bottom of the barrel because now talking to him, laying things out, it's not as bad as it is in my head.

"I'm not asking you to give up anything in your life. I'm just asking you to share it with me."

"What if I can't?" I admit to him. "What if I fall in love with you, and then I hurt you by doing something I don't even know that I'm doing?"

"You mean like this." He points at him and then at me. "I like you, Ryleigh, a lot."

"Well, I like you too, Stone," I finally admit.

"Don't say but." He holds his hand up. "Nothing good comes after but." I can't help but laugh at that. "Can we at least try?" He takes another step to me, putting his hands on my hips, and when I don't stop him, he pulls me to him. "I'm asking you to try with me. I'm asking you to be my girlfriend."

"Oh, good God," I groan, but with him here in front of me, in his arms, I feel a peace I've never felt before.

"Does that mean yes?" He puts his forehead on mine. "Will you date me?"

"I swear to everything that is holy, if you pull out a promise ring, I'm going to kick you in the balls."

"I don't have a promise ring on me." He rubs his nose with mine. "But—"

"Nothing good comes after but." I use his words against him, and I'm about to say something else, but

I stop when his mouth crashes on mine. I get up on my tippy-toes, wrapping my arms around him. His tongue slides into my mouth, and he picks me up, my legs wrapping around his waist.

He lets go of my lips, and I bury my face in his neck, kissing him once before looking at him. "You wearing my shirt?" he asks with a smirk, his arms holding me tight around my waist.

"It's comfy," I reply, burying my face again in his neck so he won't see my cheeks get pink from embarrassment.

"Is it?" He squeezes me to him.

"It is," I mumble as he starts moving to the couch and sitting down with me still attached to him.

"Did you eat?"

I sit up in his lap. "What did you have in mind?" I wiggle my eyebrows.

He shakes his head, and I can't stop the smile from filling my face, even if I wanted to. "I meant food. I haven't eaten since breakfast. I did have snacks on the plane."

"When do you leave?" I ask him as I put my hands on his pecs.

"Tomorrow morning at ten. Figured I'd get you off to work and then take off."

"So I get you the whole night?" I try not to make it seem like I'm too happy.

"You get me the whole night and some of the morning," he confirms, "but I'm good to just chill here while you work." God, this man. This fucking man. "Why don't you finish your work while I order food?"

"I still can't believe you got on a plane." I shake my head. "How did you get a flight so fast?"

"Private," he replies, and I gawk at him.

"You chartered a private plane to come see me?" The thought alone is unthinkable.

"What else was I supposed to do? You weren't speaking to me." His hands rub up and down my sides. "And my parents sort of told me I needed to tell you how I felt."

"Your parents?" My voice comes out in a shriek. "You told your parents?"

"Not really. I told them I met a girl in Chicago," he tells his story, "then my mother was like 'Ryleigh lives in Chicago' and, well, the rest is history."

"This could be very, very bad—" I start to say, but he shuts me up by kissing me. I suddenly forget what I was going to say and instead just go with the kiss. He lets me go after that so I can finish up my work. We eat way too fast, and when he steps into the shower, I'm right behind him, but not for long. I drop to my knees, taking him down my throat, where he then returns the favor. We don't even make it to the bed. He fucks me on my counter, then cleans me up. When we fall into bed, he's pulling me to him, and for the first time in three nights, I don't go to bed with a heavy heart. I don't go to bed fighting off tears. I don't go to bed wishing he was here because he is.

The next day, he wakes me up by sliding into me while he whispers, "Good morning, gorgeous." I don't even open my eyes. I just hitch my legs over his hips and go with it. It's fast, it's hard, and it's fucking perfect.

"So when I text you later, you'll try to answer me?" he asks, standing beside the car that came to pick us up this morning and will be dropping him off at the airport.

"Yes," I assure him, "or at least I will get back to you."

"I'll take it. Tomorrow, we will hash out our schedules and see what we can do."

"Sounds like a plan," I tell him, getting up on my tippy-toes to kiss him. "Text me when you get in so I know you're okay."

"See," he says, kissing my lips softly, "I knew you could do it."

"Goodbye." I slap his shoulder before walking away from him. Looking over my shoulder and waving at him, I smile like a fucking fool.

I go through security to go up to my office, and my phone rings as soon as I take off my jacket. I'm expecting it to be him, but it's my mother. "Good morning, Mother." I put the phone to my ear.

"She lives," my mother chides, and I laugh.

"She's alive and well," I confirm.

"I haven't spoken to you in a month," she exaggerates.

"It's been more like two weeks," I remind her.

"Two weeks, a month, it still feels like forever."

"I wasn't home this weekend, or I would have called you." I pull out my chair to sit down.

"Where did you go?" she asks, and I know I have to tell her before she finds out from someone else.

"I went to visit my boyfriend." Even I cringe when I say the word.

"Um, excuse me?" she questions. I hear a ringing and look at my phone to see she's FaceTiming me. I press connect, and she's sitting outside, wearing a white robe. "What did you just say?"

"I said I was visiting my boyfriend," I repeat, rolling my eyes. "It's not that big of a deal." But I know it's a big deal since I've never said those words to her before.

"Um, I didn't even know you were dating someone, let alone had a boyfriend. So it's a big deal, Ryleigh."

"Can we make it not a big deal?" I put the phone down in front of me.

"Does this boyfriend have a name?" She picks up her cup of coffee and takes a sip.

"Yes, you've met him before, it's Stone." The minute I say his name, she spits her coffee out of her mouth and coughs.

She grabs a towel from a nearby chair and coughs into it. My father opens the door and comes outside. "Are you okay, baby?" he asks. I see he's shirtless, and his hair is all over the place, so I know he just woke up.

"Morning, Pops." His face turns toward the phone when he hears my voice.

"Morning, Ry," he mumbles. "What happened to her?" He points at my mother, who is still coughing.

"I told her I'm dating Stone Richards and that he's my boyfriend." My father's mouth hangs open. "I have to go, but I'll call her later."

"You better fucking call us later," he says, emphasis on the us. "Did she say Stone Richards?" he asks my mother, who nods her head while I disconnect the phone.

I turn on my computer as I dial his number. "I'm not even gone, and you're already calling me." He laughs instead of saying hello.

"Yeah, look at me being needy," I sass sarcastically. "Just letting you know I told my parents you were my boyfriend, so the cat is out of the bag."

"That's a big step," he states, and I hear the car door slam.

"It's not a big step if we don't make it a big step. Now I have to go work," I say tightly. "Goodbye, fly safe, and call me later."

"So needy." He chuckles. "Have a great day, gorgeous." I don't answer him. Instead, I hang up and go through my emails.

I'm in the middle of reading my case file when Claudia comes in with a blue bag. "This came for you." She smirks at me. "You sure are one lucky lady."

"I guess so." I look at the bag as she hands it to me. I wait for her to walk out of my office before I open the bag and pull the white tissue paper out. Followed by a white card and a square brown box. "What have you done now?" I open the note first.

Something so you think of me.
The boyfriend.
S.

I laugh, open the square box, and gasp when I see the gold beaded bracelet with two silver squares in the middle, one with an S and the other with an R. I pick it up, my finger playing with the letters.

I pull up his number, and he answers right away.

"Twice, and I didn't even call you."

"Did you just send me a bracelet with your initials?" I'm not really asking him the question since I'm holding it in my hand.

"Well, I didn't have a promise ring, so this was the next best thing." He can't help but full-on laugh. "It's so you would see it and know that I'm thinking about you." I don't say anything. "It's also to let anyone else know you're mine."

TWENTY-ONE

STONE

I TAKE OUT my luggage and plop it on the bed at the same time the phone rings. Stopping, I see it's my father. "Hey," I greet him, putting the phone on speaker and walking back into the closet to start packing for my road trip.

"Hey yourself," he bites out. "It's been two days, and you haven't called me back."

"It took you two days to check on me?" I grab two suits and head back to my suitcase. "If that was Uncle Matthew, the SWAT team would have come barreling into Ryleigh's house one minute after midnight. You guys are slipping in your old age."

"Oh, please," he moans. "I saw you were on the ice last night, so I figured she didn't kill you."

"That she did not." I smile, thinking of her.

"That must mean she likes you?" he asks me softly.

"I hope so. She made me spend the night." I laugh.

"How is that going to work now?" I've been trying

not to think about that.

"For right now, I have no idea." I sit on the bed. "I know I'm leaving for a week. I play in Winnipeg, Columbus, and then Minnesota."

"I would never tell you what to do, but I think you need to make sure you both take time out for each other."

"I know, Dad." I inhale deeply. "I know." It comes out softly this time.

"Okay, buddy," he says, knowing I'm going to have to think it out. "Call me if you need anything."

"I will," I assure him. "Hug Mom for me."

"With pleasure."

"Ewww, goodbye." I hang up the phone, and instead of packing, I call Ryleigh, who answers after two rings.

"Well, hello, SR." Ever since she got the bracelet I sent her, that's been my new nickname.

"Hello, gorgeous." I smile. "What are you doing?"

"I'm prepping for trial, the big case I have coming up," she answers softly. "What about you? What are you doing?"

"I'm sitting on my bed getting ready to pack." I look over at the suits sitting at the bottom of the bag.

"Where are you off to?" She sounds sleepy.

"We leave tomorrow for Winnipeg, then we have Columbus and then Minnesota."

"Holy shit," she whistles out, "that sounds exhausting."

"Yeah." I get up and walk back into the closet to grab my shoes and a couple of shirts. "You have no idea." I toss everything into the bag. "How does your schedule look next weekend?" I ask.

"I have a couple of meetings during the week. That should let me know how the weekend will be."

"I have two days off between games when I get back, so maybe I can squeeze in a visit," I tell her, trying to look at the schedule and see if and when it'll fit.

"I'll check on my end also," she says softly, and I hear her yawn, "but I don't think I can swing it, to be honest. I really have to trial prep. Plus, I'm on the docket for the next two weeks."

"Go get some sleep," I urge her. "You worked until almost midnight last night."

"I think you're right," she agrees. "I'm going to shut it down. I'll call you tomorrow, SR."

"Night, gorgeous," I say and disconnect, tossing my phone on the bed.

But it doesn't stay silent for long. Two minutes later, it rings, and when I pick it up, I see it's my sister, Zoey.

"Yo," I say, putting her on speaker as I start to really pack my bag.

"Yo," Zoey says. "Yo?" she repeats. "That's the only thing you have to say to me?"

"Um…" I look at the phone while I put my shoes in the luggage.

"Don't um me, Stone," she snaps. "Do you know what I've been doing for the past two days?" With the way she is speaking, I know she's not expecting me to answer. "I'll tell you what I've been doing. Dodging Dad's phone calls because he wants to tell me how much my worth is as a woman and that I shouldn't put myself in a situationship." Her voice goes loud. "A word that took him five tries to actually get out because he didn't remember it." I can't help but laugh. "Don't fucking laugh. Every day, he sends me messages like 'You deserve the world.' And 'Don't let anyone tell you that you aren't worth the time.' And my all-time favorite, "You are perfect the way you are. Don't let them tell you otherwise.'"

"Oh my God," I say. "Well, I don't know why you're pissed at me. Mom told me about it, so frankly, you only have yourself to blame." She growls. "I'm so sorry you showed Mom a word that she spoke in front of Dad," I say sarcastically.

"You're sorry? You're sorry?" she snaps. "Why would you do that to me?"

"If it makes you feel better, it had nothing to do with you and everything to do with me."

"Yeah, I heard," she groans. "I also heard that you're dating Ryleigh." She then tsks. "You think that's a good idea? Isn't there a saying 'don't shit where you eat'? How are you going to date her, and then what happens if—"

I don't let her finish. "We're two grown adults. If shit happens, we'll deal with it."

"Yeah, but how?"

"Don't you have to think about being in a situationship? Worry about that."

"I'm not in a situationship because I, unlike you, am not dating anyone… Unless you have a friend you would like to introduce me to."

"No, sorry, I'm friendless," I retort. "But I do have to

pack. I'll let you know if I find a friend for you."

"Please do. And don't tell Dad any more new words. For fuck's sake, that's all we need is the uncles on the beach asking us about our situationship."

"Noted. Come and visit me when I come back."

"I have a job!" She hangs up on me, but not before she continues talking "this clown come visit me."

The following morning, the alarm wakes me, and I reach over and immediately snooze it, then pull up her name.

Me: *Good morning, gorgeous.*

Putting the phone back down as soon as I send the message, I close my eyes again. The alarm wakes me up again, and I have to get up this time. I dress in black dress pants with a white button-down shirt tucked in and a charcoal-gray sweater on top of it. I opt for black sneakers instead of black dress shoes. I toss my suitcase in the trunk before I head out, finally checking my phone.

Gorgeous: *Good morning, SR. Did you sleep well? I'm already at the office.*

She attached a picture of herself sitting at her desk with a coffee in her hand. I can spot the bracelet on her left wrist in front of her watch, and I smile.

Me: *You look beautiful. I'm headed out. Text you when I land.*

I send her a picture of me winking at her. I don't think she's going to answer, but she surprises me.

Gorgeous: *Looking good, SR. The things I would do to you.*

I laugh and type back right away.

Me: *Save it for the FaceTime chat tonight. I don't want to show up at work with my cock trying to come out of my pants.*

Gorgeous: *Fine, I'll save it for tonight. But just so you know, I'm bringing out the toys.*

Me: *That's not helping, Ryleigh.*

Gorgeous: *Oh, he uses my name. Am I in trouble? I am a bad girl.*

I close my eyes and see her naked in my lap, riding me the last time we were together.

Me: *Don't you have to work?*

Gorgeous: *I do, I do. Fly safe, SR.*

I put the phone away, then drive to the airport. Everyone is dragging their ass. It's almost the end of the season, and the novelty of traveling has reached its limits with everyone. The rookies included.

I carry my bag up the stairs and into the plane, going to the seat I always sit in. I store my bag before taking off my jacket and sitting down. A couple of people look up, so I wave at them. Most of them already have their headphones on when my phone starts blowing up, vibrating every second.

Looking down, I see it's the cousin chat with Matty, Stefano, and Christopher, which can only mean something big is happening.

Matty: *Is it true? Is Stone dating Romeo's sister?*

Stefano: *Oh, shit.*

Christopher: *She finally gave him a shot.*

Stefano: *STFU, Stone, are you really dating her?*

Matty: *That's what Uncle Evan told my dad.*

Christopher: *This is going to be awkward AF if they are dating and she breaks up with him.*

Matty: *What is wrong with you?*

Christopher*: I'm just saying what everyone else is thinking.*

Me: *Can we all calm down for a second? Yes, I'm dating her. She gave me a chance. It's literally been four days, so everyone needs to calm down.*

Christopher: *Already trouble in paradise.*

I shake my head.

Me: *Taking off now. Headed to Winnipeg.*

Matty: *Christopher played them last night, and they kicked his ass. The clip on the sports news showed the whole team in the penalty box.*

Christopher*: Benji got crosschecked from the back and ended up knocked out in the middle of the ice. It was a fucking mess.*

Me: *You okay?*

Christopher: *Yeah, but I've been better. Benji has a concussion, among other things.*

Even though we're family, we keep the team gossip away from the family. We reach out when someone is hurt only to know if they are okay, but it's known that we don't discuss anyone else.

Matty: *Sucks. Man, hope he gets better.*

Me: *Wheels up. Later.*

Christopher: *So who is going to tell my brother-in-law that you're dating his sister?*

I don't answer the last message. I just switch off my phone and look out the window, then throw on my own headset and watch *Jack Ryan* for the next five hours.

The minute I turn my phone on again, I see that the messages are going through.

Uncle Matthew Sr.: *You need to call me back.*

I roll my eyes and chuckle.

Dad: *Hey, so I might have told your uncles.*

I reply right away.

Me: *Might have?*

The one after is from Gabriella.

Gabby: *I hope you know what you're doing. I would hate to have to kick her ass for hurting you or your ass for hurting her. Love you.*

Then Ryleigh.

Gorgeous: *FYI, cat is out of the bag and my brother knows. Hope you landed safe!*

Me: *Yeah, figured he was going to find out. My cousins texted me before I landed. Text you when we get to the hotel.*

I put my phone away as we get off the plane. It takes an hour to get to the hotel, and when I try to call Ryleigh, it goes straight to voice mail, so I know her phone is off.

I collapse on the bed and crash, only waking at three o'clock in the morning to undress. I grab my phone and see she sent me a message after eleven.

Gorgeous: *Sorry, I was trial prepping, and we shut it down. I'll call you tomorrow. Sleep tight.*

I call her the following morning, and the conversation is literally five seconds long because she gets another phone call. That night, the game is horrible, and I mean horrible. We end up losing seven to two. Loading up right after the game and heading over to Columbus, we walk into the hotel room at three o'clock in the morning. I kick my shoes off and undress before sliding into bed.

The next day, I wake up after noon and call her.

"Well, well, well," she says. I swear the minute I hear her voice, I miss her more than I thought I did.

"Morning, gorgeous," I mumble.

"Did you just get up?" she asks me softly.

"I did. We got in last night after three. Today is an off day, so I plan on chilling in my room. I wish you were here."

"You and me both." She exhales.

"Did you get a chance to check your schedule?"

She pauses, and I know it's probably not good news. "I did, and I don't think I can swing it."

"Fuck," I swear, trying not to sound like a whiny kid. "Okay." I pretend it doesn't bother me. "We'll check again when I get home."

"Why don't you get some food, go relax, and call me later?"

"Okay. Miss you, gorgeous," I say right before I hang up.

The next night is even worse than the last game. We get handed our asses on a platter, five to zero. At this point, we aren't even going to make it into the playoffs, and it sucks hard. We rush to get on the plane, thankful that it's only a two-hour flight time.

We get in at midnight, and I text her.

Me: *Good night.*

My phone rings right away, and it's her.

"Hey," I answer, lying on the bed with an arm outstretched and another on my chest.

"Hey, you," she says softly. "I was just getting into bed."

"Same." I turn to look out the window at the night.

"How're you feeling?" she asks, and I hear blankets rustle on her side.

"I'm okay, I guess. Tired. Want to be home. Want to see you." I stop talking. "It'll be okay."

"You'll feel better once you're home." I close my eyes because will I be better once I'm home? She's still not going to be there.

"Yeah, I guess." I stop talking, and neither of us says anything. We just listen to each other breathe. "Wish you were here."

"Wish you were here," she repeats, and then we hang up. I toss my phone on the side before undressing and falling asleep.

The bus ride to the rink is quiet. No one is talking. Everyone knows how much this sucks. The minute the puck drops, it doesn't get any better. I take a stupid penalty for slashing and end up in the box, where they score after forty seconds. The second period is even worse, and we end up losing four to one.

"Can we just go fucking home?" Jay moans after the game, and the coach just looks at him.

"Flight is at noon," he snaps. "You aren't the only one who wants to get this fucking week over."

We pull up to the hotel, and no one utters a fucking word to each other. I head upstairs to my room, tossing the key card on the table along with my phone. I don't even want to text or call her. I'm so angry about it all that I need to calm down.

I'm about to get undressed when there is a knock on the door. I look over and see it's almost eleven o'clock. I walk over, not even checking to see who it is before I open the door. The Do Not Disturb sign flies onto the floor, but no one is looking at that because the only thing I see is her.

"Surprise," she says, throwing her hands into the air.

TWENTY-TWO

RYLEIGH

TEN SECONDS BEFORE he opens the door, the only thing going through my mind is *what the fuck are you doing?* But—and I know nothing good comes after but—seeing his face light up, well, it was worth all the hoops I jumped through just to be here for twelve hours. "Surprise." I throw my hands in the air, and he stands there holding the hotel door in one hand, his mouth hanging open. He's wearing dress pants with his white shirt that is untucked from his pants, his feet only in socks.

I think I count to three before he reaches forward and pulls me into his room. One hand wraps around my waist perfectly. The hand holding the door lets it go and flies to my cheek, my whole body tingles from just one touch. "You're here," he whispers, looking into my eyes. "Are you really here, gorgeous?"

I smile, my own hand coming up to cup his cheek. "I'm really here." I don't have time to say anything before his mouth crashes on mine. The kiss starts off slow but quickly escalates since we haven't seen each other in over a week. My bag slips off my shoulder and falls with a thud beside our feet, but he's spinning us farther into the room.

The only light on is the one beside the bed. "How are you here?" He lets go of my lips to trail kisses down my neck. I move my head to the side, giving him more access. "I don't care," he says, pushing my black jacket off my shoulders. "I've missed you, gorgeous," he whispers softly, my hands now moving up his chest to the buttons of his shirt.

"I've missed you more than I want to admit."

He chuckles while pulling the black T-shirt over my head, leaving me in my bra. It takes less than a minute for us to be on his bed, though his boxers are still on, unfortunately. He kisses my neck while he pushes a bra strap down, trailing kisses down my shoulder and finally taking a nipple into his mouth. "I have to taste you," he declares, and before I can answer him, he pushes my panties aside. His tongue slides into me at the same time as his finger. My eyes close, taking in the feeling of him touching me. I've touched myself while thinking of him this whole week, but nothing compares to the real thing. Nothing can compare to Stone.

My hand goes into his hair. "Oh," I pant when he sucks my clit into his mouth and slides another finger into me. "Yes." I open my legs more for him. "Right there."

He curls his fingers up, touching my G-spot, and the tightness starts in my stomach. "Did you mean here?" he asks, kissing my thigh before attacking my clit again. I don't answer him. I just push his face into my pussy. His fingers work me over, taking me right there, right where he always takes me, and I don't even have to try. I can feel the orgasm coming, making me want to open my legs wider, my hips moving to meet his fingers.

"I'm—" I don't have to say anything, or maybe I can't because the orgasm rocks through me. His fingers move faster until the end of my orgasm. I don't have time to think before he's between my legs. His knees are on the bed as he slams into me. The only sounds in the room now are of us moaning.

The fullness of him is perfect. "This isn't fair," I pant as he pulls out and slams into me again. "I didn't get to suck your cock." My legs hitch around his hips. "You got all the fun." I can't even talk because he's fucking me hard and fast. It's the best feeling in the world.

"I'll come down your throat soon enough." He grabs my hips, pulling me to his cock as if I'm a rag doll. His fingers grip my hips as he moves my body to his cock, his balls slamming my ass. "You need to get there," he urges between clenched teeth.

"Then take me there," I egg him on, "pound my pussy like you mean it."

I don't say anything else because he's throwing both legs over his shoulders. His hands go beside my shoulders, and he fucks me hard, fast, and deep. It's fucking glorious. My eyes close as I clench my pussy around his cock. "Stone," I moan, my eyes closed. I'm coming down from my orgasm when I feel another one coming. "Oh my."

"One more and you can suck my cock." My eyes open when he speaks, and I see him watching me. "I want your pussy to beg for my cum," he says, "but I want your mouth to swallow it." Just thinking of it, I'm coming again. "Yes," he hisses, his thrusts shorter and then pulling almost all the way out and slamming back into me. It's like my body is a violin, and his cock is the bow.

"You ready?" he asks me when he knows my orgasm is at the end. My throat is dry, so all I can do is nod. He pulls his cock out of me, and I sit up, taking him in the back of my throat. My hand grips his shaft, my eyes closing to take him as deep as I can get him. "You have one more in you?" I don't even know what he's asking, but then his fingers enter me. "You are so wet, gorgeous." I look up at him, his fingers working the same speed as my hand on his cock. "Look at you taking my cock." He thrusts his hips to get more of it in my mouth. "Take my cock any way I want you to take my cock," he urges, and I try to focus on his cock in my mouth, but his fingers and his words are distracting, and I can feel another one coming. It's like my body has been saving it all for this moment. "Like a good girl." The words come out in a hiss because his cum hits the back of my throat at the same time as I come on his hand. I swallow every single drop he has for me, his fingers slowing down in me at the same time as my hand slows around the base of his cock.

I open my eyes to watch him, wondering who will let

go first. "Fuck, you're beautiful," he declares, pulling his fingers out of me and sliding them into his mouth. I let go of his cock, only for him to grab my face and slide his tongue into my mouth.

"Fuck," he says, letting go of me, "I've just had the best orgasm of my life, and my cock wants you again." I look down at his cock and see it hasn't even gone down.

"You act like that's a bad thing," I joke with him, getting on my knees and taking off my bra and tossing it to the side. "We have twelve hours." I cup his balls. "When I leave here, I want to feel you still inside me." I kiss his neck, his hands coming up to pinch my nipples and then roll them. "Feel up to the challenge, big boy?"

"The question is"—his fingers are still playing with my nipples—"when you beg me to stop, will I stop?"

"You talk a big game." I kiss under his chin. "The question is, can your cock deliver?"

"Oh, gorgeous." He wraps his arm around my waist, pulling me up. "I'm going to love making you eat your words." He hoists me from the bed, and I yelp. "Time for a shower."

He walks toward the bathroom, placing me down on the counter before walking over to the white shower curtain and pulling it back to start the water. He pulls the curtain closed before coming back to stand between my legs. His mouth comes down to kiss me, and he places his hands beside my hips. One of my hands goes to his hip, but the minute I touch him, I want more, so I grip his cock, jerking it. His hands go from beside my hips to my knees, pulling them up so my feet are on the counter.

I rub him up and down my slit once before he slides into me, and there on the counter, with the hot water steam filling up the room, he makes me come two more times before we actually get into the shower.

I don't know what time we fall asleep, the both of us trying to get as much of each other as we can. I put my head down on his chest, listening to his heart beating before I drift off. My alarm rings in what feels like two seconds after I've fallen asleep. He reaches over me to slap the phone and then mumbles, but not before his knees kick my leg to the side, and he moves his hip to slide into me. "One more time," he murmurs into my neck, and I don't answer him. I just close my arms and legs around him, savoring every touch. I make a mental note of how he feels close to me. How his hair feels in my hands. How he fits into me like he was made for me.

We both groan before he rolls over to his side, taking me with him. "I need coffee," I say, and he reaches for the phone on the bedside table. One eye opens to watch him fumble with the phone. He has to release me to dial the number to room service. "Hey, can I get a pot of coffee, some French toast, scrambled eggs, bacon, sausage, and fresh fruit?" He looks up at me. "Thank you," he says, hanging up the phone. "Twenty minutes." He lies back down in bed and pulls me to him.

"That's a lot of food." I laugh as I put my hands on his chest and place my chin on them.

"I need it." He looks down at me. "After last night and this morning." I kiss the middle of his chest. "What time do you have to leave?" His voice is soft.

"My plane is at ten," I answer him, looking at the clock on the side table and seeing it's just a bit after seven.

"I can't even believe you're here," he says. "How?"

I laugh and sit up in bed, reaching over to grab the bottle of water I snatched from the desk when we got out of the shower. "I messaged Gabriella for help." I take a gulp as he places two pillows behind his head, propping himself up with his arm bent under his head. The sheet barely covers his hip and his cock. I sit next to him, crossing my legs under me with one of my knees on his uncovered hip. "She said she had a spreadsheet your Uncle Matthew makes every year when the season starts."

He laughs. "It's an Excel spreadsheet organized by month and then each month by date. No one really uses it."

"Well, it's a good thing he did that because I was able to find you right away." His hand lies over my knee. "I then called my father, who got me a private plane." His eyes open. "I didn't like that you were angry, and according to Gabriella, you sucked so bad on the ice."

I'm expecting him to be insulted by the comment, but he isn't. "That's putting it mildly."

"So I finished work last night, rushed home, changed, grabbed my bag, and said I would be in this afternoon." The tightness comes to my chest as if someone stands on top of me with one foot in the middle of my chest. I lean over to kiss his lips softly before throwing my leg over his hips and sinking down on his cock. Knowing there are other things to talk about, knowing the reality is that no matter how much I want this to work, it feels like it's impossible. Yet, as soon as I see him, all I want to do is make it work. Neither of us says anything as we come again right before the room service arrives. I slide into the bathroom while the guy sets up and then walk out, wearing another one of his T-shirts that I took from his bag to Stone in his shorts, pouring me a cup of coffee.

"Here you go, gorgeous." He leans forward, kissing me behind my ear.

"Thank you." I smile up at him, taking a sip of the coffee. I have two more hours with him, and the last thing I want to think about is when we will see each other again.

I sit in the chair, facing him at the little table in the corner of his room. He pulls off the covers of the food and hands me a fork. "Just dig in," he urges, stabbing a sausage with his fork and biting into it.

"When do you get back home?" I ask.

"This afternoon, we leave at noon." He grabs a piece of bacon. "Then I have a game tomorrow, Thursday, and Saturday." The wheels in my head spin. "Then I'm off again for another three games on the road in Canada."

"That sounds like a lot," I tell him, and he shrugs.

"It's the norm," he explains, and even though I knew he traveled with his job, the reality of it is all coming to light.

"What about you?" he asks me, and I look down at the eggs in front of me, picking up a piece.

"I'm going to be swamped for the next two months," I inform him and see the way his eyes darken over, "between new case files being handed to me and that huge case I'm prepping for trial." I swallow down the eggs that feel like they're going to get stuck in the middle of my throat. "I don't know when I'll be able to get away." The words hit me hard. However, sitting here with him having coffee after having another one of the best nights I've had, even though I'm already exhausted for tomorrow, I'm not ready to give up on this yet. My heart speeds up to the point where I let out a little cough to get the rest of the words out. "Let me check again and see what I can fit on my end."

TWENTY-THREE

STONE

I WATCH HER sit in front of me, playing with her food. "I'm going to be swamped for the next two months." She looks up, and I try not to let her know how much this news bothers me, but I know I can't hide it. My breathing comes in spurts. "Between new case files being handed to me and that huge case I'm prepping for trial." She swallows, and I can tell she's having a hard time with it. "I don't know when I'll be able to get away." She inhales. "Let me check again and see what I can fit on my end."

I push away how much that whole statement bothers me. "You need to eat," I remind her, and she looks up at me. "Chances are, you'll stay at the office late and forget to eat."

She smirks. "I want to argue with you." She holds up her fork, and I can see the heavy conversation is past us. I know we should talk about it. I know there is so much more to say, but I think we're scared of what the outcome actually means.

"Of course you do." I wink at her. "If you want to have makeup sex, all you have to do is ask for it."

She rolls her eyes at me. "Haven't you had enough of me?" She tilts her head to the side, and I lied before. Here in front of me with no makeup on, her hair hanging loose from being pulled most of the night, wearing my T-shirt, she looks the most beautiful she's ever looked.

"I don't think I'll ever get enough of you." I put down my fork and stop talking before I tell her I think I've fallen in love with her because it will be awkward if she's not there yet. I know she likes me, but I'm not sure she's at the same level I am. It's the scariest thing I've ever done.

"We'll see about that," she mumbles. I ignore the comment, not wanting the last couple of hours we have together to be us arguing about where we are, where we're going, and what we're going to do. I let her finish eating before I get up and hold my hand out to her, taking her back to bed one last time.

This time, it's like we both know it's the last time. So it's slow, keeping everything in my memory, even knowing it's never going to be as good as the real thing. We get dressed at the same time, neither of us saying a word. I pack my bag and spot her slipping another one of my T-shirts in her backpack.

Her phone pings, letting her know her driver is downstairs. Leaving my bag on the bed, I take her bag from her before walking out of the room. I slide my hand in hers as we get into the elevator and go down. My thumb rubs her hand, trying to make her feel what I feel for her.

Thankfully, the lobby is not busy, so we just walk out, and I spot the bus over to the right before seeing the black SUV waiting for her. The driver gets out. "Ms. Beckett?" he asks, and she nods at him before he opens the door for her. I hand him her bag, and he takes it, putting it across on the seat.

"We'll be a second," she tells him, and he nods at her before closing the door, walking around the SUV, and getting in on the driver's side.

"You'll text me when you land?" I ask her as my throat feels like something is lodged in it. My hand slips out of hers as I hold her hips in my hands.

Her hands go to my chest and the flap of my jacket. "I will text you when I land." Her hands nervously strum my chest. "You'll call me when you land?"

"Will do." I nod, pulling her closer to me. "Thank you for coming to visit me."

"I figured it was the least I could do." She wraps her arms around my neck, her smile filling her face, but her eyes, the smile doesn't go to her eyes, so she's faking it.

I put my forehead on hers, the pounding in my chest feeling like my heart is going to come right out from it. Instead of saying anything, I just bend my head to kiss her lips, wrapping my arms around her waist. This kiss is the perfect ending to one of the best nights. Once I let go of her lips, I lift her off her feet, giving her a big hug. "I miss you." I bury my face in her neck, and I know she heard me when she plays with my hair.

I put her down and give her one more kiss before I open the door for her. "Safe flight, gorgeous." I kiss her lips one more time.

She puts her hand on my cheek. "Safe flight, SR." Her smile is as sad as I feel. She steps into the SUV and holds up her hand while I close the door. I hold up my own hand when she puts her hand to her lips and blows me a kiss before the SUV drives away. I watch it until the red lights blend into traffic, and I can't see them anymore.

With my head hanging down, I walk back in, going to my room and grabbing my bag. The last thing I want to do is stay in the room that still smells like her. Instead, I go down to the lobby and wait for the guys to come down.

Everyone is happy to finally be going home. I get on the plane, sitting down next to the window and hoping no one sits next to me. Luckily for me, people all scatter on the plane. I close the window shade and put my head back. I fall asleep for the hour plane ride home, and once I get in my car, I call my father.

"Hey," I greet as soon as he answers.

"Hey," he answers softly, "how are you doing?"

"I have no idea, Dad," I tell him honestly. "Like, what the fuck am I thinking?"

"Where are you now?" he asks, and I can hear him moving.

"Just landed at home," I inform him, and he blows out a breath.

"Okay, I'll be there soon." He disconnects the phone, and I don't even bother calling him back because, fuck, I need to talk to someone.

I pull up Ryleigh's name and text her instead of calling her.

Me: *Just landed at home, gorgeous.*

It takes two minutes for her to answer me.

Gorgeous: *Sorry, forgot to text when I landed. Things are crazy here right now. Talk later.*

I put the phone down, feeling like there is nothing to really say. She's got her plate full. I have my plate full, and this whole thing fucking sucks.

I get home, walking up the stairs toward my bedroom, dumping my bag in the closet before stepping into the shower. I close my eyes, and all I can see is her face smiling at me, like a fucking movie going on over and over again. I get out of the shower and drag on a pair of sweatpants before going downstairs to eat something. It feels like I have the weight of the world on my shoulders.

I check my mail that is put on the side, trying to distract myself, but I'm sitting at the island looking out into space. The front door opens, and then I hear the commotion. "Is he home?" My Uncle Matthew, and even though he can be too much, I smile.

"He's home," my father confirms from the front door.

"Why does it look like someone died in here?" my Uncle Max says as the voices come closer to the kitchen.

"Jesus," my Uncle Viktor says, "can we turn lights on in here?" I shake my head, not even surprised the four of them decided to take a road trip from New York, where they are mostly based, to come and see me.

"Holy shit," Matthew swears once the light's on, and

he sees me. "What the fuck are you doing sitting in the dark all by yourself?"

"I didn't even notice," I answer him, turning to see all four of them almost dressed the same, in golf attire. I have to imagine they were probably all playing golf when I called my father.

"You didn't notice you were sitting in the dark?" Viktor asks. "Are you okay?" His voice is soft, as it always is. He married my mother's twin sister, so it's like he's my second father. They were always together. He also is a recovered addict who got traded when he was in rehab, and then met my Aunt Zoe.

"No." I look at them and then at my dad. "I don't know what the fuck I am, but it's not okay." I shake my head.

I get up from the stool and walk over to the living room and sit on the couch, putting my head back. The four of them slowly come into the room, taking their spots and waiting for me to talk. It's something they do all together. I've heard stories from Mini Cooper and Michael about how they just band together and wait for you to share your story before they tell you what you've done wrong. I rub my hands over my face, laughing because if anyone would have said that this would be me, I would have told them they were out of their mind. "What exactly are you feeling?" my Uncle Matthew starts, standing with his hands crossed over his chest, his legs apart, watching me.

"I think I'm in love with Ryleigh." I say the words out loud, looking at all four of them.

"What is wrong with you guys and thinking you're in love?" Viktor shakes his head. "Matty said the same thing."

My father is the only one sitting next to me. "When you're in love with someone, you don't think it. You just know it."

I take a deep inhale. "Okay, fine, then I'm in love with her, and it's just so fucked up."

"Why?" Max sits on the other side of me with his hands in his lap. "Also, love is fucked up. It makes you do things you can't explain."

"Like elope with my sister." Matthew side-eyes him as Max just smirks at him.

"Like marry the love of my life without her overbearing brother there." He points at me, totally ignoring the way Matthew is giving him a death glare. It's been a hundred years since they got together, and he's still not over them dating behind his back.

"Can we focus on the present and not talk about that?" my father snaps. "Why is it so fucked up?"

"Because I live in Nashville and she lives in Chicago, and I hate that I can't see her when I want. I hate coming home and she's not here. I hate that every single time I'm with her, all I do is fall more and more in love with her, and I don't know if she feels the same. I hate we have so few hours to spend with each other when we finally see each other. I hate I feel so totally fucking helpless, and I have no solution for it." I look at the four of them, thinking one of them will have the answer to this. But they just look at me, and at one point, I even see

Uncle Viktor grimace. "Thanks for all your help," I bark. "Good talk."

"What is it you want us to say?" Matthew says. "You both have careers. She's a fucking ADA. Did you think she could come whenever she wanted?"

"I didn't think of that, obviously." I glare at him, and he laughs at me.

I look at my father. "How did you do it?" I ask him. "How did you do this whole long-distance thing?"

"It fucking killed me. I hated every single second of it. But unlike Ryleigh, I was lucky, your mom was able to work from anywhere she wanted unless she had to go meet clients. But she usually did that when she knew I was traveling, so we wouldn't lose that time together."

"Great." I put my head back. "So basically, I'm fucked."

"Not exactly," Max chimes in. "There is one thing you can do." He looks over at Matthew, who closes his eyes.

"Don't say it," Viktor says to Max.

"Why?" Max retorts. "Evan did it." He then turns to me. "You ask to be traded."

TWENTY-FOUR

RYLEIGH

I STEP OFF the elevator with my coffee in one hand and my phone in the other. "Good morning, Claudia." I smile at her as she waves at me, picking up the phone that's ringing.

I walk down the hallway toward my office, looking around to see who else is in. I lean my head to the right, wondering if Kristal is in. Both of us walked out of our offices last night at ten. Both of us dragging our asses, mine especially since I didn't really sleep two nights before. I was running on caffeine, energy drinks, and peanut M&M's, and since I've been back from that impromptu trip, it's been balls to the wall. But I filed the brief that I've been working on for my big drug case and the trial is in a week. I can check that off my to-do list.

I look forward to getting some much-needed sleep in the next couple of days. My head automatically goes to Stone and the last message he sent me yesterday morning.

SR: *Sorry, I had an impromptu visit from my father*

and uncles. Call me later.

The message ate me up inside. It was so stupid that I was jealous of his family members for being able to spend time with him. Forget the fact the plane ride back home was the most horrible plane ride ever, and I blamed my puffy eyes and nose on allergies when I walked in. I don't know if anyone believed me, but no one questioned me. I've never once since I've been here suffered from allergies. But that was my cover story and that's what I was going with.

Seeing Kristal isn't in, I walk into my own office, going to my desk, putting down my coffee and my phone, before walking over and shrugging off my jacket. "Good morning." Kristal dips her head into my office. "I thought for sure you would be at home working."

"I thought about it, I'm starting trial prep today to get ready for next week. It's easier to do it here," I tell her, and she nods at me.

"Wish me luck." She holds up her fingers, crossing them. "I have a hearing in an hour regarding a motion that I filed and I hope the judge grants it."

"All the good mojo." I smile at her as she rushes to her office.

I pick up my phone to call Stone, who answers after three rings and sounds out of breath. "Hey, gorgeous."

"Hey, are you busy? You want to call me back?" I ask him, turning to look out the window.

"No, I'm just on the bike," he says. "I have practice in an hour, so I have to get off anyway. How did you sleep?"

"Good," I reply, instead of saying, "I slept horribly because you weren't here and I kept thinking about how this whole thing is going to work because you live there and I live here." "You?"

"Yeah, good," he says, and I can tell from his tone that he's disconnected a bit. Sort of like he's unsure about everything, and he's not the only one. "You have a busy day ahead of you?"

"I do." I lean back in my chair. "Don't you have a game tonight?"

"I do, and then we take off for three games, coming back next week. Have you checked your calendar?"

"I did. I don't think I can swing it by next weekend. I'm in court all next week, after we present closing arguments, the jury will deliberate, and they could come back with a verdict at any moment. I have to be close by." I close my eyes, knowing if the roles were reversed, I would be pissed.

"I can't do anything in the next couple of months," he says. "Between being on the road and the home games, everything is crunched together. There are also the playoffs we have to worry about."

"We'll talk about it later." I push it aside, knowing we both have to head to work, and worrying about this now is not something we need.

"Yeah, I guess so." His tone is as frustrated as I feel.

"Have a great day. Call me later." I try to sound upbeat, but somehow, even I know I sound defeated.

I hang up the phone, putting it down on my desk before grabbing the coffee I brought to work. I take a long sip of the coffee, trying not to think too much about it because all I've been doing about it is realizing that the two of us just can't work, and if it will work, it will be a long-distance relationship. Now that I've gotten to know him, been with him, woken up with him, shared time with him, I know I don't want that.

There is no time to think about that, so I turn on my computer and prepare for trial. There are so many things to do in order to get ready for next week. It's crunch time for me; everyone handles the way they prep things differently.

With me, I always start with reading the brief again before starting on my opening arguments, then reviewing depos, witness statements, and evidence.

I open the brief, grabbing my cup of coffee to take a sip. I'm in the middle of putting down the cup when I freeze in my tracks. I'm shocked when I see a mistake, and it's not just a little mistake like a typo. It's a fucking colossal mistake.

My body feels like it turns to stone, my neck gets hot as I put the cup down. "No-no-no-no-no," I chant over and over as I pull up the case law I cited in the brief. I close my eyes for a second when I see it's a colossal mistake.

I pick up the phone right away and call Gary, my boss and the district attorney. His secretary picks up after two rings. "Hi, Ryleigh, how are you?"

"I'm good," I say, but really I'm the opposite of good. My stomach feels like it's going to be sick, my heart races so hard and fast I don't even know if I can talk without freaking out. "It's urgent that I talk to Gary."

"One second, he just got off the phone," she says, putting me on hold. My leg bounces as I wait for him to pick up.

"Ryleigh," Gary greets when he picks up the phone, "what can I do for you?"

"Gary," I hiss, "I fucked up on the Robert Phillips case."

"Define fucked up," he prods, his voice tight as I proceed to tell him what I fucked up with the case.

"Did you call Brenda?" He mentions the judge's assistant.

"No, I called you first to inform you," I answer softly, waiting for it.

"I'm not going to sugarcoat shit for you, Ryleigh. This is a huge fuckup." There is nothing that he is saying I don't agree with. "Off the record, I'm going to say you probably made the mistake because—" My spine goes up because I'm thinking exactly what he is thinking as to why this happened. All of this is because I was so fucking tired from traveling. My head was thinking too hard about when the next time I would see Stone was to focus on the case at hand. "Your briefs have always been too long. You have to remember what you learned in law school; trial briefs should be short. While I appreciate all your hard work, this case is a winner. All the evidence is in our favor. It's a slam-dunk case, while your error certainly doesn't derail the case, it definitely isn't a good thing and it's a terrible mistake for an attorney of your caliber to make." I can hear the disappointment in his voice. "You better call Judge King's judicial assistant, Brenda, and see if you can schedule an emergency hearing. It's better to admit your error to the court before Judge King finds it." Just the thought of Judge King finding it before my admission is too much for me to even imagine. Not only could I be sanctioned, but this might cost me my promotion to becoming a district attorney, and the most devastating blow is I could lose my job, which has me on the verge of having a panic attack.

"I'll call her right away," I assure him. "I'll let you know."

"You do that," he says, hanging up on me.

I hang my head for a moment, trying not to kick myself in the ass just yet. There is one more important phone call that has to be made. I press the button for my assistant, Tanya, who picks up right away. "Can you come here, please?" I ask her, and she is at my door before I hang up. "Please close the door."

She comes in, closing the door behind her and stands there looking worried. "There is no easy way to say this, and I can't bury my head in the sand. I fucked up on the Phillips brief I sent to Judge King." I say the words, and she gasps out in shock because I don't make fucking mistakes.

"If you can call from here?" I ask her and she nods her head, coming over to my side of the desk and picking up the phone.

She knows I'm a stickler for knowing everything, so she puts it on speakerphone, and I whisper, "Thank you."

She smiles sadly at me, making my stomach feel even

worse. "Judge King's office."

"Hi, Brenda, it's Tanya Digirmo from Ryleigh Beckett's office." She looks down at the phone.

"Hi, Tanya, how are you?" Her voice is cheerful.

"I could be better. I'm sorry to request this at the last minute, however this is urgent and I need to schedule an emergency hearing." My hands tremble when she asks to schedule the hearing, now not only will my entire office know that I fucked up, it's going on record that I fucked up. "It's regarding an error that was discovered in the trial brief filed regarding the Robert Phillips case. The case number is JF325386."

"Oh," she says, "I can schedule the hearing at eight forty-five a.m."

"Thank you." I take a huge deep inhale, swallowing down the bile that worked its way up. She hangs up the phone.

"Thank you, Tanya," I say softly. "Can you close the door on your way out?"

She walks out without asking me another question, leaving me with my eyes on the brief open in front of me. The emotions that come out of me are all over the fucking place. I'm pissed I've put not only myself but also my team in this position. I'm angry with myself for worrying about things I shouldn't even be thinking about. I close my eyes, the stinging of tears coming to me, but I push them away. There is no time for feeling sorry for myself. I have too much to do, but the first thing I do is correct the mistake in the brief.

Then I start prepping for the trial. I don't step out of

my office the whole day, and finally, when my stomach rumbles, I get up, seeing that it's just after eight o'clock. I grab my things and leave the office since I'm the last one in there. When I'm in the car, I see Stone has tried to call me twice and sent three messages.

I pull it up and respond.

Me: *Major fuckup today. Have an emergency hearing in court. I'll call you when I can.*

I look out the window, hating that I want him here so I can talk to him, then mad at myself because if I wasn't so focused on him, maybe this wouldn't have happened.

I get home at the same time my dinner arrives and eat it at the counter before heading to bed. I barely sleep that night, getting up before my alarm and going into the closet. I take off his T-shirt before grabbing my dark blue pants and a white silk button-up top with a baby-blue jacket. I put on my low-heeled shoes and grab my bag on the way out. The phone vibrates in my hand, and I look down.

SR: *I am so sorry. I hope you have a better day today. Let me know if I can do anything.*

I don't answer him. Instead, I put my phone in my bag and pray that I won't throw up in the middle of court. The whole time I'm in the car, all I can do is try to control my breathing. I breathe in and out, my chest tightens, making me clear my throat a couple of times. My hands are clammy, and I'm sure my knees are fucking weak. But I have to push all that aside and walk in there with my head held high. I rush toward the courtroom, gripping the bag in my hand as tight as I can. My nails dig into my palms as I make my way over to the courtroom.

Pulling open the door and seeing the courtroom empty, I walk up to my side of the courtroom, putting my bag beside my chair. I don't know how long I'm in here because all I can do is tell myself to calm down. At this point, my armpits are fucking sweating, and it's pushing heat to rise up the back of my neck. The door opens and the defendant's lawyer walks in, looking at me and nodding before heading to his side of the courtroom. "Morning, Ms. Beckett."

"Morning, Mr. Bradley," I reply, hoping my voice doesn't crack. The bailiff walks in followed by the court reporter, who takes her seat and waits for the proceedings to start.

The door to the side opens, and Judge King walks out wearing his black robe. "All rise." I push away from the desk and stand. I've been in his courtroom more than a couple of times. He's tough, but he's also fair.

"Please be seated," Judge King says, and we both sit down. "Ms. Beckett." He looks at me. "How are you doing?"

I try not to make Mr. Bradley see how much this is affecting me. "I'm good, Your Honor. Thank you for having me in on such short notice." I put my hands on the desk instead of in front of me so he won't see them shake. I start to feel like I'm being sent to the principal's office after I've been caught cheating, except this is so much worse. "I'm here today because there's an error in the trial brief that I filed."

"Excuse me?" He isn't the only one shocked. "The

one I started reading?"

"It came to my attention yesterday morning when I was in the middle of trial prep." I go on to explain to him how I somehow fucked up the brief. I ignore the need to look over at Mr. Bradley to see if he's gloating.

"I have to say I'm very surprised by this." He just looks down at me. "You've appeared in my courtroom before and your skills have been up to par."

"I've corrected the error and will refile immediately once I get back to my office."

"While this isn't irreparable damage, the court will not forget what you've done here especially since you have aspirations of becoming a district attorney, Ms. Beckett." He picks up his gavel. "Court adjourned." His words are harsh, but I wasn't expecting anything less. He was beyond pissed I've wasted his time since he started reading the brief and now has to wait for me to send the correct version.

I'm already standing when the bailiff says, "All rise." I wait until Judge King walks out of the room before I grab my bag. Luckily, more people have entered the courtroom, so I avoid talking to Mr. Bradley. The last thing I need is for him to gloat. I walk out of the courtroom and opt to work from home today. I'm not sure I can face the office, knowing that the word will get out. News like this spreads like wildfire, and even though none of us judges the other, our pride makes it seem like that.

That night, when Stone calls me, I answer. "Hey," I answer softly, looking at his face. His eyes look darker than I've ever seen them.

"Hey, you okay?" he asks, and I have to wonder how bad I look.

"Not really." I don't know why with him I open myself up like I have to no one else, not even my parents. "This has been a clusterfuck of two days." I wipe the tear I've finally allowed myself to shed. "I fucked up." My voice trembles. "So fucking bad I—"

"Gorgeous," he says softly, and it just makes me want to be with him so much more. I can feel his arms around me. I wish I could crawl through the phone and be with him. "Shit happens."

"I should have known better," I admit. "I should have double-checked or even triple-checked." He listens to me beat myself up.

"Are you done yet?" he asks, and I just look at him. "You are the smartest person I know." He smiles. "You admitted you fucked up. Now you get back up and be the badass I know you can be." I sniffle. "I hate that you are crying, and I can't do anything about it."

"It's okay, you have to be a hotshot hockey player." I roll my eyes, and by the end of the phone call, I tell myself that tomorrow is a new day.

I go all day with my head focused on my opening statement, only getting home a bit after nine o'clock to a huge teddy bear at my front door with a big blue card in the middle. I open the card to see the words.

Gorgeous,

I'm sorry I can't be there to hug you, but he can take my place for now.

SR

I smile before dragging it into the apartment and straight to my bedroom. For the rest of the week I'm so focused on the case I don't even know what day it is. With Stone traveling in Canada and then coming home, our conversations have been all through text.

The day of the trial, I wake up with a text from him.

SR: *Go and show them what you're made of.*

I smile, getting dressed in a blue pantsuit before heading down to the courthouse. The nerves hit me right away in my stomach. I get to the courtroom and walk in, my head in a different mindset than the last time I was here. I walk over to my table and pull out my chair, sitting down. I open my bag, taking out my folders and placing them all in the order with the witnesses who will be called. I look over to see Mr. Bradley arrive with his client, Robert Phillips. He smirks at me as he takes his seat next to Mr. Bradley.

I don't have a chance to think about it by the time the bailiff says to all rise. I put my hands on the desk and mumble to myself, "Let's do this."

For the next four days, I eat, sleep, and breathe the trial. I got a break over the weekend but all I did was think about the trial and how it was going. I need to win this trial so I reviewed everything over and again. Making sure I didn't leave anything out, making sure that every single point was made. I briefly talked to Stone on Saturday but I wasn't focused on our conversation and I told him that I would call him back. On Monday, when the closing arguments are done, I look over at the jury as they listen to Judge King give them instructions before they file out.

I'm back at the office the next day, waiting on the jury's verdict when Stone calls. "It feels like I haven't spoken to you in forever."

"That's because you haven't," he says. "Last time we spoke was three days ago and you said you would call me back."

"Sorry," I say, "court life. Are you home?" It dawns on me that I have no idea what his schedule is because it's been that long.

"I am. We have a game tonight and then another tomorrow before I head out to Tampa, Fort Lauderdale, and then Washington." He trails off, and I'm waiting for the dreaded question. "When will we see each other?" I think he's gone easy on me since I've been in court, but if I were him, my patience would be growing thin. It's been over three weeks since I've seen him last, and that visit was for less than twelve hours. The phone call goes silent, both of us thinking it but neither of us saying what should be said. Instead, we skate around the issue all the time. "Okay, I'll let you go."

"I'll call you later," I say before he hangs up.

That night, I have to stream the hockey game on my computer. My heart literally skips a beat when I see him on the screen. I can't help the smile that fills my face, and my hand reaches out to touch the screen, just to touch his face.

The next day, late in the afternoon, I'm in my office when my phone rings, telling me the jury has reached their verdict. I rush toward the courthouse, my whole body a pack of nerves. I know that I gave it everything I had. I stand in the courtroom while the jury comes in, and I listen with bated breath as Judge King asks them, "Have you reached a verdict?"

"We have, Your Honor." The jury foreman stands up. I listen to the judge giving her the instructions, and then I hear her. "In the case against Robert Phillips." I trail off until I hear, "We, the jury, find the defendant not guilty." I close my eyes and try not to sit down in defeat, willing myself not to break down in the courtroom.

The judge thanks the jury for their time, but all I can hear are those two words. Not guilty.

I walk out of the courtroom in a daze, texting two people, my boss and then Stone, the same message to both.

Me: Jury just came back with a not guilty verdict.

I put my phone away, heading home right away. I shut the door behind me before I collapse at the door. Lying on my side, I watch the house turn pitch black. My whole body, which was on the go for the past two weeks, has now given out. I have no energy to do anything, not even move from the front door. I wait until I can muster up that energy to just get undressed. Leaving my clothes at the end of my bed, I slide under the covers, the tears streaming out of my eyes like a river. My pillowcase is soaked, but I just lie in it, looking at the stars outside my window. The moon rises in the sky, and I just lie here. The silence of my breathing fills the room when I hear tapping on my front door. I get up on my elbow, looking over to see it's just a bit before midnight. I listen and again hear the tapping, so I get out of bed. My head feels like it weighs a million pounds, and my eyes feel like they weigh seven hundred pounds. I walk toward the tapping again, this time looking out of the peephole and seeing him standing there. I unlock the door in shock and disbelief, not sure this is really happening or maybe I'm dreaming again.

He stands there wearing a black suit and white dress shirt, the top two buttons open, holding a white box in his hand. "Stone?" I ask, not sure what is happening.

"Gorgeous," he says, his voice music to my ears. When he comes in and wraps his arms around me, I collapse into them. He carries me, holding on to me with one hand toward the bed. He places the box on the bedside table before sitting on the bed. I crawl into his lap, hoping I can become one with him. That's how good it feels to be in his arms again. He smells of his fresh soap, but most of all, he smells of home to me.

"Are you really here?" I ask through tears and sobs.

"For the next six hours I am." He wipes away a tear.

"You came all this way for six hours?" I ask, shocked, and all he does is smirk at me.

"I would have come all this way for an hour." He kisses my lips softly. "I figured you haven't eaten, so I brought you cupcakes."

I smile and wipe my cheek with the back of my hand. "Cupcakes?"

"Well, according to my sister, Zoey, and most of my female cousins, when one is sad it's either cupcakes or ice cream, and considering I was on the plane for an hour and a half." He reaches over to grab the white box he was holding in his hand. "I ordered them on my way to the game when you texted, and I rushed here as soon as the game finished."

I blink twice before I say anything. "You finished the game and then came all this way?" I repeat. "And you brought me cupcakes?" He nods, and if there is any doubt in my head about how I feel for him, here at this moment, I know I have fallen in love with him.

TWENTY-FIVE

STONE

"I CAN COME to the airport with you," she whispers when the alarm rings six hours after I got there, even though neither of us have slept. I kiss the top of her head, squeezing her body to me. The heat from her naked body goes through me. Seeing the words on the screen that she lost the case made me feel so helpless. I've never in my life felt that helpless before. I also knew I had no choice but to get the ball rolling. I got off the ice and hustled my ass out of there in under twenty minutes. I told them I had a family thing and couldn't do media. They didn't ask any questions, just nodded their heads. Besides, they have twenty other people to ask. The plane ride had to be the longest. I kept checking my watch every two minutes. It was horrible. When I got here right before midnight, I didn't know if she would be sleeping, but when I saw how destroyed she looked, all I wanted to do was hold her to me and give her my strength. Then she sat there in the middle of the bed, wearing my fucking T-shirt, as I fed her cupcakes.

"You still have two hours before you have to get to work." I look over at the clock, seeing that my car will be downstairs in ten minutes. "You need your sleep." I don't want to, but I have no choice but to pull away from her. The cold air hits me right away where her head was lying on my chest. She sits up in the middle of the bed, holding the sheet up to her chest. After I fed her a cupcake, she kissed my neck, and without saying a word, she undressed me, and I made love to her. It was soft and slow, and we savored every minute. I get up and get dressed as she walks me to the door. I kiss her longingly before I have to leave. My feet drag as if I'm wearing cement boots.

Even when I walk out of the door and into the waiting car, my body that was filled with heat now feels like it's on ice. My chest, which stopped aching for six hours, now starts a low, throbbing pain. I get on the plane and shut my eyes, dreading the whole day. Unlike when I was going there, the plane ride is over in the blink of an eye. When I get home, I send Erika, my agent, a text to call me. It's time to do something about this situation. It's time to end the torture. It's time for us to be in the same fucking space. She doesn't waste any time calling me back.

My finger presses the green button, putting it to my ear. "I want to be traded to Chicago." I come right out and say the words instead of saying hello.

"What?" my cousin, Cooper, who is also Erika's husband, shrieks. "Chicago? Why the hell would you want to go to Chicago?"

"Give me the phone," Erika snaps, and I hear some rustling going on until it's her on the phone. "Sorry, you know him, always wants in on my phone calls."

I laugh because the two of them were best friends, and when he got divorced, they started hooking up, and since then, I think they have about twelve kids. "Whatever, I don't care. I need you to see if you can get me traded to Chicago."

"Stone." Her tone goes serious. "You have one year left on your contract with Nashville, and we've been working on extending it."

"Things change." Both my legs start to bounce with nerves. My heart rate climbs, racing now. My mouth gets dry, and my hands start to tremble. "Things change," I repeat softly.

"Oh my God, this is because of Ryleigh," Cooper pipes in from the background, as if he just solved a mystery. "That's why he wants to be traded to Chicago," he deduces. "It all makes sense." Then he shouts even louder, "Why don't you come to Dallas? We are all here!" Yes, but Ryleigh isn't there I'm about to say, but I stop myself.

"Cooper Grant!" Erika yells at him, moving the phone away from her mouth. "Can you go and do something besides annoy me? Like take care of our children?" Then her voice comes back to me. "Sorry."

"Do you think you can make it happen?" I ask her, waiting, holding my breath, knowing it's not going to be easy. I mean, I know this. I'm captain of the team.

I've been here forever. This is my second home, but the reality is now, she's not here.

"I can see from my end but, Stone, we have to be realistic." I close my eyes, somehow knowing this fantasy of me being traded will come true.

"Please, Erika, you have to try," I beg her softly.

"Okay." Her voice lowers to match mine. "I'll do what I can."

"That's all I can ask you to do," I say. "Tell my cousin to shut his mouth about this."

"He knows better than to open his mouth!" she shouts, more to Cooper than to me. "I'll call you when I have something."

I hang up the phone and collapse on my bed until my alarm rings seven hours later. We are playing back-to-back games before leaving for three days, but then we'll be home for ten straight days. I get into the shower before getting dressed in another suit and packing my bag. The phone rings when I get in the car. "Hi," I greet softly when I see her name.

"Hi," she says, "I haven't heard from you since you texted you landed."

"I crashed as soon as I got in, and then I had to pack," I tell her. "How was your day?"

"Good, I worked a half day and then came back home," she tells me.

"Did you eat anything?" The worry fills my voice.

"I did because you sent me food." She laughs. "I don't know how you do it."

"One can do a lot in a twenty-minute car ride." I laugh

with her. "You got the soup?"

"I got the soup and then the snacks. Then the pizza and sushi." Her laughter is like a kick in the stomach. "I have enough food for the next two days, so don't send any more."

"What about cupcakes?" I tap the steering wheel.

"Demolished those as soon as you left this morning. I thought red velvet was my favorite, but that lemon blueberry." She gasps. "That might be the best thing I've ever tasted."

"Ever?" I joke with her.

I can see her roll her eyes at me even though I'm not with her. "Obviously, your dick will forever be the best thing I've ever put in my mouth. So I guess lemon blueberry is a close second." She shrieks, "You know what we should do?" I can hear a joking tone in her voice, and I know she's feeling just a touch better. "I should eat it off your dick."

"Oh, that sounds like the best thing you've ever said." I laugh with her.

"Better than 'fuck me harder, Stone'?" The two of us are howling with laughter. "Or 'you're so big'?"

I stop the car and put it in park. "Okay, fine, it's a close second or third." I get out of the car and slam the door.

"Guess you're at work. Call me later if you can."

"We leave as soon as the game finishes." My stomach tightens when I know I'll be even farther away from her. "I'll call you tomorrow. Get some rest."

"Will do, SR," she assures me and then disconnects.

The game that night is brutal. I end up in the penalty box three times, and I'm benched pretty much most of the third period. We end up only losing by one goal, and when I get onto the plane, Jay sits next to me. "You okay?"

"Yeah, just off tonight, I guess," I tell him, and he nods. "I'll be okay."

"You let me know if you need anything," he states, and I just give him a chin up before turning and looking out the window. The two games on the road are better. I end up with four points.

When we finally get back home, I toss my bag into the closet and text Ryleigh.

Me: *Home for the next ten days.*

I try to give her hints about how I want her to come and see me. Even though we are home for ten days, we have games every other day, and the coach has called practices on the off days. We're close to making the playoffs and all need to give our best effort.

Every single day, I wait for Erika to call me. Every single day she doesn't, I lose more and more hope. Forget the fact that Ryleigh hasn't even mentioned anything about coming to visit me.

We talk every single night, and every single night, I end the night telling her I wish she was with me. Then I hang up. After the first five days, my mood goes downhill, and after the seventh day, our conversations get shorter and shorter.

Finally, after nine days, Erika calls me back. "Hello," I answer after one ring.

"Stone," she says, and I try to see what her tone will tell me, but it's neutral.

"What did they say?" I cut to the chase. I don't want to know how she's doing. I don't want to know how Cooper is doing. All I want to know is the answer.

"I'm so, so sorry," she says, and I close my eyes. "I tried everything I could. Nashville would not budge, even if I asked for first-round picks. They wanted to hear none of that."

"Okay." The defeat hits me right away. "Well, I tried."

"We can try again in June when the season is officially over." She tries to give me hope.

"Sounds good. I have to go." I hang up the phone and toss it to the side.

This literally feels like you are in the Stanley Cup Finals, and it's game seven, and you lose. Everything that you wanted was within reach, but you just couldn't grasp it. It literally fucking sucks.

I try not to show it in my tone when we speak later on in the day, but she picks up on it right away. "Is everything okay?"

No, my head screams. "Yeah, just tired is all."

"Well, why don't you get some sleep?" she urges me, and it just makes me madder than I already am.

"I'll do that," I confirm. "I guess I'll call you tomorrow."

"Okay," she says softly, "sleep tight, SR."

"You too, gorgeous." I hang up the phone and the urge to take it and throw it against the wall is strong.

"What the fuck am I going to do?" I ask the empty

room. "How much longer is this going to even go on?" The thought alone is too much to bear, but the reality is I already feel like I'm losing her. She hasn't once even mentioned coming to see me. She hasn't once told me she misses me. She hasn't once sounded frustrated about the situation.

This woman who stopped my heart the first time I laid eyes on her has got a hold of my heart in a way I can't even describe, and little does she know, I would give it all up for her. Everything I've worked for in my whole life feels futile now. Everything I've busted my ass for feels like it's been for nothing. Everything without her in it is lifeless.

TWENTY-SIX

RYLEIGH

HE HANGS UP the phone, and all I can do is stare at it. The picture of us on the hot air balloon from my screen saver now flashes. I close my eyes before tossing my phone on the side of the bed that he sleeps on when he's been here. The teddy bear he sent lies down on his pillows while I wear his T-shirt.

I lay my head on the pillow and pull my knees to my chest, blinking away the tears. I have never in my life cried more than I have in the last two fucking weeks. After losing the trial that, according to my boss, was a slam dunk, I've been keeping my head down and plowing through with work. I don't even work from home anymore. I show up every single day, afraid to even skip a day in case he comes into the office and sees me not there. The last thing I need is to go away to see Stone for a few days and then he shows up. I can't do it. I just can't. I know he's dropped some hints here and there, mentioning he's home for ten days. Trust me, if it were up to me, I would have been there on day one, but I just can't leave when I want. I just can't. That's not to say I haven't tried. Fuck, have I tried. I've gone through my calendar and even tried to take off and see him on the weekends, but it just couldn't happen. And when I could go, he was leaving to go on the road for three days.

It's like the universe handed me this amazing gift on a silver platter. They gave me this brand-new sparkly gift. But then at the same time they went ahead and snatched it right back saying, "Joke's on you, you can't really fucking have it."

Even though I try not to let it get to me, I have to admit that everything these days fucking sucks. Which fucking kills me because my work was my life. It was the most fucking fulfilling thing I've ever done. I loved going to work. Now it's just fucking blah. I want to say it's because I fucked up and my ass is now on the line, but it's more than that.

The next day, I show up at the office bright and early and fake a smile to everyone before sitting at my desk. I'm literally going through the motions each day, and I catch myself during the day staring either at the computer screen or out the window. I keep looking for the answers. I keep wondering if this is worth it. I keep trying to tell myself that it will be all right.

For three straight days, his tone has been off. For three straight days, I pretend it's not there. For three straight days, I fall asleep with tears in my eyes while I look at the picture of both of us taken a couple of months ago, yet it feels like it's in another lifetime.

On the fourth day, I don't know why, but I fucking snap. "What's wrong?" I huff. "You've been weird the last couple of days." Or for the last three weeks.

"Have I?" I don't know if he's asking me or testing me.

"You have." I try not to flip out. "What's wrong?"

"Well," he starts, and I'm not sure I want to do this. Maybe we should just do what we've been doing, ignoring the big elephant in the room. "I asked to be traded." I gasp in shock. "To Chicago."

I close my eyes. "What? When?" I sit up straighter in bed, my heart hammering in my chest.

"About a month ago." His voice that was weird for the past couple of days now sounds broken. "I had my agent try to perform a miracle, but it didn't work out." My eyes close as I listen to his words as they sink in.

"Stone." I just say his name, only because a lump has now formed in my throat. This man, who I've let see the side of me not one other person has ever seen. The man who sat with me in his arms as I sobbed after losing the court case. The man who I thought was going to go away after we were together that first time.

"Yeah, I know." He sighs. "I knew it was a long shot, but I had to try something." Again, I stay silent. "Ryleigh, would you be willing to move to me?"

The question shocks me. "Um…" I hesitate. "It's not that easy."

"I know it's not that easy. Nothing these past couple of months has been easy."

"I can't move to you." I close my eyes while I say the

words. "I've worked my ass off to be where I am and to start all over…" Tears roll down my cheeks. "I just can't."

"I figured that too." His voice is broken, just as I am. "Worth a shot to ask, though." He laughs bitterly. "Forget I asked."

"Stone," I whisper.

"I'm going to go and get on the bike," he informs me. I look at the time, seeing it's after nine o'clock. He never works out this late.

"Okay," I mumble, "I'm going to head to bed."

"Sleep tight, gorgeous," he says right before he hangs up, and the phone slips from my hands onto my bed.

"He wants me to move to him," I repeat the words. "I can't move to him. How would that make me look?" I swallow down the lump in my throat while my stomach pushes it right back up. "Moving for a man? What if I move and then I hate my job? Or what if I move and then we break up? Or what if I have to rely on him? This is not the woman I am. So what if my job sucks lately. It's just a bump in the road." I lie back down on my pillow, looking over at his teddy bear.

"He was going to move to you." The words come out of my mouth, and it feels like someone has kicked me in the stomach as the air escapes my whole body. "He literally was going to leave his home for you and move to a city he's visited once or twice." I put my hand in the middle of my chest, trying to calm my racing heart and rub away the pain forming. "That's insane."

I can't help the way my hand moves as I grab my

phone to call my mother. She answers after two rings, her voice is cheerful, "Hello, my daughter."

"Mom," I whisper, my voice cracking.

"Ryleigh," she quickly says, "are you all right?"

"I'm not sure," I say honestly. "Can you talk?"

"Of course," she says softly, "talk to me."

"Stone asked to be traded to Chicago." I say the words, and even though we know nothing about hockey, she gasps. "They didn't approve it or whatever. I don't know the hockey lingo, but he asked me to move to him."

"Okay," she says, unsure of where this is going.

"I can't move to him, Mom," I quickly declare. "That would be insane."

"Would it?" I don't even know how to answer her. "Would it be the end of the world?"

"Yes," I hiss, "it would be the end of the world. Look at everything I've done to get where I am."

"Well, does all that work just go away?" She doesn't give me a chance to answer. "Ryleigh, just because you move doesn't make your success go away."

"I am not moving for a man," I snap. "I won't."

"So why are we having this discussion?" she asks me the million-dollar question. "Why are you even thinking about it? Why does this even bother you?"

Because I fucking love him, I want to shout, but I don't. "You're right." I pretend I'm okay. "Thanks for the talk."

"Anytime," she says to me, instead of telling me I'm just bullshitting myself.

I hang up the phone and put it aside. Put aside

everything that just happened. Put aside all the thoughts I'm now having. Put aside how empty I feel without him here.

The following morning, I'm off the elevator and smile at Claudia, saying hello. I'm arriving later than anyone else. I spot a couple of people I know, and Kristal comes out of her office and waves at me before walking into someone else's office.

I walk into the office and sit at my desk. My hands tap the desk in front of me before I pick up my phone and make one more phone call.

TWENTY-SEVEN

STONE

WE SKATE OFF the ice, every person with their head hanging down. The reality of the season hits us all at once. We are not making the playoffs. It's mathematically impossible for us to make it. Bottom line, we needed to win the game tonight, and we missed the opportunity.

Walking into the locker room, no one is saying anything. I put my helmet on top of the shelf and then toss my gloves beside it before I turn to sit down. I grab the water bottle beside me, taking a sip of it. "We did everything we needed to do out there," I state, and a couple of the guys look up at me. "It's tough. It feels like we have let each other down. I know I could have been better, and it's hard. I also know everyone in this room will think they could have been better, but we win as a team, and we lose as a team." I get up, take off my jersey, and toss it in the bin in the middle of the room.

The coach comes in with his hands in his pockets. "Before the media comes in here and fucks with your heads, I want to say something." I sit. "We will look back at tonight's game and won't like the game we played. But I want to say something. It has nothing to do with our top pair, top line, or third line. We know that we are capable of more as a group. So we learn from this." He looks around the room. "Are we clear? We still have two more weeks and five games. I don't want to see anyone dragging ass on that ice."

"Yes, Coach," we all say in unison before Jay laughs.

"We did good, guys." He looks at me. "Even you, Richards."

I toss my head back and laugh before I take off my elbow pads. "Thanks for the vote of confidence." I hold up my fist for him to fist-bump me, and when he does, he smirks at me.

The coach was not wrong, the press came in, but we decided we were going to go down as a team, and that is what we did. The minute I get into the car, I look down at my phone, and I'm not surprised about the texts on the screen.

Uncle Matthew Sr.: *Tough loss. You'll get 'em next year. We'll train harder this summer.*

Uncle Max: *This fucking sucks. Call me to bitch.*

Dylan: *Next year, yeah?*

Michael: *I'm sure you've gotten the texts, so I won't hash it out. One step closer to summer vacation.*

Grandpa Cooper THE OG: *Tough loss out there, my boy. Doesn't define you, remember that.*

I smile because no matter how many of us play hockey, he literally watches every single game, maybe not that night, but he is always up to date. He also always texts us.

Dad: *Proud of you always.*

Mom: *I'm also proud of you.*

I laugh because they probably sent the texts at the same time.

Zoey: *Dude, what the fuck is up with your game? I don't know a lot about hockey, but that did not look good.*

I chuckle because she is not wrong.

Then I read the group text with my cousins.

Christopher: *If it makes you feel better, we won't make the playoffs either.*

Matty: *Chin up.*

Stefano: *This is why I don't play hockey.*

Matty: *This is why? It's not because you suck?*

Christopher: *Now we all have to deal with Dylan, Tristan, and Xavier saying their team is better.*

Matty: *They made the playoffs; I'm going to say they are.*

I turn off the phone because the one person I wanted to hear from didn't text me. I want to say I'm surprised, but I'm not. It's not like she knew tonight was a big game. Our chats lately haven't been deep and meaningful.

Ever since I asked her to move in with me, over three weeks ago, it's been awkward between us. Forget the fact we haven't seen each other; we haven't even made the effort. I really couldn't, but she could have, and she didn't. I was thinking of just showing up at her place, but I didn't think she would want that either. Things have just become weird between us. Even the conversations are few and far between. The texts are starting to dwindle also.

Not bothering to turn on any lights when I get home, I go straight to my closet to get undressed. Kicking my shoes to the side and taking off my pants, I fold them and place them on the hanger with the jacket over them.

Getting into bed, I grab the remote off the side table and turn on the television. The sadness of tonight makes it hard to fall asleep. I avoid watching *SportsCenter* to relive the game. I'm sure it'll be on the front of the local newspaper tomorrow. I turn off the television and look off to the side, my eyes getting used to the blackness when I picture Ryleigh's face smiling at me.

I've never been in love before or wanted someone who feels like she doesn't want me back. I close my eyes, only to open them five hours later. I get out of bed and head to the shower before walking to the gym.

I know I should calm down before I call her, but my hands pull up her name on my phone. Calling her, I listen to the phone ring. One side of my head tells me to *hang up the phone*, while the other side of my brain tells me that *it's about fucking time*.

She answers after four rings and sounds out of breath. "Hey," she says, "can I call you back?"

"Yeah," I say before I hang up the phone. I wait five minutes, which turns into an hour, and then finally, six hours later, the phone rings, and I see it's her. "Hello."

"Sorry, the day got away from me. I just walked into my place."

I'm pissed, and it's beyond dumb at this point. "Story

of my life, I guess."

"Excuse me?" she says, shocked.

"What is this?" I ask her, my neck warming up from the question.

"I don't understand?" she says softly.

"This, me and you. Or is there even a me and you?" I don't wait for her to answer. "We can't really call this a relationship, can we?"

"I don't know wh—" I cut her off.

"Yeah, I know. I think we both don't know what this is. For me, it's a relationship. But then the reality is that maybe it isn't one."

"Stone," she whispers.

"I mean, let's be real." My stomach tightens. "Were you even trying to be committed to me?" The question makes me want to vomit. "I've been constantly telling you that I've missed you. I've been constantly trying to tell you how I feel, but all I've gotten is the runaround."

"Can we just for once—" she says, and I snap.

"Yes, can we just for once say it like it is?" I close my eyes, and the lone tear escapes me. "It was a fling, I guess a long-distance fling. I was in it more than you were, and I was hoping in the end you would want me just as much as I want you. I was wrong. I shouldn't have started this thing; I know that now. I should have left you alone."

"Stone, please, it's no—" she cuts me off, but I don't want to hear it.

"It's not what?" I cut her off again. "Are you going to start with the 'it's not you, it's me' bullshit? Because I think it's past that. It's been over six weeks since we've seen each other. It's been over six weeks since you lost the case and not once did you offer to come and visit me. Not once did you say 'Hey, should I come down this weekend?'"

"I have a job," she bites out, "you know it's not easy for me to just leave."

"Oh, trust me, I know you have a job. An important job." I take a deep breath. "Let's be real for a second and say what needs to be said. Let's finally say what we both know is coming. We are just prolonging the inevitable."

"And what is that?" Her voice comes out monotone.

"In the past four months, you know what I've learned?" I ask, but I'm not waiting for her to answer. "I've learned I've fallen for a girl who puts her work before me, and that's okay. It's fine. What I also learned is I can't do this long-distance bullshit. It's too hard. I want to come home to you, and I've gone out of my way to try to make it happen. I spoke to my agent about being fucking traded, and when I asked you to move to me, you wouldn't even think about it. I think your words were, 'I won't.'"

"Stone, can you let me say something?" she pleads.

"No." I shake my head. "Because there is nothing left to say. You live in Chicago. I live in Nashville. It was a stupid idea to even think we had a chance. There isn't anything left to say. We get over this fight, and then what, continue what we're doing? It's not good enough anymore. Not for me and not for you." I wait for her to tell me she misses me also, that not seeing me is killing her just as much as it's killing me not to see her. I wait for her to give me anything to make me think it's not just me who is invested.

"I'm sorry."

"Yeah, I've gotten a lot of sorrys over the past couple of weeks," I breathe out, not listening to anything she has to say because I'm angry, but more importantly, I'm fucking heartbroken. "Take care of yourself, Ryleigh," I say softly. "I hope you find someone who can make you happy." The thought alone is enough to kill me. It's like you cut my veins and left me to bleed out. "I hope he knows how fucking lucky he is." That's the last thing I say to her before I hang up the phone. This time, I bend my elbow up over my head and throw the phone across the room, making it hit the wall before it falls down and shatters, just like my heart.

TWENTY-EIGHT

RYLEIGH

A KNOCK ON the door makes me look up. "Are you ready?" My mother sticks her head into the room, seeing me sitting on the bench at the end of the bed. Since my brother bought a house here in Dallas, my parents thought it was a good idea for them to own a house in Dallas.

"Explain to me why we are going to the hockey game tonight?" I grab one white sneaker, bending to put it on and tuck in the laces.

"Because we came to visit Romeo and his in-laws are playing," she reminds me, tilting her head to the side. "At least, I think they're playing." She throws her hands in the air. "There are so many of them, I'm sure at least one is playing." She laughs as I stand and walk over to the mirror to look at myself one more time before we leave. I opted to wear black tights with a loose white T-shirt. I pluck the jean jacket and tug it on before I pull my hair out of the back of it, letting it hang loose.

"Good?" I ask my mother, who smiles at me.

"You look gorgeous." The minute she says that word, the hurt comes hurling back at me. It's been a month since our last phone call. Since he broke my heart and left me. A month since I've heard his voice. A month since he was last mine.

"Don't use that word," I mumble, and she wrings her hands. "Anything but that word."

"Okay." She doesn't ask questions. She hasn't asked a question since I called her and just said "it's over." I didn't say anything else; I really wasn't ready to share, not then and still not today. She knows that when I'm ready to talk about it, I will. But the wound is still raw. In fact, every single day I think the wound is going to be better, but every day it feels like I'm being cut open and gutted once again.

I walk over to the bedside table, taking my phone off the charger. The screen saver is changed to just the view from the hot air balloon. It seemed stupid to have him as my screen saver when we weren't dating anymore. It also hurt too much to see his face every time I looked down at my phone. That doesn't mean I don't open my camera roll every day to see his face. I don't need to; he's in my dreams every single night, even if I don't want to dream of him. Putting the phone in my back pocket, I walk out of the room with my mother.

My father waits downstairs in the living room. "Romeo and Gabriella will be here in two seconds." He gets up, and I see he's wearing black jeans, a white shirt, and a black leather jacket with his black boots. "You look—" he says to me, and my mother puts her fingers on his mouth.

"She looks nice, doesn't she?" Her eyes go big, giving him a sign for something.

"She does," he agrees, and then we hear the horn honking. "Let's go." He waits for my mother and me to walk ahead of him.

Gabriella gets out of the front seat and heads to the back seat, giving it up for my father. I slide into the car beside her and then my mother comes in, closing the door. "Can't we take two cars?" I ask, struggling to put on my seat belt.

"Do you know the mess that parking is here?" Romeo asks.

"How the hell would I know the parking situation in Dallas?" I shriek. "I don't even have a car in Chicago. I use Uber everywhere."

"It's easier to get in and out with one car," Gabriella says softly. "We have the family pass to park in the other side of the parking lot where the players do, but it's still a mess."

"Got it," I say, looking ahead at the road. They are not joking about the traffic getting into the arena.

We park in the family parking lot and get out. My heart starts to race a bit. "Hey," I say to Gabriella when we are away from my parents, "by any chance is—"

"No." She shakes her head. "He's not here. I asked."

"Okay." I try not to sound happy or disappointed. "I know it's going to be weird to see him at these things, and I know it'll eventually happen." I smile at her. "But I just wanted maybe a heads-up."

"I know," she says softly, "I wouldn't blindside you like that."

"Thank you," I say as we follow Romeo and my parents. She's never asked me what happened between Stone and me. I also don't know if he told her or not. The only one I've talked to about it was Romeo, only because he wouldn't leave me alone until I told him.

He was the one who got on a plane the day after I told my mother, showed up at my house, and demanded to know what happened. He learned I wasn't going to tell him anything, so he camped on my couch with me until I was ready to share what I did. He was the only one who knew I quit my job the day Stone broke up with me. He was the only one who knew I was looking for a job in Nashville. After he asked me to move in with him, I started looking for jobs. I didn't want to tell Stone because I didn't want to get his hopes up. But now that we aren't together, I won't be moving to Nashville, so I'm taking my time to decide where I want to go. Eventually, I'll have to tell my parents I quit my job, but right now, they just think I'm on vacation.

I'm nervous to see the family, but the nerves go away once I walk in the room and see his uncles Matthew, Max, Viktor, and Justin. They all hug and kiss me, just like they did the last time I saw them before Stone. Not one of them brings him up, and I don't know if I'm thankful or sad.

It's only when I turn around and see Evan does my heart sink. He turns and spots me, coming over to me right away. "Hi," he says cheerfully, "you look gorgeous." The minute he says those words, I blink away the tears. He must see them, but pretends he doesn't. While he hugs me and kisses my head, he asks, "You okay?" I smile at him, hoping he sees that although I'm not okay, I'm trying to be. "Zara is around here somewhere. She will be mad if she doesn't see you."

"I'll go say hello to her," I assure him. "It's nice seeing you." He smiles at me before he joins the rest of the guys.

I look around the room with its couches and spot Zara, who sits with her sisters, Zoe and Allison, and sisters-in-law, Karrie and Caroline. She spots me and gets up right away, coming over to me. "Hey." She opens her arms for a hug. "It's so nice to see you here." She acts like nothing happened, which makes me happy. I thought things would be awkward, but it's just like every other time.

"Thanks. I'm down visiting my parents," I share when Gabriella comes over with her twin, Abigail, who is dressed head to toe in Dallas stuff, while she holds the hand of her little boy, who's also wearing a Dallas jersey.

She hands me a baseball hat. "Apparently, we have to wear these," she says while Zara squeezes my arm before walking back to her seat. I put the hat on, and then everyone stops talking when the roar of the crowd starts. "I think they're on the ice," she states, bumping her shoulder into mine. "You okay?"

"I thought it would be weird," I admit to her. "But I don't know if anyone knows we dated besides his parents and, well, my parents."

"Everyone knew," Gabriella confirms. "He made sure everyone knew."

My stomach rises to my throat, and I breathe out through my mouth and inhale through my nose. "Well, I'm glad no one is holding a grudge."

"You need a drink," Gabriella declares. "Let's get some shots before we head out to watch the game." I walk over to the bar at the left side of the room as she pours six shots. A couple of her girl cousins come over and take the shots with us.

I'm waiting for one of the girls to ask me what happened, but no one does. The game ends with Dallas winning, and the crowd is electrifying. And standing with Stone's family without him here is more painful than if I was home alone, looking at pictures of him. Feeling him all around me but not having him here is horrible, and with each drink I have, the pain gets worse.

When we finally get home, I head to my bedroom, the tears coming nonstop as I slide into bed. The following morning, I don't even bother looking at myself in the mirror before I head down to the kitchen. My father stands by the counter with the blender going, and I wince.

"Why is that so loud?" I ask as I grab a cup of coffee.

"How much did you drink last night?" he scoffs. "You look like shit."

"Tyler," my mother hisses at him, "what is wrong with you?"

"Her eyes are all puffy." He points at me.

"I have allergies." I avoid looking at them. "Started this year." Neither of them calls me out on my bullshit.

"We leave at noon," my mother announces when I'm about to sip my coffee.

"Leave at noon for what?" I swear I sound like a whining kid.

"Family lunch. We spoke about it in the car on the way home."

I'm about to argue with her. "Was I awake?"

"You were blinking your eyes, so I assumed you were awake." She grabs her own cup of coffee, bringing it to her mouth. "I think I heard a grunt."

"Why do I have to go?" I ask, and they both stare at me.

"That would be so rude," my father scolds. "They know you are here with us and then you aren't going to show up?"

"Ugh, fine," I concede, walking out of the kitchen, "but this is it. I'm not doing anything more."

"Duly noted!" my father yells while he turns the blender back on.

I stay in my bedroom, watching television until I have to get up and get dressed. Going over to my open bag in the closet, I get on my knees and toss clothes around until I spot my white jeans. Getting up off the floor, I shimmy my way into them before I snatch up my thin, long-sleeve black sweater and bra. I put the bra on and then the sweater, pulling up the sleeves before tucking one side in the front. I brush my teeth and put a bit of cover-up on to hide the dark circles I have under my eyes.

"Mom," I shout from my bedroom door, "can I borrow your Converse sneakers?"

"They're by the front door," she replies. I run down the stairs to get them.

At one minute past twelve, we're in the car and going to someone's house. When we pull up, there isn't even parking on the street. "Where did all these cars come from?" I mumble as we park and walk down the street toward the house.

"It's starting to get so hot," my mother huffs. "I can't wait to head to Montana."

"Girl, same." I look over at her, smiling as we walk up to the door.

My father rings the doorbell, and I look over at him. "Why are you ringing the doorbell?"

"We aren't just going to walk in," he sneers at me.

"Dad, do you not hear the hundred people in that house?" I point at the door. "They probably don't even hear the doorbell."

"Then walk in." He holds out his hand, and I'm about to do it when the door swings open.

"You guys didn't have to ring the doorbell," Matthew says, holding the door open, "you just walk in."

"See, told you," I tell my father. I kiss his cheek at the same time that my phone buzzes in my back pocket.

"Go on in." Matthew points at the door that leads to the foyer. People are everywhere.

Kids run after each other, laughter all over the house. I spot Gabriella, who has a frown on her face. She spots me and rushes over at the same time I give her father a kiss on the cheek.

"I just texted you," she hisses, and I laugh, pulling the

phone out of my pocket.

"I didn't know you two were coming," Justin says from beside me, smiling at whoever is behind me.

But I stop midway because I hear it. The voice that is usually in my dreams or in the videos I took from the hot air balloon. "Figured why not." I turn and look over my shoulder, and there he is, standing in the middle of everyone in dark blue jeans and a white T-shirt that I know feels like silk on my skin.

"Sorry, I just found out," Gabriella apologizes from beside me, but I don't know if I heard her or not over the ringing in my ears. He doesn't know I'm here either as people approach him and hug him. The smile on his face is big, but his eyes are not as bright as when he used to smile at me. "Why don't we just get out of here?" Gabriella whispers, but I'm stuck in this spot, my arm still halfway with my phone when he turns and our eyes meet.

TWENTY-NINE

STONE

I WALK UP the steps to the house just as the door closes. Christopher stops the door with his foot in front of me. "Whoa," he calls, and the door is swung back open with Uncle Matthew standing there. The smile on his face fades just a touch. "Are we not invited?" Christopher asks with a chuckle.

"Of course you guys are invited," he assures us. For the first time in my life, I see him flustered, which means he's up to something or someone just told him a secret, and he's doing his best to keep it. Until he sees Uncle Max. "I didn't know you two were coming?"

"It was a last-minute decision," Christopher replies, hugging him. "Besides, if I had to sit in this one's house"—he points over at me as I walk up the steps to the front door—"one more minute and watch him watch the fucking trees grow, I was going to take a fork and stick it in my eyeball."

"Hey," I defend, "we worked out too." Christopher

glares at me before he walks into the house.

"Surprise," I say softly, going in for a hug.

"Yeah, Stone—" he says, and I hold up my hand.

"I know, I know. I didn't call you back." I take a deep breath and run my hands through my hair before I put them in my back pockets. "It's just." I shrug, not wanting to bring Ryleigh up.

Fuck, for a whole month, I've been fighting with myself to call her or get on a flight and go to her. I can honestly say I've never been more devastated in my whole life. "In other news, I got the vacation plans." I take one hand out and slap him on his arm. "Count me in."

I turn to walk into the house when he calls my name again. "Stone." I look over my shoulder at him. His eyes are worried, but I don't have a chance to answer him before my mother is in front of me.

"This is a surprise," she says, hugging my waist as I wrap my arm around her shoulders.

"Christopher made me come," I admit before my Aunt Zoe comes over to me, giving me a hug and a kiss. I smile at her. "Hey." She reaches up to touch my cheek, and I make the mistake of looking up.

My eyes lock with the ones that have haunted my dreams for the past month. The eyes I search for every single night before I go to bed. The eyes I look for in crowds. The eyes that are the key to my soul. She stands there in as much shock as I'm in, her arm midair with her phone in it. I take her in. Her eyes look tired, and my fingers literally tingle to touch her face. Her mouth opens in an O as she stares at me. Gabriella is beside her saying something to her, but her eyes are on me. I spot her father and mother moving to stand beside her. Romeo stands behind them. The glare on his face is directed solely at me, and I have no problem with that. I also know that before the end of the day, we'll have words. The room bursting with noise two seconds ago is now so quiet you could hear a pin drop.

"I think the food is ready," My Uncle Matthew's voice booms out, and even he's a little surprised with how loud he is. "Let's go eat." He nods to Tyler, who does a chin up to him before turning and taking Ryleigh away from me. He puts his arm around her shoulders as they make their way with everyone else toward the kitchen. My heart contracts in my chest as she gets farther and farther away from me. The talking slowly starts up again.

"Son, you going to be okay?" my father whispers from beside me, and it feels like my knees are going to give out.

"Yeah," I answer, taking a deep breath in and looking up to see Christopher standing there watching me while his mom talks to him. One ear is on their conversation, another on making sure I'm okay. My uncles Max, Viktor, and Justin hang with my cousins Cooper, Michael, and Dylan, who are also around, pretending they are having a conversation, but in reality, everyone is making sure I'm okay. "I need a second."

I look at my Uncle Matthew. "I tried to warn you."

"It's fine," I say. "I just need a second."

"I'll wait here," my father says.

"There is no need for that, Dad," I try to reassure him. "I'm fine. It'll be okay."

He looks into my eyes. "I'll wait here," he repeats, and all I do is nod. My throat feels like a golf ball is stuck right in the middle.

I walk down the hallway toward the bathroom, closing the door behind me, before putting my head back and closing my eyes. "What the fuck is she doing here?" I rub my hand over my face before pushing away from the door and going to the sink. I turn on the cold-water faucet and lean both hands on the counter, my head hanging down. I knew I would one day have to see her. I knew one day this would come. I just didn't think it would be this soon.

The moment I saw her, I felt like my heart was ripped out of my chest. It was empty and hollow, yet at the same time my heart felt like it started beating again.

The minute I hung up the phone with her, I trashed my phone. I took a day before I called my father. It took him less than four hours to be at my house, just him. He sat with me, watching television, pretending that I didn't lose the love of my life. He stayed for two weeks, and my mother joined him after two days. They rode the rest of the season out with me until I kicked them both out. We had to get back to our routines. It was time to face the reality of it.

When Christopher came down to spend a couple of days, I could tell he was also going through something, but neither of us brought anything up. Instead, we hit the gym twice a day, skated for hours each day, and just pretended it was all okay.

I fill my hands up with water, splashing my face twice, then grab a white towel and dab my cheeks. "It's going to be okay," I say to my reflection. Opening the door, I walk out and spot my father waiting for me.

"You okay?" he asks, and I stand in front of him.

"No," I admit, "I'm not okay."

He puts his hand on my shoulder and squeezes. "You want to get out of here?" I think about it for a full minute before I answer him.

"No," I say because the thought of leaving, knowing she is here, is worse than staying here and loving her from afar, "it'll make a scene if we do."

"Who gives a fuck?" he hisses. "No one cares."

"I do. Let's just grab something to eat."

"Okay." He squeezes my shoulder again. "But if at any time you want to leave, all you have to do is say the word." I don't say anything except to nod at him.

We walk back out to the foyer and see that it's empty. Everyone is back to normal. Or at least pretending they are. We walk into the kitchen, and I say hello to my aunts before grabbing a plate. My eyes try not to do a sweep of the room to see where she is.

I spot her sitting between Gabriella and Romeo, her head down as she looks at her plate, the fork in her hand pushing things away. I wonder if she's as affected as I am, or does she even care. I walk out and go the opposite direction from where she is, spotting Christopher sitting at a table with Dylan. The two of them look like they are having an intense conversation. When I pull out a chair and sit down, they both stop talking. "You good?" Dylan looks at me and I just shrug.

"That was fucking brutal," Christopher says. "Swear to God, I had no idea she was going to be here."

"It's fine." I grab a water bottle from the middle of the table. "It had to happen sometime," I mumble while Maddox comes to sit next to Dylan, who leans over and grabs him around the neck in a chokehold and kisses his head.

"Dad," he grumbles.

"Love you, kid," Dylan says to him, letting him go. "Don't forget it."

"What's with the mullet?" I ask Maddox, who just smirks. His hair is shorter on top, shaved on the side, but long in the back.

"It's the fashion," Dylan answers for him.

"Mullets are back in style?" I ask, trying not to look over and see Ryleigh.

"Apparently," Dylan confirms, "I had the same hair style when I was eight, except it was called hockey flow."

"Who didn't have that haircut?" Christopher interjects. "I think my third, fourth, and fifth grade picture had that haircut." We all laugh at him as we start talking about the game last night.

I glance over at her a couple of times, and each time she looks quiet and withdrawn. Each time I silently hope she looks over at me so I can look into her eyes.

I push away from the table that went from the four of us to at least fifteen people all squishing in. "I'll be back," I announce, walking with my head down. This is too much for me. Even though I want to be in the same room with her, I can't do it.

I make my way to the front door, planning to just get an Uber and text Christopher that I left. Someone grabs my arm, and when I look over, I see Romeo. "A word," he says, and even though I want to rip my arm out of his hand, I just turn to face him, his hand falling off mine.

"You get one minute," I tell him, standing with my feet apart and my hands by my sides.

"I'm not going to need a minute," he hisses, looking around to make sure no one else can hear us. "You're fucking stupid."

"Is this what you wanted to have a word with me for?" I roll my eyes, not admitting to him I'm fully aware of how fucking stupid I am. Stupid to have fallen in love with her. Stupider to have let her go.

"You should have never messed with her." He advances a touch, and I see my uncles Matthew and Max waiting and watching in case they have to step in. They aren't the only ones; my father stands with Tyler. Their eyes are on us, but they're too far away to hear what we're saying.

"Fuck you," I say to him, "I'm never going to regret that." I shake my head. "I didn't care back then what you thought, and I don't care now." His jaw clenches. "You think this is easy for me?" I ask him. "You think I don't feel like I've lost a piece of me?" I advance. "You know nothing."

"Really?" He crosses his arms over his chest. "Did you know she was going to give it all up for you?" he says, and I take a step back as if he just punched me in the face. "She was giving up on all her dreams for you." He points a finger and stabs my shoulder. "For you, she was giving it all up." He shakes his head, and I'm speechless. "Guess you didn't know that, did you?"

With that, he turns around and walks away from me, past our fathers and out the back door toward Gabriella and Ryleigh. Toward the woman who is my home.

THIRTY

RYLEIGH

"ARE YOU READY to get out of here?" Romeo asks when he comes back from the bathroom, his hands balled into fists beside his legs.

"I think so," Gabriella says, looking at me.

"Are you coming with?" she asks. Even if she hadn't asked me, I would have left with them anyway. Either that or I would be calling an Uber.

"Lead the way," I say softly, trying not to look up to search for him. Ever since he walked into the room, my heart has been searching for him. I forced my eyes to focus on what was in front of me and nothing more. Even when we sat down to eat, all I could do was tell myself that I was fine. That it was fine. That him being here didn't matter to me, but I was lying to myself, just like I have been for the past month. I didn't eat a thing. Instead, I pushed shit around my plate and counted down the time until I could get the fuck out of here and away from him.

I tuck my hair behind my ear, looking down as I start to walk out of the room when I hear whispering. My eyes move up to see what everyone is whispering about when I see him coming for me. I stop breathing, literally holding my breath as he gets closer and closer, his eyes fixated on me.

I want to run away from him, but my feet feel like they're stuck to the floor, and my body feels like it's turned to marble. The blood in my body halts, making everything in me freeze. He stops in front of me, our fingers grazing each other, before he turns his hand around to grab mine. Anger shoots through me. Why can't he just let me fucking be? He leans down, and I silently gasp as his lips go to my ear. "I know I never told you this." His breath and softness of his voice sends shivers down my spine. My heart feels like it's going to jump out of my chest. "But you deserve to have this, to know." I don't move a muscle as he tells me, "I love you." The three words I've said to him every single night in my dreams when he comes to hug me. The three words I've yearned to hear from him. The three words that shatter my heart. Then he kisses me right behind my ear where he used to always kiss me.

If I thought him breaking up with me broke my heart, I was wrong. This right here, knowing he loves me, knowing I love him, it's earth-shattering.

He squeezes my hand once before he lets it go and turns to walk away, taking everything I love with him. "Well, fuck me, I guess." The words come out of my mouth so fast and so loud, he stops walking and turns to face me. Everyone around us is watching the drama unfold.

I didn't want this. I never wanted to do this here in front of everyone. Especially after they pretended the two of us in one room together wasn't awkward AF.

My body radiates anger that he's done this to me. "You made me fall in love with you, even when I didn't want to." I don't even try to stop the tears as I shout the words. "You sent me chocolate and opened my doors." I feel I'm just rambling, yet I can't stop the words from coming out. "You knew I didn't want to date you. I ignored you and ignored you and what did you do?" He knows I'm not asking him the question. "I'll tell you what you did. You torpedoed your way into my life. You made me want you. You made me need you. You made me miss you. You made me go against everything I thought I didn't want." My breathing comes in pants as I try to calm my racing heart. "You fed me cupcakes and made me feel important." My eyes look into his, and I see a reflection of how broken we both are. "You don't just get to leave without having a conversation with me. I had everything I ever wanted, and then without you there, it felt like I had nothing."

"You are the most important thing to me!" he roars, his chest rising and falling, filling out his white T-shirt. "I tried everything in my power to be that person for you. I wish things could be different."

The words make me bring my hand up to my mouth as I silently cry, my body shaking when I smell him. I look up at his chest and then up to his face. His hands come up and hold my face, his thumbs rubbing my tears away as they fall. "I hate it when you cry." His voice is soft. "I'm so sorry, gorgeous." My nickname on his lips has to be one of the last words I ever want to hear in my life.

"Why couldn't you just listen to me?" My body basks in his touch. My body goes from ice cold to warm from his heat.

"When?" His eyes search mine, trying to find the answers.

"Before you walked away from me. Before you walked away from us. Before you just threw us away." I take a deep breath. "Did you know that morning I walked into my office and handed in my notice? I quit my job to be with you." I hear gasps from beside me, and I know it's my parents. I also see the shock on his face. "I had nothing but you, and it didn't matter because we were going to be with each other, and I was going to get a job. I kept telling myself it was going to be okay, but then you were gone." My hand comes to my stomach, trying not to get sick. "I gave up everything for you, and in the end, I didn't even have you."

"What?" he yells.

"You stupid, stupid man," I mumble, shaking my head.

"Why didn't you tell me?" His hands now fall from my face, and I want to snatch them back.

"Why didn't I tell you?" I snap, repeating his question. "I tried. I tried so many times, but you wouldn't listen to me. You just assumed the worst because you're an asshole who is so consumed with your own wants and needs that you didn't think about how I was feeling." I put my hands on my hips, and I know at the end of this, it's going to be over. "You broke up with me without even a second thought. You asked me to move to you as if it was that easy." He just looks at me. "I had a career. I just couldn't up and jump on a dime for you." The anger makes my voice rise. "You think I didn't want to come and visit you?" I don't even take a breath. "You think I didn't try my best to come to you? It wasn't that easy, Stone."

"You didn't even—" he says, but just like when he broke up with me and didn't give me the time of day, I'm not giving him the time of day either.

"I didn't what? Run at your beck and call? I slept with that fucking teddy bear every goddamn night," I yell at him, "because he was a part of you! I slept in your fucking shirt because it felt like I was near you. I didn't have to say the words because my actions did."

"I'm sorry," he says, taking a step closer to me. "I'm so, so sorry."

"Yeah, well, sorry doesn't get me my job back," I tell him. "Sorry doesn't fix things between us."

"What would fix it?" His voice is soft and broken at the same time.

"I don't even know," I say, taking a deep breath before walking past him and away from him. I have to zigzag my way through people who are all around us, avoiding looking at anyone as I get the fuck out of here.

THIRTY-ONE

STONE

I WATCH HER walk away from me, zigzagging through everyone I know and love to escape me. "I am so fucked!" I shout, throwing my hands up, but she doesn't stop moving. "Don't you walk away from me, Ryleigh." She continues walking, but that doesn't surprise me since it's her. "You are the love of my fucking life!" I roar, and she finally stops and slowly turns around. People move out of the way so I can get to her, but I stand on my side of the room, and she stands on her side. "You are the love of my life," I repeat, this time quieter, "and I'm going to marry you."

She folds her arms over her chest and glares at me. "Don't you fucking dare propose to me right now."

"You'll know when I'm proposing to you," I tell her, walking past everyone to go to her. "I'm sorry I didn't listen to you. I'm sorry I let you go. I'm just plain sorry that my stupid ass let you go." I stand in front of her. "I'm going to make you mine." I grab her face. "I'm going to make you mine today and every single fucking day after this." I bring her face to mine, smashing my lips on hers.

"About fucking time," Uncle Matthew says from behind me.

I let go of her lips, my thumbs rubbing her wet cheeks. Her eyes open slowly as she looks at me. "Will you come with me so we can talk?" I kiss her softly again. "In private."

"You want to do it in private?" Matthew laughs. "After all of that?" I look over at him, and he has his hands on his hips. "We're all invested in this now."

"Why don't we give them some privacy?" my father urges.

"I think they said everything they had to say," Tyler says, his eyes glaring at me. "Ryleigh, are you ready to go?"

"She's not going anywhere," I declare, trying to sound as respectful as I can, but no fucking way is she going away from me.

"Is that so?" Romeo asks.

"Perhaps everyone needs to calm down a little." Christopher holds up both his hands, earning him a glare from Romeo. Christopher then looks at my Uncle Justin, who nods and goes to stand next to him.

"I think that we all need to give them a bit of space," he finally declares, looking at Romeo and his father. I know he probably doesn't want to go toe-to-toe with his son-in-law and father, so I step up before anything else gets said or things start happening.

"I'm really sorry this played out in front of everyone."

I slip my hand in Ryleigh's, and I'm expecting her to snatch it out of mine. "Now, if you will all excuse us." I look over at Ryleigh. "We're going to get out of here."

"Might as well just go with him, and then you know." I look over and see Jessica, who looks at Ryleigh. "Call us or come back."

"Jessica," Tyler snaps.

At the same time, Romeo groans, "Mom."

"What?" She throws up her hands, getting frustrated with it. "They need to talk." She points at us. "And they need to do it in private, without all the eyes." Her finger then points all around the room.

"And opinions," my mother interrupts.

I don't wait for anyone else to say anything. Instead, I walk with her out of the house, and by some miracle, she follows me. Only when we are out of the door and it's closed behind us does she pull her hand from mine. "You don't have to do anything," she says. "It's over, no one is watching us."

I stop in my tracks and turn to face her. "You think I give a shit if people are listening or watching?" I ask, but I don't wait for her answer. "I don't give a shit. The only reason I wanted to leave was so I could hold you in my arms, on my lap."

"What?" she gasps in a whisper.

"I don't care who hears this conversation. I don't care if we do it in the middle of game seven of the Stanley Cup. I don't give two shits who hears this conversation." I smile at her softly. "I just want to do it while touching you." I slip my hand back into hers and pull her down the driveway and across the street, walking up the driveway.

"Where are we going?" she asks as we walk up the steps to the front door.

"My house," I inform her, putting the code into the front door. "This whole block is ours." I motion with my finger up and down the block. "Well, not ours but every single one of the houses on this street and in the cul-de-sac belongs to one of my family members. My Uncle Matthew found a developer, and we all bought houses."

"That sounds like your family," she mumbles as I open the door and wait for her to step in before locking the door behind her. "Where do you want to do this?" She looks around.

"Naked with you in my arms." My mouth doesn't give my brain a minute to think. "But I'll settle for the living room."

"Good choice," she huffs, walking down the hallway toward the family room. "How many houses do you own?"

"A few." I shrug. "It's an investment."

She steps into the sunken family room, turning to face me. "I don't really think there is anything else to talk about."

"There is a whole lot of stuff for us to talk about." I close the distance between us, putting my hands on my hips. "Like the fact you gave up everything for me."

"I didn't give up everything for you." She glares at me. "I gave it up for myself."

"So you didn't quit your job to move to Nashville and be with me?" She's about to argue with me, but I hold up my hand and touch her cheek with my thumb. "Why didn't you tell me?"

"I didn't want to get your hopes up, in case it fell through." Her voice goes higher. "How would you have taken that, Stone?" she asks. "Do you even know what that did to me?"

"Yes." It's almost a whisper. "Your job meant so much to you."

"Obviously, not as much as you since I gave it up," she says.

"So now what?" I ask.

"Now, nothing. Now, we go on with our lives. You were fine, anyway."

"Why would you think I was fine?" I ask. "I was the opposite of fine."

"Well, you look fine," she mumbles.

"Are you saying that you're fine without me?" It hurts my heart to ask her that question because what do I do if she says she is fine without me? What if she really is done with me? "Because I'm not fine without you." I grip her hip. "I will never be done with you. Never." She looks down, and I close the distance to her. "I meant what I said before." I lift her chin with the other hand. Only when she looks at me do I continue. "I'm going to marry you. We're going to have babies together. We're going to fight, and you will always be right." I wrap the arm that is holding her hip around her. "Living without you has been the worst time of my life. I felt like I was dying every single minute of every single day. I refuse to live like that again. I know what it feels to have you in my life, and I know what it feels like not to have you in my life. I never ever want to do that again. So, Ryleigh…" I exhale, stepping into her.

She puts her hands on my chest, right over my heart. "I'm not fine without you," she admits, blinking away the tears in her eyes, but one escapes and rolls down her cheek, stopped by my fingers. "After you broke up with me, it was too late to turn back. I had already given my notice at work, and they were bringing in someone new. I was days away from meeting with a couple of firms in Nashville, which I called to cancel. One called me back the next day. It's a firm that specializes in family law and I spoke with the owner who told me to take some time for me. He told me to take some time for myself, and that I had an office waiting for me when I was ready. After that, I packed up some clothes and headed to my family's home in Montana. Some nights, I would sit outside by the firepit and think back to every memory we had together. It would hurt, the agony of loving you and not being able to have you."

"I should never have let you go." I put my forehead on hers. "I should have listened to you."

"Yeah, you should have." She sniffles. "It would have saved us a lot of heartache."

"You could have shown up," I tell her, "with your bags."

"You could have gone skating without skates," she snaps, "and hot feet." I chuckle at her joke but only for a minute. "You hurt me, Stone." Her voice is like a whisper. "Like no one has ever hurt me before."

"I'm going to spend the rest of my life making it up to you," I vow to her right before I kiss her lips softly. I haven't touched her in a month, so the soft kiss I want to give her quickly turns into serious tongue.

Her hands move from my chest up to my neck, and she slides one into the back of my hair. "Forever." I let go of her lips for a second, only to consume her again. "For the rest of my life." I pick her up, and she wraps her legs around my waist. "I will show you how much I love you." I walk toward the steps, her arms going around my neck. "I will never ever let you go again, Ryleigh."

She stops moving when I say her name, her arms dropping from around my neck as I stop at the top of the landing. "What did you just call me?" I look into her eyes. "Did you just use my name?" She shakes her head.

"Gorgeous," I say gently, and her face goes soft.

"Say it again." She wraps her arms around my neck tighter, burying her face in the crook of my neck. "Say it again and again."

"Gorgeous," I repeat, heading down the hall to the primary bedroom. "Gorgeous." I squeeze her tighter. "Gorgeous." I walk over toward the bed, turning to sit on the edge. "Gorgeous."

"Yes," she mumbles from my neck.

"I love you," I say softly as she unwraps her arms, "so much more than I can say."

"Do you now?" She tries to hide the smile on her face. "Well, it took you long enough."

I throw my head back and laugh as she leans in and kisses my neck. "You know what else is taking you too long?" she asks. "Getting me naked." I smirk at her. "I thought you missed me."

"More than you will ever know." I pull her shirt up, and her arms go in the air as I peel it off her and toss it to the side. Her hands lunge for my shirt, balling it in her fists as she pushes it over my head.

"What the…?" Her eyes fly to the black ink under my left pec, where my heart goes toward my ribs. "What is this?" Her fingers slowly trace it.

"It's the coordinates of the first time I kissed you and fell for you," I tell her. "I'm going to put our wedding day under there, and then every time we have kids." Her eyes fly up to mine.

"You were serious," she says, "about the whole wedding thing."

"Why would you think I was joking?" I put my hands on her hips. "I wasn't joking, just like I'm not joking when I say we're going to Chicago tomorrow and clearing out your place." Her mouth hangs down. "And then you're going to move in with me."

"Just like that?" she asks.

"Just like that," I state. "I don't know if you are aware, but you were made for me."

EPILOGUE ONE

RYLEIGH

Two months later

"IT'S SO BRIGHT outside," I hiss as I put my black sunglasses on. "Why is it so bright?" My head throbs as we walk out of the lobby and toward the path that leads to the beach.

"Because it's the sun," Stone deadpans beside me, trying not to cackle.

"It's so hot," I moan as we walk toward the pool. "Why is it so hot?"

"Gorgeous, it's almost three p.m." His thumb rubs my thumb. "Peak hours in the sun."

"It's so hot," I huff as we walk past the empty pool. "Where is everyone?"

"They are having a beach party today," Stone explains, and then I hear the music.

"Why is it so loud?" I ask, and he laughs.

"Well, apparently, yesterday you, Zoey, and Gabriella

told my Uncle Matthew his beach was lame."

I stop mid step and turn toward him. "What?" I put my hand to my mouth.

"Not only was it lame but it was boring with a capital B," Stone continues.

"I told you not to let me drink," I hiss and hear screaming and cheering.

"Yes, yes, you did. Then you told me you're a grown woman who can make her own choices, and just because you live with me doesn't mean I control your life."

I close my eyes because I might have said that.

"Well, I am." I avoid prolonging this conversation because, well, tequila, rum, sun, and all that sugar—it's no wonder I got drunk.

"Oh, trust me, I know," he goads as he walks behind me a step. "You made sure you told your father to tell me that I'm not the boss of you."

I look over my shoulder. "You're not." We walk through the shaded trees that lead to the beach, and when we finally walk out, I stop in my tracks. It's like a party on the beach. There are couches and beach beds everywhere. Wood poles holding white tarps block the sun and give you shade. A DJ on an elevated stage busts out tunes while people are dancing and lounging. People are scattered everywhere, which isn't surprising since it took three planes to get us all here.

This time it is a family beach vacation, except this year everyone from Sofia's family is here also, including my parents. So what they did was buy out a whole hotel. I'm talking about every room bought out by Matthew or

Casey.

"There they are." Gabriella points at us when we make it to the loungers. She's lying on the bed with her sunglasses on too. "The whole day is almost done."

"We just got here," Romeo says, flopping down beside her, and she turns to glare at him.

"I'm not talking to you. I'm talking to your sister and my cousin." She points at us.

"I need some food," Stone announces from beside me, looking around.

"The buffet is over there." Romeo points to the side where the dining room is.

"Do you want anything to eat, gorgeous?" he asks, and I look up at him.

"Yes, a cheeseburger with fries." I smile at him, and he leans down and kisses me on my lips.

"And some tequila," Romeo adds. "How about a piññaaaaaaa coladaaaaa?" He sings the words, making Gabriella and me both groan.

"Where's Zoey?" I look around and spot her in a bikini with her sunglasses on her head.

"Why does she look so fresh, like she didn't crawl to bed at three o'clock?" Gabriella takes off her sunglasses to look at her.

"Because she didn't," Romeo states. "She left the two of you trying to do the tango at midnight. The only ones crawling were you two."

"Hmm." I put my hands on my hips. "I remember more people than that."

"Well, considering you had seven personalities last

night." Romeo points at me. "I could see it."

"You're going to let him talk to me like that?" I look at Stone.

"Now you want me to talk for you?" He smirks, then looks back at Zoey.

"Who the fuck is she talking to?" He puts his hand over his eyes to shade the sun so he can look at the guy about six foot one with brown hair, wearing shorts that go to mid-thigh and an open button-down linen shirt.

"I think that's Nash," Romeo says.

"Who the fuck is Nash?" Stone asks, his eyes staying on Zoey as she puts her head back and laughs.

"He's Caine's brother," Romeo replies like he should know who Nash is.

"Who the fuck is Caine?" Stone asks, not moving a muscle as he watches them interact.

"Sofia's cousin Grace's husband's brother," Gabriella informs us, using her hand to go through the people. "He got here last night."

"Why is he so close to her?" Stone wonders out loud as Nash leans in to tell her something in her ear and puts his hand on her arm.

"Not fun, right?" Romeo teases, and I look at him and roll my lips. "Imagine sharing a wall."

"Oh, stop, it wasn't that bad," Gabriella says, laughing.

"We changed rooms at two o'clock in the morning," Romeo sneers.

"Well, if you would have taken care of your woman"—I cock my hip to the side—"then you wouldn't have had time to listen to us."

"It sounded like you were using a megaphone," Romeo declares, getting up. "Right there! Right there! Right there!" He tries to mimic me.

Stone claps his hands together and laughs. "She was on the bed fully clothed and thought we were having sex."

"We did!" I gasp.

"Gorgeous, I was in the shower, and when I came out, you asked me if it was just as good for me." He grabs my hips and pulls me to him. "You were also half on the bed and half on the floor."

I don't bother answering him because my parents join us.

"Oh my God, we thought you guys were never going to come out of your room," my father says, wearing just shorts and sipping something from a pineapple. "It's almost dinner."

I roll my eyes, but no one can see me since they're covered. "Honey, leave them alone." My mother sits at the end of the bed, wearing her own bikini and cover-up. "Remember when we first got together?" She snickers. "We stayed in the room for twenty-four hours straight."

"I'm going to be sick." Romeo sits up, putting his hand on his stomach.

"What?" my mother shrieks and takes a drink from her own pineapple. "It's not a crime for us to have fun with each other." She looks over at my father and winks.

"Is there any sweet tea left?" I turn to Stone. "I need to pour it in my eyeballs and hope it goes to my brain."

He just laughs as he kisses me. "I'm going to eat." He

looks at Romeo, who shrugs and gets up to join him.

"Wait for me," my father calls, joining them as they walk over to the food.

"Move." I push Gabriella, who moves over to the other side. "I'm exhausted."

"I thought you were going to rest and relax." My mother looks at me. "You start your new job as soon as you go back." In the past two months, I've completely moved to Nashville. The day after we got back together, Stone and I went back to Chicago, where I packed up all my clothes and made the move.

"I was celebrating getting a new job, Mother." I take off the tank top I had on. A week after I moved in with Stone, although I already had the job, I went in for a formal interview. It was strange when you get a job and are like, I already have a family vacation planned. They didn't even bat an eye and expect me in the office as soon as I return. I never thought I would be excited about family law, but I'm looking forward to it. But more importantly, I'm excited to be with Stone.

Five minutes later, Stone comes back with a plate for me. "Here you go, gorgeous." He hands me a plate with a loaded burger and some fries, then a bottle of water. "I'm going to eat with my cousins."

"Okay," I say as he kisses me before bending to kiss my neck. "Have fun."

"Hurry up and eat," Gabriella urges. "Just looking at that food makes me want to yack."

I take a bite of the burger and hand it to her. "You'll feel better." She grabs it from me and takes a bite. We pass it back and forth to one another.

"Look at how cute that baby is." My mother points at one of Gabriella's aunts holding a baby in her arms. "No pressure, you two, but I'd like one."

"Well, go get one." Gabriella points at the kids. "No one will notice one missing."

I snicker, and my mom looks at me. "I'm not kidding. I would like a grandchild."

"Congratulations," I tell her. "I don't know why you're looking at me. I literally just got a boyfriend. You should be looking at this one." I point my thumb to Gabriella. "It's been a while over there."

"Well," Gabriella hedges, and I sit up.

"Oh my God, you are not."

"Of course I'm not. I was drinking with you last night," she reminds me. "I also might want one soon." She looks at me. "Don't you?"

"I like practicing to make them," I joke, looking over at Stone and seeing he's now without a shirt and walking to the water with his cousins. "I mean, look at him. What's not to like? He's all that and his package." I put my fingers to my mouth. "Chef's kiss."

"And I'm going to barf," Gabriella declares. Getting up, she tosses her sarong on the bed. "Now I'm going to go into that crystal blue water."

"I'm coming. I feel like if I stay here, my mother will want to harvest my eggs." I look at my mother. "Go hold a baby and get it out of your system." I toss my own sarong down. "I love you, Mom." I kiss her cheek. "But not now."

"Ugh, fine," she huffs and gets up, walking over to where the baby is.

I spot Stone sitting in a chair with all his cousins around him. "I'm going into the water," I announce. "Don't forget to put sunscreen on the tattoo."

"I did, gorgeous," he replies. I think he's going to sit there, but instead, he gets up and comes over to me.

"I can't believe you put numbers on your body," Christopher says. "Imagine if you hadn't gotten back together." He shakes his head. "How would you explain that? It's the coordinates for when I fell in love with another woman."

Stone puts his arm around my shoulders and pulls me to him. "Nah, I was always going to end up with her."

"Yeah. I saw that coming, especially after you waited six months to ask her out," Christopher jokes with him.

We walk into the warm water, the waves softly hitting our legs as we get waist-deep. He then ducks under and pulls me to him. I wrap my legs around him as he buries his face in my neck. "My mother wants a grandbaby," I say softly.

"Yeah?" he says as we wade in the water.

"Yeah," I repeat softly.

"How do you feel about that?" he asks but kisses my lips before I answer.

"I've never given it much thought. Have you?"

"Yeah," he answers without skipping a beat because that's Stone. Always one step ahead of me.

"How many do you want?" I ask, expecting to feel out of sorts talking about this. I would expect my mouth would be dry. I would expect my heart to race a little. What I don't expect is not to have any anxiousness about it.

"However many you want to give me," he answers softly. "It's all in your court, gorgeous."

I can't help but smile. "I'm going to need you not to be so perfect, SR." I kiss him and then bury my face in his neck as we just float in the water. Neither of us says anything as I put my head on his shoulder, watching the madness on the beach. I spot a couple of the kids running to the water and then running back, and I can see it in my head. Our kids doing this in five years, and I can't tell you how okay I am with it. "Two, at least," I say, and he tightens his arms around me, "but I want a girl for sure."

"Anything you want, gorgeous," he says, and I slowly unwrap myself from him.

"Just not now. I mean, we can practice," I say as we walk out of the water, and I see the water glistening on his body. "We can actually go right now and practice if you want."

He chuckles, and the sound sends shivers down my body. "Did you guys bang in the water?" Christopher comes up to us. "No one wanted to send the kids in."

I gawk at him and am about to answer when I look around. A couple of the phones start to ring, including Christopher's in his hand. "Why the fuck is Coach calling me?" I don't know what's happening, but I can sense it's not good from the way Matthew Sr. is coming our way. "Hey, Coach," he greets with a smile that quickly fades as he listens to the coach. Matthew and Max are fighting to get to Christopher, whose face goes as white as the snow on a winter day. The phone slips out of his hand as he whispers, "Benji's dead."

EPILOGUE TWO

STONE

Six Years Later

I PARK MY car in the driveway, getting out and jogging up the front steps to the house. I enter the code 0708 into the pin pad before I walk into the house.

The cold air hits me right away as I see two pairs of little pink Crocs tossed to the side, and I can't help but smile. My two girls. Aspyn, who is four years old going on twenty, was conceived on our honeymoon, literally. And Dalia, who is two and going into her terrible twos.

After Ryleigh moved in with me, it took two months to ask her to marry me. I wanted to do some big grand thing, but it was in the middle of her arguing about all my T-shirts ending up in her drawer when she huffed and threw them at me. But she went into my drawer, grabbing all of them, and when she threw them at me, the square box with the engagement ring I was saving hit the floor right at her feet. So there in our closet, around all my unfolded T-shirts, I slipped the ring on her finger and said, "Are you happy now? You ruined the surprise." To be honest, I expected her to take the ring off, but all she did was nod, and, well, we ended up fucking on top of all those T-shirts. It was glorious.

Neither of us wanted a long engagement, so at Christmastime, with every single one of my family members and a couple of friends in attendance, we tied the knot.

I toss my keys on the table by the door and walk in, seeing our frame hanging on the big wall. Ryleigh gave it to me as a wedding gift. It's the moon phases, along with the coordinates on the day we got married. Along the way, we've added one for Aspyn and one for Dalia. I can hear voices.

Ryleigh's voice is soft. "If you eat all your veggies, then you can have two jelly beans."

"Okay, Mommy," Dalia agrees, her voice full of joy.

"But, Mommy," Aspyn says, and I close my eyes. "How about if I eat two pieces, I get two pieces, and if I eat four, I get four?"

"How about if you eat all of them, you get two?" she counters, and I want to laugh because it's like watching a tennis match between them. Ryleigh is the best mom to our girls. She had some reservations when she was pregnant, thinking she didn't know if she could do it, but she hit the ground running. She always knew what to do. Even when she went back to work after four months, she took Aspyn with her to the office unless she had to be in court. Not only did she like family law but she was the most cutthroat out of them all. There was one thing in the world she hated, and that was a deadbeat parent. She went for the kill every single time.

"Hey," I say, rounding the corner.

"Daddy!" Aspyn and Dalia both shout my name. I walk over to Dalia first because she is closest to me on the stool sitting at the island.

"How is my gorgeous girl?" I kiss the top of her strawberry-blond hair. She looks exactly like my mom but with Ryleigh's eyes.

"I'm getting jelly beans," she announces happily as she sticks her plastic fork through the broccoli.

"Lucky you." I move over to Aspyn. "How is my gorgeous girl?" I ask her as I kiss her head.

"Mommy doesn't want to give me any jelly beans," she says, looking at me with my exact eyes. She looks exactly like me, but she's her mother's twin in attitude.

"She doesn't?" I ask, looking over at Ryleigh, who glares at her and clenches her jaw.

"Yes." She puts down her fork and turns to me. "She said she's only giving me two jelly beans for"—she turns around and counts the pieces of broccoli she has on her plate—"ten pieces of broccoli. That's not fair. She's being unreasonable."

"You know what's not fair and unreasonable?" Ryleigh asks her. "Zero."

Aspyn now pushes her plate away. "I don't want any." She gets off her stool. "I'm full."

"Aspyn Richards," Ryleigh orders, "upstairs and get in the bath."

"I'm going," she huffs, almost stomping up the stairs.

"All done," Dalia announces, unfazed by the showdown between her mother and sister.

"That's my good girl," Ryleigh praises, going over to the cabinet and grabbing two jelly beans for her. Dalia walks over to her as she holds them out for her. "Here you go, my love."

"I'm going to give one to Aspyn," she says, putting one in her mouth and running toward the stairs with the other. "Aspyn, I have a jelly bean for you."

"She better take it and not make her feel bad," Ryleigh grumbles, and I walk over to her.

"Hi, gorgeous." I wrap my arms around her and pull her to me, bending to kiss her lips. "How was your day?"

"Well, considering I spent the whole day in a showdown with your daughter," she huffs but still wraps her arms around my neck, "it was exhausting." My hands wander down to her ass, grabbing and squeezing it. "Why? Why is she like that?"

I can't help but laugh. "You mean combative?"

"This is not funny. It's like everything is a debate." She looks into my eyes, and all I can do is smirk.

"It'll get better," I assure her.

"Better?" she huffs. "It's getting worse as she gets older. She's getting smarter with her comments, and honestly, sometimes she's so good I want to be proud, but I can't show her how proud and irritated I am."

"Mommy," Dalia shouts from upstairs, "can I take a bath?"

"How about you go take a bath?" I urge her. "I'll put

the kids to bed, and then I'll join you."

"I'm only saying yes because I deserve me time." She gets on her tippy-toes. "Also, my parents are in town and taking the kids all weekend long."

"All weekend?" I wiggle my eyebrows. "Naked weekend it is."

"I was thinking of maybe perhaps checking into a hotel," she suggests.

"But then I can't fuck you on the kitchen counter when I want to lick whipped cream off you." I kiss her neck. "After you ride my face."

She pushes me away from her. "Go and wash our children." She walks toward the stairs. "And make sure your cock goes down. I don't need another conversation with Aspyn on why she shouldn't ask every male person we know if his penis is gross and big."

I can't help but laugh. "Michael's girls wanted to know if he satisfied Jillian sexually, so it could be worse."

"Of course it can with your family." She jogs up the steps, and I make my way up the stairs to the kids' bathroom.

I spot Dalia getting undressed and start the bath. "Don't go in there until I come back."

"I know, Daddy, or I'll die," she repeats the dramatic words my father told her when she went in the tub without him.

I walk over to Aspyn's room and find her on her bed reading. She may only be four, but she's reading at a second-grade level. "Bath time," I say, and she looks up.

"I took one this morning, and I didn't sweat," she tries

to say, and I hold up my hand.

"Did you go outside today?" She nods her head. "Did you touch a cell phone, a door handle, a pencil?" She nods again. "Then it's bath time."

"Fine, I'll wash my hands." She gets off her bed. "Then I'll be clean."

"What about your feet?" I ask, and she looks over at me.

"Fine, I'll shower and wash my feet and hands."

"Works for me," I tell her, knowing for today I won. She gets in the shower while Dalia gets in the bath. In an hour, both of them are in bed, asleep. I walk into our bedroom, taking off my shirt and making my way to the bathroom.

I open the door and spot Ryleigh with her hair piled on top of her head. She's standing at her side of the sink, putting cream on her face while she wears one of my white T-shirts.

"Hi." I walk to her and grab her hips, bending to kiss her neck. "You smell amazing." My hands move up her hips to cup her tits.

"Do I?" I watch her smirk in the mirror. "There is a surprise for you," she says, motioning next to her.

"What is it?" My eyes go to the long white stick, knowing what it is. My eyes go from the stick to the mirror and back to the stick.

"I think you know what it is," she teases, and my hand leaves her tits while it reaches out to grab the stick, the word Pregnant in the middle of the screen.

"Is this a joke?" I ask, and she turns to face me.

"Yes, because let's joke about bringing another child into the world," she retorts, and all I can do is look down at the stick in my hand. "I literally just lost my baby weight."

"What baby weight?" I snap.

"I had like five pounds left," she explains as I toss the pregnant stick into the sink.

"Have I told you I love you?" I grip the shirt with my hands and pull it over her head, leaving her naked in front of me, stepping in the middle of her legs. "Have I told you I love our life?" Her hands go to my hips. "Have I told you that you are my everything?"

Her hands go up to touch the side where my tattoos are. "You'll have to add another to this one."

"I know." I smile, my chest feeling fuller than it has ever felt before. "I love you, gorgeous," I say softly, and she looks at me with tears. "Thank you for giving me the world."

"Thank you," she whispers softly, kissing the middle of my chest, "for showing me what love is." She tilts her head back. "Especially for that sex tour."

I can't help but laugh at her as she pulls my pants down over my hips. "I need you." She grips my shaft in her hand, putting her feet up on the counter.

"Whatever you need," I confirm as I slide inside her. "Whatever you need."

Eight months later, she gives birth to our baby boy, who comes out fit to be tied. "Oh my God, another one who will go head-to-head with me." She shakes her head, looking down at our son as he looks up at us, his eyes blinking and taking everything in. "Why do all of our children come out looking nothing like me?" she cries. "It's like my genes didn't even try."

"Gorgeous," I say as I hold them both in my arms, "what are we going to name him?"

"Leo," she says, "like a lion." She looks at him. "What do you say, little one, are you a Leo?" He opens his mouth as if to agree with me. "Yup, Leo it is."

MEANT FOR HER

Christopher

I came from the biggest hockey family in the NHL. Records were set by my grandfather, my father, and now my brother.

I was taught to love the game, but more than that, I learned early on the men you play with are your family.

You get on the ice every night and protect them, celebrate the wins, and pick each other up when you fall.

So when we lost Benji, I stepped in to help his wife and kids, but this pull I feel when it comes to them is something more than I can even understand.

Dakota

My life was perfect until six months ago.

Gone was the husband I thought I knew and in his place was a stranger.

I saw him change before my eyes.

Then he was gone, leaving me and our girls alone. I wanted nothing to do with anyone or anything that took him away from me.

But no matter how many times I've told his best friend I don't need help,

he's there doing things for us, and the worst part is I want him to.

Made in the USA
Coppell, TX
15 December 2024